CHANGES

A Randall Lee Mystery

Charles Colyott

PRAISE FOR *CHANGES*

"Charles Colyott is a fresh and bold new voice on the mystery scene. Just when you think it has all been done before, here comes Randall Lee."

--Scott Nicholson, author of *Liquid Fear*

"Charles Colyott's novel, *Changes*, is a stunner. A thrill-ride from start to finish that will stay with you long after you've finished the last page. The characters are unique in detective lore, the situations are mesmerizing and together they draw the reader into a world quite unlike anything previously encountered. Read this book to learn, laugh, and fall in love with a brilliant young writer's work."

--Lisa Mannetti, two-time Bram stoker nominee and winner, *The Gentling Box.*

"With slick action reminiscent of Barry Eisler, and witty dialogue in the league of Jeff Strand, Charles Colyott creates a thriller all his own. The compulsively readable prose of *Changes* will keep you reading long into the night, and when you're through, you'll be hoping for another thriller starring the sometimes troubled acupuncturist/Tai Chi Chuan expert, Randall Lee."

--Glen Krisch, author of *Brother's Keeper, Loss, Where Darkness Dwells*, and *The Nightmare Within*

ISBN: 1493708023
ISBN-13: 978-1493708024

DEDICATION

For Ken Colyott (I think he would've liked this one) and for Cara, always

SPECIAL THANKS

Sifu, Tom, Alex & Scott and the NOLA crew

CHANGES
A Randall Lee Mystery

1

Yu Bei: Preparation.

I fell into the stance effortlessly and stood until my breath came slow, quiet, and easy. I focused on the feel of stale air on my skin, the flash of dust motes gleaming golden in the sunlight, and the stink of rotting fish from the dumpster down in the alley. Cardboard boxes still lined the walls of my apartment, stacked in random, leaning columns; I ignored them. Cobwebs caught the light and shone against the dingy ceiling; a wayward water beetle scrabbled along the floor, looking for a meal or, perhaps, a way back to its home. And through the open windows, guttural shouts in Cantonese, bits of conversation in lilting Mandarin, and heat: oppressive, humid, Midwestern heat. I pushed the distractions from my mind.

Qi Shi: Begin.

I start to move, searching for the stillness in motion, the motion in stillness. The postures shift from one to another without pausing, without breaking. 'Grasp Sparrow's Tail' to 'Single Whip,' flowing into 'Lift hands'. I moved through them, my mind quiet, almost peaceful. It was a refreshing change.

If someone asked me why I still practiced Tai Chi, after everything, I'm not sure I could give them an answer. I would probably say that it was comforting or relaxing, or maybe I would quote some study about the health benefits of the practice, but none of that was it, not really. I just kept on doing it.

The ringer was off on the phone, but I heard the answering machine whir to life in the kitchen. A voice, incoherent and low, muttered something gruff and clicked loudly as the caller hung up. I pushed it out of my head, something to handle later, after. By the time I began the first 'Cloudy Hands' set, my arms felt heavy, inflated, and numb. Sometime during the third section of the form, the damned machine started muttering again - more incoherent male voice, a bit more urgent and pissy-sounding this time. Whoever it was, they would just have to wait.

After closing the form, I glanced at the clock. Fifty-five minutes from start to finish, and my muscles knew it. My thighs and calves burned and glistened with a layer of sweat. I went to the fridge, grabbed a beer, and took a long pull from the glass bottle, relishing the wave of chills that started in my throat and stomach and spread outward through my body.

I listened to my messages. Both were from some cop, a Detective Knox, and he said he wanted to ask me a few questions. About what, he didn't say. I called the station, spoke to the detective, and told him he could meet me in twenty minutes.

I showered but didn't bother to shave. After running a towel through my hair, I bunched it into a ponytail, and got dressed - loose, black drawstring pants and a white tank top. I slipped on my battered black Converse All-Stars, grabbed a cardboard box from the kitchen table, took another beer from the fridge, and left.

A flight of steep, narrow stairs lead down to street level to my shop. As I emerged from the relatively cool, dim entryway, I shaded my eyes from the sun and once again cursed my particular migratory choice. I couldn't have picked someplace like San Francisco. No, it had to be St. Louis… The city with the shittiest excuse for a Chinatown I've ever seen. I like to call it China-street.

I unlocked the front door of my shop and went in, greeted as ever by the familiar sour stink of herbs and the cloying, medicinal smell of antiseptics. A stack of bills littered the floor by the mail slot. I kicked them into the corner, halfway under a bookshelf, dropped the box on the counter, and went in the back room to start a pot of coffee. I don't drink the stuff much myself, but I keep it around for clients. I've never known a cop to turn down a free cup of coffee.

I was drinking my beer and checking my appointment book when the cop showed up. I knew him immediately from the bad suit; somebody needed to tell this kid Miami Vice was cancelled ages ago. He was a youngish guy, maybe mid-thirties, very yuppie. Very clean-shaven. Either that or his face hadn't figured out how to grow hair yet. He walked in, looked around as I finished scribbling notes on the calendar, and finally said, "I'm looking for Mr. Lee?"

"That's me." I said.

"*You're* Randall Lee?"

I nodded.

"And this is your place." He said.

It wasn't really a question, but I answered it anyway.

He frowned, probably thinking that there must've been some sort of mistake. I was used to the reaction.

"I guess," he said, rubbing his bare chin, "I just figured you'd be more…"

I raised an eyebrow.

"…Oriental," he finished.

I took the box from the counter, slid my fingers under the thick brown packing tape, and pulled.

"*Things* are oriental, Detective. People are Asian. As you say, I am neither. Just another *Gwailo* like yourself."

He put his hands on his hips, probably in an attempt to look powerful or intimidating. He just ended up looking pouty.

"How long you been a cop?" I asked.

"Why?"

"Curious, that's all."

"Almost seven years." he said.

I glanced at his shiny badge, prominently displayed, as it was, on his belt, and said, "And a detective?"

"Two months."

"And you've been working *this* neighborhood for those two months?"

"Mostly, yeah." He said.

I nodded and said, "How's that been working out for you?"

He sneered a little. "Y'know what, pal? I don't really need any shit from you, alright?"

"What exactly *do* you need from me, Detective?" I said.

His face clouded. I couldn't tell if it was anger, embarrassment, or, most likely, a little of both. Conflicted as he was, I figured it might take a while for him to spill it. So I carried my box over to the shelves of herbs and began unpacking.

"Look, the department doesn't typically enlist the help of civilians but we're a bit short on resources at the moment…"

I brushed Styrofoam peanuts from the packing list and gave it a quick once-over.

"…and we've got a situation right now… are you even paying

attention?"

I looked up at him, hefting a bag of Siberian Ginseng, and said, "Absolutely, but you'll excuse me if I work as we talk? I'm a little busy."

"There was a murder last night. A *Chinese* prostitute." He said the word slowly, with emphasis. Smartass. I was starting to like him a little.

"So?" I said.

"So nobody's talking to us 'white devils', and we got nobody on the force who speaks Chinese."

I looked up. "How is that possible?"

"We only ever had a few to begin with. A couple joined Homeland Security, and Joanie - she was the last one – she's on maternity leave."

"So… you need a translator." I said.

"Well, yeah, but we were hoping to find somebody *they'd* talk to. Y'know, one of *them*."

"I could show them my jade secret decoder ring." I said.

He frowned and said, "You're kind of an asshole, you know that?"

"I get that a lot, yeah."

He stared at me for a minute.

He turned to leave.

As he reached for the door, I said, "Alright, Detective, my first appointment's not till two-thirty. That gives us a couple hours."

2

Knox drove a white, unmarked sedan. The big boxy thing may as well have had a giant speaker on the roof blasting the theme to Cops, though; nobody but a cop would be driving that thing around. The interior smelled. It reminded me of a time when I was a kid and somebody puked in the school bus.

"Your car smells like baked-in vomit," I said conversationally.

"Thanks," he replied. "Man, I could really use some coffee. You want some coffee?"

"I made some, actually…forgot to offer you any, though."

"Am I supposed to say that it's the thought that counts?"

I shrugged and said, "So, what happened to her?"

"Who?"

"The girl we're asking around about. You got ADHD or something?"

"We're looking into it."

"The girl or the ADHD?"

"*The hooker.*" he said. He wasn't as amused as I was, apparently, with my wit. I was pretty used to that.

"I know I'm not a cop," I said, "but isn't it usually sort of obvious how somebody was killed?"

"Yeah. Usually."

"But not this time?"

"No."

He stared out the window, presumably at a couple of kids playing in the parking lot of an old, boarded up Church's Fried Chicken.

"Why not?" I said.

He looked at me. "Why you wanna know so much? All you have to do is ask the questions and tell me the answers. Just translation, that's all."

I shrugged. "Hey, you came to me for help, detective. If I don't know a bit about what's going on I might not translate so good..."

He made a snuffly-sighing sound and tapped his fingers on the steering wheel. "Alright, but you don't say shit to anybody about this, got it?" he said.

"Sure."

"...She was *blue*."

"It's my understanding that's a time-honored tradition among corpses."

Knox glared at me and sighed. "I'm not talking about regular dead body blue. She was...really fucking blue."

Okie dokie.

"And naked, but no marks on her anywhere. No sign of struggle, no sign of sexual contact. Her hands were balled up real tight, fingers all bunched up like fucking claws."

"O.D.?" I said.

"No sign of a needle or anything else. Preliminaries say her blood was clean. Plus... and you tell this shit to the papers and I'll kick your fucking ass... Her eyes were filled up with blood...from the inside, y'know? Same with her nose and mouth... it was like something inside her...popped. Coroner said he'd never seen anything like it."

Interesting.

"Still," I said, "you called it murder... if you can't even tell how she died, how can you be sure?"

"She was laid out."

"What do you mean?"

"You'll see," he said.

It was the last thing either of us said before we hit the east side. Knox had to swerve to avoid hitting a pair of feral dogs fighting over a scrap of garbage in the street. An eighty pound crack whore shambled along the sidewalk, weaving like a zombie. Paint peeled from an ancient billboard that proclaimed that Jesus was the answer. I felt like I must've missed the question.

"You ever see that movie Escape from New York?" Knox said. "Kurt Russell, John Carpenter...y'know that one?"

"I don't really see a lot of movies," I said.

"It's one of those post-apocalyptic deals. New York's a big prison. Anyway, parts of that movie were filmed right along here."

I can't say I was surprised. Post-apocalyptic was right. We passed a block of abandoned buildings, collapsed structures, and burned wreckage. The 'Taste of Asia' spa sat wedged between a strip club and a porn shop. A pervert's oasis. It was a squat, shoebox-shaped building, decked out with neon and amateurish paintings of half-nude geisha girls on the door. A painted sign on the side of the building proclaimed that, "This establishment is not responsible for damage to your property or person. Enter at own risk."

We decided to risk it. We went inside.

The place smelled like cheap cherry air freshener, but underneath was the stink of sweat, cigarette smoke, mildew and mothballs. I recognized the madam despite her caked-on face paint. She'd been in to see me a few times about her arthritis. She spotted me with Knox, looked at the floor, clasped her hands, and bowed.

In Cantonese, she said, "Doctor Lee? What a surprise… what brings you?"

I told her.

She nodded, wiped an invisible tear from the corner of one pasty eye, and turned to walk away. She gestured for us to follow.

A few cops milled in and out of the various rooms. I caught curious looks from some of them. I felt the irrational urge to smile and wave, but I refrained.

The madam led us to one of the back rooms. The bitter tang of ammonia stung my nostrils. I covered my nose with my hand - for all that helped - and followed Knox inside.

"They took the body early this morning, but we've kept the rest of the scene the same." He said.

The massage table, the only furniture in the small room, was covered with white silk. The floor surrounding it was blanketed in single bills of Monopoly money. Yellow scraps of paper painted with red ink hung from the walls. I read the characters on several. They were mostly insults, gross descriptions of bodily functions, that sort of thing.

Several small jars lay around the room. I knelt by one and realized that the smell came from them: they were filled with piss.

Lovely.

I wondered whose piss it was and whether there was a way to fingerprint waste products. Then I realized that I was wasting time. Sometimes I annoy even myself.

I called to the madam and asked what she knew about the scene. Her observations weren't much different from my own. Her theory on the girl's death, however, tripped me up momentarily. I disagreed with her, but she kept on repeating herself. I turned to Knox.

"Could I see the body?" I asked.

"No. Why?"

I stared at him and blinked.

He shrugged uneasily and said, "Is it important?"

I kept on staring.

"You can stare at me all day, but that's not going to get you in to see the body."

"What if I told you that I might be able to give you the cause of death?"

He shrugged again and said, "Alright, alright…Why the fuck not? It's all a clusterfuck anyway. I'll call ahead, make sure they know I'm bringing you."

We went outside. I took a deep breath of the (relatively) fresh air. We got in the car and headed for the morgue.

Knox said, "What'd the madam say? The point of you being here, y'know, is to translate. So fucking translate."

I took a deep breath and said, "She didn't have much to say. Superstitious nonsense, mostly. But listen, detective, whoever killed this girl set everything up like a mock funeral. They did it as an insult. Taoists believe that if a person isn't properly buried their soul cannot rest. Whoever did this… they didn't just want her dead. They wanted her damned."

3

Knox stopped me before we went inside. I figured I was in for a lecture on police procedures, but that wasn't it at all. "Listen," he said. "The thing you need to know is that this isn't a real great area."

I looked across the street, to where somebody had nailed a dead raccoon to a tree, and said, "Really?"

"My point is that this isn't exactly a high-profile investigation. And Childerson, well, he's…" he searched for the right words for a minute, but ultimately decided to let me find out for myself.

I'd only been to one other morgue, but apparently they're all more or less the same. Sterile, yet somehow dingy. Always that one fluorescent light that flickers away, threatening to go out. The smell - not just the formaldehyde that gets in your skin and hair and clothes, but that other smell. The one reminiscent of meat.

And the cold. You never forget that cold. It gets in your bones, and you can't shake it.

The M.E. was fat, jovial, yet a little sickly. A little too cheerful, too smiley. Yellowish teeth. This was the infamous Childerson. He clapped Knox and I on the shoulders and led us to a steel table in the center of the room. Lights perched overhead like metallic buzzards; trays surrounding the table held numerous, wicked-looking instruments which shone dully in the cold, artificial light.

Then there was the body. Knox hadn't been kidding. The girl was really fucking blue. Not the typical pale bluish cast that most corpses had. She looked like a smurf.

"Most dramatic case of cyanosis I've ever seen." Childerson said, seeming to read my thoughts, "Comes from a lack of oxygen in the blood."

I leaned in for a closer look.

The girl was young… maybe twenty. She was fine-boned, with big eyes and full lips. Delicate hands, long fingers. She must've been quite beautiful in life. I felt guilty looking at her.

"What's her name?" I asked.

Childerson looked at me like I'd just asked him if I could have sex with her corpse. He glanced over at Knox, who shrugged and waved a hand impatiently.

"All we managed to get from Madame Chong was that she called herself 'Mei Ling'. I kinda don't think that's her real name, though."

Knox asked about the cause of death. Childerson turned his considerable bulk toward the detective. I took the liberty of grabbing a pair of rubber gloves from a box on one of the steel trays, and I slipped them on.

"Early evidence would suggest asphyxiation." Childerson said. "From her skin tone and the state of her eyes, I'd say it's looking like it's probably from a crushed larynx. Probably her pimp that did it. Same old bullshit."

I put a thumb lightly on her closed eyelid and slid it upward, exposing her eye. The pale green iris swam in a sea of red - every blood vessel had burst.

"I'd place the time of death at sometime early yesterday morning." Childerson continued. I had just opened her mouth to examine her tongue when he turned and screamed, "What the fuck do you think you're doing? Don't fucking touch her - you're fucking up the evidence, you asshole!"

I ignored him for the moment. Mei Ling's tongue was a bloated black slug that barely fit inside her mouth. I pulled up her upper lip; her gums were the same – blackish, swollen almost to the point of bursting.

I stood and faced Childerson. "Your evidence? The astounding amount of evidence to suggest that she suffocated from a crushed throat? That evidence?"

Childerson puffed up like an obese blowfish and got up in my face. "That's right."

I looked at Knox. He watched us with a sort of detached interest.

"You asked for my help. Do you care about how the girl really died, or are you content with this asshead's throat crusher theory?"

Asshead protested.

"You got something he hasn't got?" Knox said skeptically.

"Yeah. I've seen something like this before."

Childerson said, "Oh, bullshit."

I turned to him and said, "Did you actually examine her? She's been here since early this morning, and you don't know anything about her, do you?"

"She's a fucking dead whore. Case closed."

"She's somebody's daughter," I said.

He tried to stare me down, but a drop of sweat rolled into his eyes. He blinked the sweat away and sighed loudly. "Alright then, let's hear your theory, fucko."

"Tell you what: I'll lay it all out for you. You do your tests. Fifty bucks says I'm right and you're an idiot."

Childerson crossed his huge arms and said, "You're on, asshole."

I stepped to the other side of the table, allowing them access to the body as well.

"Knox, you said there were no marks on the body. That's not true. And this is not cyanosis."

Childerson laughed. "She's fucking *blue*… what else could it be? Too much time at Willy Wonka's?"

"No. She's bruised. From head to toe."

They looked at each other and Childerson laughed again. I held up a latex-clad finger and said, "Let me explain."

Childerson sneered at me; Knox frowned but waved me on.

"I want you to press lightly inward," I said, "here and here." I pointed to the ribs directly beneath Mei Ling's breasts. Childerson reached out a hand, rolled his eyes at me, and pushed on the girl's chest. The color immediately drained from his face and his eyes widened. Knox looked from the M.E. to me and back, and then felt her ribs for himself.

"Jesus Christ…what the hell happened to her?" he said, pulling his hand back quickly. Human chests shouldn't be squishy.

"Certain martial arts have very specialized, almost legendary, strikes. As Mei Ling here realized what her client really wanted, she would have inhaled to scream for help. The killer then struck," I extended both of my palms slowly outward in a pushing gesture, "both sides of the ribs, simultaneously. With sufficient internal energy and body coordination, this compresses and shatters the ribs. The lungs pop like balloons and crush the heart. The blood - with no place else to go - shoots outward, and temporarily soaks into the muscles and tissues. This girl died within an hour of being discovered; by tomorrow morning the blood will already start pooling on the underside of her body."

I slid the gloves from my hands and tossed them in the trash.

Reaching in my pocket, I took out my wallet, slid a business card out of it, and handed it to Childerson.

"Business hours are on there. Feel free to drop off my fifty bucks any time."

I headed for the door.

When I realized Knox wasn't following, I checked my watch and said, "My first appointment's in twenty minutes. I gotta go."

Knox nodded absent-mindedly.

"I rode with you, man." I said, hoping to jog his memory.

He looked up at me as if he'd just woken up.

"Let's. Go. Please." I said.

As we headed out, I looked over my shoulder at Childerson. He was still staring at my card.

'Fucko,' indeed.

4

Once we were in the car, Knox said, "How the hell did you do that?"

"What?" I said. Coy as a schoolgirl, that's me.

"How did you know all that?"

"It's part of my job. Knowing things. It's what separates me from somebody like Childerson. There are other things I *think* I know, but I wasn't positive…and I wanted my fifty bucks…" I was mostly guessing about all of it, but there was no way I was admitting that to Knox, and certainly not to Childerson.

"What other things?" he asked.

I slipped a plastic bag from my pocket, drew a decent-sized slice of ginseng from it, and popped it in my mouth. The root tasted earthy, slightly bitter, and a little sweet.

"Well," I said, "I'm pretty sure Mei Ling was pregnant, for one thing."

"No shit?"

"If Childerson would get on with the exam, we'd know soon enough. Also, I think it's pretty clear this wasn't a random thing…"

"Right. This was planned… an assassination?"

"Seems so. Which would suggest certain things." I said, "Bad, bad things."

He was silent for a minute. I kept on chewing.

"Okay, I give up." he said.

"What?"

"What things? What did you mean?"

"You've got a dead Chinese girl, a hooker. Probably a contract killing. The killer is proficient in martial arts, specifically, a Chinese martial art. Are you seeing a pattern?"

Knox slipped a cigarette in his mouth and muttered, "It's all way fucking Chinese…"

"True. So you've got prostitution and murder for hire. Who's likely to be involved?"

Knox's face lit up. I half expected him to raise his hand and say, "Oh! Oh! Me! Pick me!"

"Triads," is what he did say. Give the man a cookie.

"But look," he said, "this is St. Louis...there's very little Triad activity around, and they've always kept things quiet, always handled things themselves. So why attract all the unwanted attention over some hooker?"

He parked in front of my shop and turned to look at me.

I chewed the ginseng some more and said, "That's an excellent question. I'll leave that to you to figure out. I get paid to poke people with needles, so this is all way above my pay grade. But this was all very interesting, and I'm glad I could help out. See you around, Detective."

I got out of the car and fished my keys out of my pocket.

Knox rolled down his window and said, "Hey, Lee… you busy tomorrow?"

"Why?"

"Might need some more translating." he said.

"I'll be around." I said.

5

The girl sucked air through her teeth and hissed, "Ow!"

"Tender?" I said.

She squirmed on the table and said, "Uh, yeah."

"What happened?"

She lifted her head to look at me and said, "Let's just say that platform boots and cobblestone streets don't mix."

My hands slid from her swollen knee down her smooth, shapely calf to her ankle. I moved her foot gently.

"Sore?" I asked.

"Yeah, but nothing like the knee… I landed right on it when I fell."

"The good news is that it's not that bad. The bad news is--"

She winced and said, "You're gonna turn me into a pincushion?"

I nodded and went to the cabinet for my supplies.

This was Tracy's first visit. Well, as a patient, anyway. I'd seen her once before, when she came through the neighborhood with a friend. There are a few semi-touristy locations down the block from me: a rundown chop suey shack, a video rental store trying to cash in on the success of Jackie Chan and Jet Li, and HK Trading, a small grocery that carried incense, hell banknotes, and the sort of silly, mass-produced crap that westerners think of when they think of "the Orientals" - soapstone Buddhas, tiny gongs, that sort of thing.

Tracy and her friend had been amazed to find that I wasn't selling any lucky bamboo kits, but they were more amazed to see that I was not Asian. I remembered her smile, her funky hair and clothes, and the way she snatched one of my business cards with her black nail-polished fingertips. I couldn't tell you a single thing about her friend.

When Tracy called to make an appointment, she made it very clear that she hated doctors, and that she really wasn't too keen on needles either, but I was used to that. Needles, I've heard, lie somewhere just below public speaking and death on the list of most feared things.

When I returned to her side, I said, "I promise you this won't be nearly as bad as you think it'll be… nothing ever is."

She bit her lower lip and nodded. I tried not to notice the lip-biting, because Tracy was a very attractive girl… outstanding facial structure, big, dark eyes, full lips, a figure that a pin-up model would kill for, long, *long* legs. Really cute feet. And I'm not into feet at all. In fact, I haven't paid any attention whatsoever to any part of a woman in a long time.

I haven't wanted to.

A lot of that is because of Miranda, I know, but the rest of it is that I'm mostly used to dealing with elderly people. They love to inform me of their bowel issues. That is no fun. But being paid to attend to this young lady's legs? Hell, I would do that for free.

I opened an amber jar, poured its smelly contents into a basin, and soaked some thin gauze strips in the liquid.

"What's that stuff?" she said, wrinkling her nose.

"It's an herbal mixture that's good for joint pains. I'm going to send some home with you and I want you to use it, even if it does smell like cat pee, alright?"

She laughed and nodded.

"On the bright side," I said, "unlike some of the prescription stuff you could get, this stuff will not cause weight gain, projectile vomiting, or persistent rectal seepage."

She giggled again. I felt this absurd swelling in my chest, this ridiculous, almost overwhelming giddiness because *I* made her laugh.

It was probably heatstroke.

I took a strip of gauze, shook out the excess fluid, and laid it on her injured knee. I crisscrossed several more wet strips around the joint before wrapping her leg in a fresh, dry bandage.

"How's that?" I asked. "Not too tight?"

She shook her head and said, "It feels neat… and all *cold* inside."

I nodded and took a packet of needles from the glass jar at my side.

"Shit," she said with a frown, "I was hoping you'd forgotten that part."

I unwrapped the packet and tossed the paper in the trash. With my left hand, I measured out the *cun* distance from her kneecap toward the outside of her leg. I held the needle lightly in my right hand and looked up at Tracy; her eyes were squeezed tightly shut and she was biting her damned lip again.

I situated the tip of the needle directly over the spot, and held my left hand up a few inches from her face. Simultaneously, I snapped the fingers of my left hand as a diversion and lightly tapped the needle home.

"You okay?" I asked.

Without opening her eyes, Tracy said, "Yeah. Just tell me before you do it okay, because…"

"First one's in, kiddo."

She opened her eyes and looked. "Oh… Oh, wow."

"Cool, huh?" I said.

She watched as I inserted the other needles. Once she'd convinced herself that it really didn't hurt, she allowed herself to relax. As I worked, she said, "So… do I call you doctor, or mister, or, like, master, or what?"

"You can call me Randall." I said, twirling the first needle a little.

"Okay, but what's your title?" she said.

"Well, I'm a doctor of traditional Chinese medicine, but that doesn't mean much here in the good ole U.S."

She cocked her head sympathetically and said, "I guess the powers that be want that whole medical school thing… seven years of schooling or whatever it is."

"Maybe," I said, "but, I spent ten years with my teacher before I was ever allowed to even sit in with a patient."

"Jeez," she said, "did you start when you were a little kid?"

I grinned and said, "I'm older than I look."

She flashed a quizzical look and grinned back.

When we'd finished up, there was a part of me - the bad part - that was thinking about telling her that part of her treatment involved taking her out to dinner, but luckily I was spared that moment of impropriety by the arrival of my next client.

Mrs. Lhung.

A sixty-eight year old Cambodian woman.

With bowel issues.

Christ.

6

That evening, after the rest of my appointments, I settled in to dinner. My dining room consisted of a folding card table and chair, but I made the most of the evening – microwaveable Ramen noodles and Miller Genuine Draft.

I like to keep it classy.

As I ate, I thought about Mei Ling. I wondered why anyone would've wanted to kill her. I wondered how a girl like that got into the life to begin with. How had life failed her? No answers sprang to mind, so I thought about Tracy, and her exquisite legs, instead. That carried me through the rest of dinner. I finished my beer, rushed through a little Tai Chi, and went to bed.

I only woke up a few times during the night.

Only twice did I scream.

Thank heaven for small favors.

In the morning, I got up, threw some cold water on my face, and did some stretching. Once I was loose, I practiced the form - slow to make up for the hurried practice from the previous evening. I focused on releasing the tension from all of my muscles. It was a struggle not to fight against gravity, to let go and allow the movements to happen. I don't know if it worked, but it kept my head quiet, and sometimes that was good enough. I finished up, showered, and was getting ready to go downstairs to the shop when the phone rang.

It was Knox. He asked if we could meet in the park across the street. I said sure. I didn't have much else to do - only two appointments, later in the day, and neither of them were with attractive young women, so I could do with a little diversion.

I walked down to HK Trading, picked up breakfast, and strolled over to the park. Knox was messing up his nice suit sitting on a park bench. As I approached, he said, "Didn't know what you'd want, but I brought you some Dim Sum or whatever, just in case."

"Yeah? I brought some of your native cuisine, too," I said, tossing him the box of donuts I'd bought.

"Nice." he said. "Did you *think* about bringing coffee?"

I opened the paper sack I was carrying, took out a Styrofoam cup, and handed it to him.

"Well, damn. I feel special."

"You should," I said.

He opened the box and took a glazed donut as I sat down.

"So what's up?" I said. I popped a ground pork dumpling into my mouth. It was chewy, undercooked, and packed with enough MSG to make my brain bleed. He must've picked them up from the chop suey shack.

Knox took a bite of his doughnut, dabbed at the corner of his mouth daintily with a napkin, and said, "Childerson checked out the girl…"

He took a fifty-dollar bill from his inside coat pocket and handed it to me.

"He also said the girl *was* pregnant. Oh, and a special message just for you… he said, 'Go fuck yourself.'"

I pocketed the money, blew on my coffee to cool it, and said, "Classy."

Knox nodded and said, "So, you want to tell me what that shit was that you and the madam were arguing about yesterday?"

"What? Oh, right. It was nothing."

"Bullshit. She kept repeating that shit to our boys all night… '*Deem mock, Deem mock.*'"

I took a jelly donut from the box and said, "*Dim Mak.*"

"Whatever. What's it mean?"

I shrugged and said, "It's hocus pocus, nothing but an old Chinese superstition. 'The Death Touch'… supposed to be some secret deadly art. Y'know, where you touch certain energy points and cause a person to die hours later… they say that's what got Bruce Lee… Madame Chong said that's what killed Mei Ling. I already showed you how she died, though. So it's crap."

Knox seemed to think about that as he popped the rest of his donut in his mouth. He dabbed his mouth again, tore open the plastic lid of his coffee, and took a sip.

"Why?" I asked.

"Got the call this morning. Chong's dead. Heart attack, we think."

"…Shit."

"Yeah. And it looks like the case dies with her."

"What? Why?"

"These massage joints… they get girls fresh off the friggin' boat in California. Ninety percent of 'em are illegals. They stick 'em in a parlor and rotate 'em out to another place whenever a new group arrives. Keeps things moving, keeps the girls from getting any kind of criminal record in any one spot, and keeps things more or less anonymous."

"A kind of slavery, then."

"Basically."

"And with Chong dead, there's no way to find out who Mei Ling was."

"Pretty much. The girl's a ghost. No records of her anywhere. Frankly, no one in the department is going to lose a minute's sleep over a couple of dead Chinese hookers."

After our cheery breakfast, Knox went his way and I went mine. Before he left, he slipped me a copy of Mei Ling's file, in case I could come up with anything else, and made certain I knew just how much trouble I'd be in if I was caught with confidential evidence files.

Touched by this show of camaraderie, I went home, tossed the file on my desk, and got ready for work.

Mrs. Lim had pain from an inflamed gallbladder, and Mr. Yeung was quitting smoking. All told, it was about two hours out of my day. The rest of the time I spent thinking about Mei Ling. Something about all of this stunk like the back alley behind HK Trading, and that was pretty goddamned stinky.

That girl was too pretty, too damned *clean*, to be giving twenty dollar hand jobs out of some chop-socky shit-hole on the east side. Besides, she would've started showing before long and that would've been the end of her brilliant career.

The whole ceremonial aspect of the scene bothered me too. Did it mean that Mei Ling was a Taoist, or was the killer? Or both? I'd known a lot of Taoists, back in Hong Kong, and they were the most peaceful people I've ever known. Did this guy really hate her that much, or was the room made up that way for someone else's benefit. Was she made into some sort of example?

Then there was Chong.

I checked my files. Turns out, she'd been in to see me a total of eight times in six months. The last time was three weeks ago. Minor arthritic pain in the hands, hips, and feet. In Chinese medicine, we take a pulse diagnosis to gauge the strength of each organ. I'd noted the pulse diagnosis for each visit, and there was no mention of any weakness or imbalance in the heart. In fact, there didn't seem to be much of anything wrong with her besides the arthritis. Must've been all that clean living.

I called the station and managed to catch Knox. I asked him for a double or nothing shot with Childerson. He told me to meet him in twenty minutes.

The morgue was as upbeat and cheerful as it was the last time I'd visited. Childerson was just as fat. Madame Chong's body occupied the steel table this time around. She'd seen better days. Knox distracted Childerson with sports talk while I gave the body a quick once-over. I noticed a dullness to some of the skin on her face. I touched her lips briefly and rolled my fingertips together.

"Any preliminary findings?" I asked.

Childerson was rambling about the size of some cheerleader's tits.

I repeated myself.

"Wha…?" he said. "Nah. Nothing, yet."

"There's that sterling work ethic I know and love." I said.

The man adjusted his straining belt against a tidal bulk of gut flesh and crossed his arms. Brownish pit stains peeked out from underneath his arm fat.

"I suppose you're going to throw out some bullshit theory about ninjas and *chi* and shit like that, right?"

"Ninja are Japanese." I said.

"Whatever. You gonna show me which aura points the killer whacked to magically cause an elderly woman to have a massive coronary?"

"Sure." I said. "And it's really comes down to just one point."

"Oh, really."

"Yep, this one." I said, raising the woman's arm and pointing to the puckered hole situated neatly between folds of skin in the crook of her elbow.

The M.E.'s face fell. He immediately started sweating. It wasn't pretty.

"Maybe it's my mystical new age bullshit talking," I said, "but that looks an awful lot like an injection site to me. What do you think?"

He nodded. Droplets of sweat hit the floor with loud little splats.

Even his sweat was fat. Whoa.

"Now, I'll leave the details to you and your medical expertise," I said, "but you and I both know that just about anything could have been shot into this woman's veins, right?"

He nodded again. The tile floor received another flash flood.

"Awesome. You might want to try X-raying her before you slice her open, alright? And if you don't have the cash on you right now, I understand. You can always have Knox drop it off later."

Childerson gathered his senses; it only took him a second, which was a surprise. With an arrogant certainty he said, "You still don't know she was murdered… an injection site by itself means nothing."

"You're right," I said, "but the adhesive residue on her mouth is an interesting coincidence."

I touched Madame Chong's wrists and felt the same stickiness.

"Maybe she just likes self-bondage." I shrugged and grinned. "You never know with these kinky old broads and their weird hobbies."

"And what, exactly, do you expect we'll find through x-raying a corpse?" Childerson said.

"Honestly? I think our boy here got a little sloppy with the duct tape. I think he moronically picked the most obvious injection site on the body. But I'd be willing to bet that he wasn't stupid enough to pump an old woman full of crank or Drano or arsenic or something that would show up right away and stand out. It looks like he wanted it to look like a heart attack, and he almost fooled you already, so keep an eye out for things that don't belong."

"Like what?" Knox said. Mostly, he'd just let me and Childerson bark at each other, but now he was interested.

I shrugged. "Something natural. Potassium, maybe. Or even air. That would be the easiest way. Hard to catch too, I'd imagine."

"Shit." Knox said.

"Actually," I said, "Shit was a favored poison of the aforementioned ninja, way back in the day. Antibiotics pretty much put a stop to that, though."

"What the fuck are you talking about?" Childerson said.

"Never mind me. Get to work on that x-ray." I said.

Knox and I left him to simmer in his own considerable juices. We went outside.

The detective lit a cigarette, took a deep drag, and blew out a lung full of carcinogens. He picked at his thumbnail for a moment and said, "So there are two killings. One flashy, one not-so-flashy. Mei Ling was planned out. An organized, ritualistic assassination… Chong was a relatively sloppy rush job. Why?"

I thought about it for a minute. I knew he was talking to himself, but I shrugged, and said, "Different killers?"

"Yeah. The first guy was pretty slick. In and out without drawing attention to himself. Unless he did draw attention but the girls are too scared to talk… and the other…" he stopped and turned to me.

"How the hell do you know all this shit?" Knox said.

"I'm observant, I pay attention, and I used to watch Quincy reruns all the time."

We stopped near our cars. Knox took a toothpick from a plastic box and began gnawing on it. This guy seemed to have a serious oral fixation.

"Y'know what I don't get?" he said, "Why are you doing this? I mean, you didn't give a shit about any of this when I came in your store…now, suddenly, you're all gung ho. What's that about?"

"I don't like bullies." I said.

He leaned against his car and said, "Oh, so you're just a Good Samaritan?"

"No, but if I can do my part without inconveniencing myself…why not?"

The expression on his face was hard to read. He wasn't exactly happy, I knew that much, though I didn't know why.

I wished him luck on his search, got into my car and went home.

7

I checked the cupboards and the fridge - sad. Really sad.

So, at nine thirty at night, with a couple beers in me, I decided to hit the market, assuming it was still open. I walked. It was a nice night, and all the beer on my empty stomach made everything pleasantly ridiculous.

They say that St. Louis used to have a Chinatown, until the city demolished it to make room for a new baseball stadium. So my sad little China-street was made, and it never blossomed into anything bigger. When I came to the city, I picked the location because it felt a little like home and I thought the locals might appreciate my skills. Truth was, I could've moved into one of the ritzy white business districts and raked in the cash, but I'm not the new age healer those types want. I hate that whole racket. So this modest, hell, rundown little neighborhood was my home now, and I figured I'd get out and see it a bit more. Since alcohol makes everything better.

HK Trading closed at ten.

I checked my watch: ten till. I was in luck.

I went in, inhaled the smells of fresh fish, dried herbs, and incense, and nodded to the elderly man behind the counter. We didn't know each other really, but I'd shopped there enough that we did that weird stoic male nod thing. A wall-mounted television in the corner played a grainy kung fu film. From the music - a Chinese folk song called 'On the General's Orders' - I knew it to be a Wong Fei Hung movie, but it didn't look like one I'd seen.

I grabbed a bowl of ready-made soup and a few packages of noodles. I saw a bin filled with durian melons and, on a (very) drunken whim, grabbed one.

For those not in the know, the durian is a sort of Hong Kong delicacy. It is a hard, spiky, football-shaped fruit with a sweet, almost buttery taste. It's very, very healthy. On the downside, it smells like rotting garbage threw up in a honeydew melon, and that honeydew melon then took a shit. Really.

I grabbed a six pack of Tsing-Tao, because I was going to need it if I honestly thought I was going to eat that durian, and took my stuff to the counter. The old man was ringing everything up when I heard the doorbell chime.

A group of wannabe thugs came in, giving me and the old man a heavy case of the stink-eye. The shopkeeper grumbled and began bagging my groceries; he put the spiky durian in its own plastic shopping bag so that it wouldn't crush the noodles. I appreciate that kind of good customer service.

The kid in the front of the group, I assumed he was supposed to be the leader, looked like he'd just fallen off the boat from Hong Kong... Circa 1985. Greasy golden skin, bad teeth, really shitty mullet. He wore a white t-shirt with a bad iron-on Scarface transfer (a picture of Al Pacino and his "little friend"), an honest-to-god pair of parachute pants, and high-top kangaroo sneakers.

His crew wasn't dressed much better. A couple of them even sported headbands.

I nodded to them. It didn't hurt to *try* to be friendly.

He sneered at me and pushed past; as he did, he muttered something to his friends about "the stupid American *Gwailo* bastard." That, I thought, wasn't fair. I mean, I'd had to go through the whole immigration process myself. I don't doubt I had it a little easier; being Caucasian, male and speaking English gets you pretty damn far in this world, but still.

I should've let it lie, but there was that whole matter of being drunk enough to eat fruit that smelled like poop, and, well, I am not always as mature as my years would suggest. In fact, drinking – especially alone – usually brings out the worst in me.

I called out to them. As they turned, I gave them my most charming smile and - in Cantonese - suggested that they might enjoy having sex with each other's mothers. The leader turned a bright shade of red and got in my face.

Kind of... He was about a foot shorter than me.

I glanced at the shopkeeper. He raised his hands and backed away; he didn't want any trouble, and I didn't blame him. He'd probably dumped everything he had into this place; I'd have to try to keep the damage to a minimum.

The kid sprayed a number of Cantonese curses, and a good deal of spittle, in my face. He smelled like curry and garlic mixed with a wicked case of body odor. He probably still smelled better than my desert. That thought made me giggle.

Just say no to alcohol, kids.

I cut him off mid-spittle stream and said, "What's your name?"

He spat, "Scarface!"

I looked at the picture on his shirt. "Ah."

The kid turned a different shade of red and - in broken English - said, "Fuck you, motherfuck. You want ass-kick, you come right to place!"

In Cantonese, I said, "I believe the word you were looking for is 'motherfucker.' And the rest of that was just a train wreck. Insults and threats are tough if you don't have a good grasp of the language. Like this:"

Then I told him that his mother contracts turtles.

I know it doesn't make any sense, but apparently, that's a really big deal. I read it somewhere on the internet.

He spouted out something unintelligible and shoved me as hard as he could. I didn't move. He succeeded in sliding himself back several feet, though. By the look on his face, you'd think *I* attacked *him*. His hand flew to his waistband and came up with a balisong – those flippy little blades that Americans incorrectly call 'butterfly knives.'

Grinning a crooked, yellow-toothed grin, he began flipping the mobile handles of the knife. His dexterity and speed was impressive.

I leaned on the counter and admired the display for a minute before wrapping my fingers around the handles of my plastic grocery bag. I turned and swung the bag like a mace. The spiky football-sized durian fruit splintered the bones in Scarface's hand and sent the balisong spinning across the floor. He yowled in pain for a second before I twisted, rocketing the makeshift weapon into his teeth. They looked like they needed to come out anyway.

He fell on his back, groaning, and bled for a while.

Scarface's friends kept looking from him to me and back again. They didn't want to abandon their fearless leader, but I could tell that they weren't overly anxious to take an ass-kick either.

I told them to take 'Scarface' – now a little more aptly named - and get the hell out.

Wonder of wonders: They did.

As the last of the gang left the store, I turned to the old shopkeeper and asked if he was alright. He called me a stupid American *Gwailo* motherfuck, and told me to never come back to his store again.

I took my remaining groceries - the durian split when it hit Scarface's teeth, and the market was flooded with the scent of hot, shitty melon stink - and left.

So much for my understanding of the culture.

8

The next morning, I got up, had some green tea, and checked my appointments for the day - I was pleasantly surprised to see that I had a follow-up with Tracy at six fifteen.

Something to look forward to, anyway.

Since coming to St. Louis, I'd more or less neglected my daily practices. I decided that I'd been lazy for long enough. I went to my practice space – my empty living room - sighed at the boxes, as if they would unpack themselves, and assumed the basic preparation stance. Feet shoulder width apart, spine straight but relaxed, arms loose at the sides, head held as if suspended from above. I inhaled, pulling my stomach inward, and exhaled, relaxing it outward. My eyes drifted closed, and I let the room disappear.

In its place, I imagined a field of wildflowers. The sun warmed my face; a light breeze blew past, ruffling my hair. As I breathed in, my wrists floated up while my elbows sank down. My arms formed a circle, a posture called 'Embracing the tree.' I released the tension throughout my body and simply allowed myself to stand – the simple art of *Zhan Zhuang*, 'Standing Stake' *chi gong*.

After a while, my body felt heavy. My legs seemed to push down into the earth. The real activity, though, happened inside - Surges of fire and ice intertwined and danced along the nerves of my spine. They echoed outward, down my arms and legs, sparking at the tips of my fingers and toes. Streams of force flowed down the surface of my skin, into my pores, to collect in my lower abdomen.

The whole thing sounds like the kind of new age crap that I hate, but the practice is actually very beneficial, its results very tangible.

When my eyes fluttered open, an hour had passed. My arms and chest felt like I just bench-pressed a Buick. My legs shook.

I did some light stretching and went straight into the 103 posture Yang style long form. As I went through the movements, my mind wandered again to the girl, Mei Ling.

I wondered if Knox was having any luck.

I wondered why I cared.

I wondered if I'd ever get around to unpacking.

It was nearly noon when I finished practicing.

On a whim, I went to my computer, got online and looked up 'Taste of Asia'.

After sifting through a handful of restaurants and porn sites, I found it. Turns out, they were a chain. San Francisco, Vegas, Houston, St. Louis, Miami, New Jersey, New York. I clicked the buttons for each location and skimmed through the photos of young women dressed in silk robes, their postures alluring, their eyes dead, looking for any pictures of Mei Ling.

No such luck.

I sighed and closed the window.

9

Tracy arrived just before six, wearing a sleek little black dress that could cause a twenty car pileup, thigh high fishnets, and stiletto heels.

When I regained the power of speech, I said, "...so, your knee is doing better?"

She smiled a little and said that, yes, it was feeling fine.

"Um... It's going to be hard to do much work on your leg," I said, "with you in those stockings."

"Oh, should I take them off?" she said.

I felt my face heat up and it pissed me off. I'm an adult for god's sake, not some horny teenager. I opened my mouth to speak, but incoherent gibberish fell out of it. She giggled and went into the treatment room. I thought of what she was doing, of the lucky stockings that got to slide down those thighs, and felt the need to sit down. Perhaps, I thought, if I were really good in this life, I could be reincarnated as Tracy Sandoval's stockings.

When she called out that she was decent, I went back too.

Her legs were crossed at the ankle, her dress slid up to mid-thigh. The vast expanse of skin made the edges of my mind crackle and buzz with a kind of pleasant static. They were very high quality thighs. And I was becoming increasingly uncomfortable.

I sat near the foot of the exam table and put one hand just above her knee. I pressed my fingers gently into the soft tissue, feeling for any swelling. Most of what I felt was a ridiculously strong case of butterflies in my stomach.

"Can you move it?" I asked.

She nodded and bent her knee. I pretended not to notice the momentary flash of black lace accentuating the perfect, pale crescent of her ass.

Instead, I worked at two very difficult tasks – swallowing and breathing.

"Is there any pain?" I croaked. "Any stiffness or soreness?"

Yes.

"No." she said. "It feels great."

Yes, yes it does.

I cleared my throat, fumbled her file from the desk, and made some notes in the margin. I thought of Mrs. Lhung's thighs, riddled as they were with varicose veins, and attempted to regain my composure and professionalism. I kept looking at the box in Tracy's file marked Date of Birth. Twenty-six was hardly a child, but still…

I stopped that line of thought right away. The room felt very hot.

Tracy sat up, slid those long legs over the side of the table and said, "Everything okay?"

"Um?" I said. Smooth. Real smooth.

"I said, is everything alright?"

"Yes." I said. "Sorry, I'm just a little out of it today. My *chi* must be on vacation."

She laughed and said something but my heart thrumming in my ears blocked most of it out.

I finished the notes in her file and walked out to the front room while she put her stockings back on. I thought of herbs to occupy my mind in some kind of positive way. She came into the front room, paid for her visit, and was almost to the door when she turned and said, "Mr. Lee?"

"Yes?"

"This is probably, like, against the rules and stuff… but… would you ever maybe want to… have dinner with me?"

Gulp.

"Uh," I said, being a terrific conversationalist, "dinner?"

Yes, Randall. That meal that happens in the nighttime.

Jesus.

Tracy winced. I saw her teeth closing in on her bottom lip and looked away before I had an aneurysm or something.

"Yeah. I'm being inappropriate aren't I?" She said. "I'm really sorry. It's just…"

She continued on with apologies she didn't need to make, but I didn't hear them. There was too much of a roaring thrum in my head. I knew I had to be the adult here. To take the moral high ground. I couldn't start dating patients… if I did, Mrs. Lhung would want a shot, and I prefer not to know my date's gastrointestinal history.

But before I could muster the maturity to say no, my mouth opened and said yes.

10

Her middle name is Ann.

She said that she's a Scorpio. I didn't know what that meant until she told me. She listed off a number of characteristics common to Scorpios, and blushed fiercely when she mentioned that Scorpios, apparently, make great lovers.

Yikes.

Things were going too fast. It was all just too much.

I asked her for her birthday. In Chinese astrology, she was born in the year of the snake and I told her so.

"If I'm a snake," she asked, "what are you?"

"I was born in the year of the rabbit." I said.

She flashed a sexy, evil grin and said, "Snakes eat rabbits."

I slammed another cup of plum wine. It provided a handy excuse for the color in my cheeks.

She'd picked Wong's BBQ for dinner. It was just two blocks from my shop, but I'd never been there before. I really can't remember if the food was any good or not. The company was terrific. The wine was pretty decent too.

She told me that she was a bartender at a club downtown, some place I'd never heard of called the Outer Limit. She'd majored in dance and art in college; clearly a practical girl. Her father taught history; her mother, literature. Her favorite bedtime story as a child was The Odyssey. She told me how she used to look up at the night sky, as a child, looking for all the constellations from the myths, like Orion. She said that the city lights blocked out most of the stars. She said she missed the stars and shrugged, embarrassed, as if what she'd said was stupid. As if I wasn't entranced by every word she said.

"Your turn," she said, grinning.

"Hm?" I said, sipping wine.

"Don't play innocent. Spill it. C'mon…"

"What do you want to know?" I asked.

She cocked her head and stared at me. "For starters, how does a white boy from St. Louis grow up to be an acupuncturist and all that?"

"First off, I'm not *from* St. Louis. I just moved here around six months ago. I was born in Hong Kong."

Her eyes widened. "Whoa, really?"

I nodded.

"So you learned all your stuff there?"

"Yeah. My dad was a tax attorney for a big multinational import/export company. My mom died when I was five. I spent a lot of time cooped up in the apartment, with not much of anything to do. When I was old enough, I'd sneak out. The kids in the bay were tough; I didn't know it at the time, but a lot of them had already been recruited into the Triad youth gangs…"

"Hold it. Silly American question - what's a Triad youth gang?" she said.

"Triads are organized crime syndicates. Chinese mafia. They like to line up their recruits early. Anyway, those kids didn't like any 'white devil' like me hanging around. So I used to get beat up. A lot."

"Why didn't you just stay home?" she asked.

I shrugged. "I guess it was just one of those dumb boy things… even bad attention was better than nothing. Plus I had this weird idea that sooner or later they'd have to respect me for taking their crap, y'know? I've never claimed to be very bright.

"Anyway, this one day a group of the guys chased me until I couldn't run anymore, and they kicked the crap out of me. One of the kids had an aluminum baseball bat, and he hit me in the stomach a few times…"

"Jesus!" Tracy said.

"…Yeah, well, they quit when I started spitting up blood. This old woman saw what happened, and when the boys all left, she made her husband carry me inside while she went for help.

"Turns out a famous doctor, Wu Cai, lived in the neighborhood. He came and checked me out. Did some acupuncture, some massage, gave me some herbs… that sort of thing. He did so well that I was able to hide the whole incident from my dad. So I started hanging out at his house a lot. Bugging him to show me stuff. Finally he did."

She leaned forward and said, "He started teaching you acupuncture?"

"No." I said, "He started teaching me how to stand."

"What?"

"Yeah. He said that if I wanted to learn from him, that's what I had to learn. How to stand. So I'd show up at his house at seven in the morning and just stand by his front door. Whenever he felt like it, he'd come outside, adjust my posture, and go back inside."

"How long did you have to stand like that?" she said.

"Oh, I didn't have to stand there at all. He made that very clear. He wasn't looking for students; he didn't care if I was there or not. But the longer I was there, the more I saw, and the guy was like a magician. He could do stuff I'd never seen anybody do. I wanted to learn to do what he did.

"So I stood there. Ten hours a day, six days a week, for six months. Finally he let me come inside…"

"What did he teach you then?" she asked.

"Nothing. He just let me stand inside. The kids had caught on to the whole thing, see, and they'd started showing up to make fun of me and throw rocks and stuff."

"Damn! What a bunch of little asshole delinquents."

I shrugged. "Most of my ninth year was that way. Get up, sneak out, stand until dusk, and sneak back home. When summer rolled around again, Wu wasn't correcting me anymore. In fact, he didn't really pay much attention to me at all. I was starting to get discouraged. Since the weather was nice, he made me stand outside again, and the bullies were coming around again. I was determined not to let them get to me, so I just pretended that I didn't notice them."

"Didn't they bother you?"

"Yeah. But I bothered them more, by not reacting. Then one day something funny happened."

I stopped to take a drink.

"What? What happened?" she said.

"A couple of the kids tried to shove me, and nothing happened."

"What do you mean, nothing happened?"

"I mean they pushed, and I didn't move. And the harder they pushed, the *more* I didn't move. It was like they were trying to move a building."

She smiled and hunched her shoulders. "So they left you alone?"

"No, they punched me in the face."

"…Oh."

"Master Wu brought me in, fixed me up, gave me some soup, and sent me home. The next morning instead of my normal standing, he showed me a different posture. He also made me do this weird exercise where I would just turn my waist and let my arms kind of flop around… I didn't understand why at the time.

"The next time I stood outside, the bullies came again. Following Master Wu's instructions, I released all the tension from my body and just became loose. When one of the kids pushed my right shoulder, my body rotated around my spine –like a revolving door - and he got socked in the gut with my left fist. When another kid punched at my face, I raised my arm the way I'd been taught for the new posture, and he just sort of bounced off it. That went on until they were all too hurt or tired to keep it up, and *then*, yeah, they decided to pick on somebody else."

"What was he trying to teach you, though? I don't get it." she said.

"To be still. In stillness, he said, all things are possible."

"Is there, like, a rulebook of cryptic shit that these teacher guys are supposed to say? Because damn. I'm Mister Miyagi-ed out."

I smiled and said, "Look at it this way – Master Wu spent his life learning and perfecting his knowledge. He didn't want to give even a shred of that to someone who wouldn't fully appreciate it."

The waitress came and set the check on the table. Tracy moved to grab it, but I intercepted.

"Hey, I asked *you* to dinner, remember?" she said.

I gave her a wide-eyed, innocent look, slapped down enough cash to cover the bill and tip, and said, "What?"

She glared playfully and rolled her eyes.

We sat, finishing our drinks, until, blushing fiercely, she said, "So…what now?"

The blushing was contagious, apparently.

Christ, what was I supposed to do, ask 'her place or mine'?

My cell phone rang. Saved by the proverbial bell.

Knox shouted in my ear, "Lee? We need to talk." I heard bad techno music in the background. Never a good sign.

I turned in my seat and said, "Detective, I'm at dinner right now, could I call you back?"

"No. We need to talk now, Lee, or I'm sending a squad car."

I frowned.

"What's going on?" I asked.

"That's what I want to know."

He rattled off an address and asked if I knew it.

I didn't, but I told him I could find it.

He said, "Look for the sign, you can't miss it."

11

After quickly excusing myself from dinner, clearly disappointing and confusing poor Tracy, I went to my car, shook off the plum wine buzz, and drove.

Knox wasn't kidding about the sign… a lump formed in my throat at the sight of the giant, leering neon beaver.

Who was dead now?

I parked and walked in the ornate brass doors. A doorman stopped me and, over a thumping bass line, asked for my I.D. and a ten dollar cover charge. I told him that I was here to meet Detective Knox on police business; he didn't care.

I flashed my license, watched him do the standard double-take, slapped a ten in his hand, and entered the club.

The music rattled my teeth and the lighting was a do-it-yourself epilepsy kit. Young women in various states of undress writhed on stages, molesting customers, or wandered about in search of an easy mark.

Knox hunched over the bar. I managed to get to him without getting overly pawed. Sliding onto the stool next to him, I said, "What's going on? You screwed up my date."

He took a long drag from his cigarette and stared at me.

I waited.

He stared some more.

I felt the urge to burst into tears and confess something, but I kept it together somehow.

"If you wanted to hang out and stare at strippers, all you had to do was ask…"

"Where were you Saturday night, between eight and midnight?" he said.

"Home. Why?"

"Anyone around to back you up on that?" he said.

"No."

He nodded, blew smoke from his nose, and flagged down the bartender. He ordered a six dollar beer and an eight dollar shot of whisky.

"Asked around about you," he said, lifting the shot, "and it seems you're some sort of kung fu expert."

He took the shot; his eyes never left mine. He didn't flinch at the bite of the liquor.

"I wouldn't say I'm an expert."

"Modesty? From you?"

"I know. Weird, huh?" I said.

He smirked and drank some beer. Knox lit a new cigarette from his old one and said, "We have a problem."

"We do?"

"Oh yeah."

"As in, you and I?"

"That's right."

"Tell me about it. Maybe I can help." I said.

Knox stamped the cigarette out on the bar and turned to face me.

"I have this dead hooker, see? She was killed by some obscure-ass Chinese kung fu technique… one that you knew about, no less. I have a dead madam. Somebody taped her to a chair and injected air into her veins… again, you knew...

"Now, I like you, Lee. I do. But put yourself in my shoes for a second… It's all pretty fucking fishy, right?"

"So, wait… You're trying to say that I did it?"

"No, I'm asking you – if you were in my position, what would you think?"

I waved to the bartender and ordered a beer. When she left, I said, "I'm not the only martial artist in town, y'know."

Knox closed his eyes, rubbed the bridge of his nose wearily, and said, "Last night a kid was taken to the E.R. at Barnes. Broken hand, broken jaw, lost a bunch of teeth. His friends gave a description."

"He had a knife. What was I supposed to do?"

"What did Mei Ling have?"

I sneered at him. "Oh, screw you. If I did it, why the hell would I offer to help you out?"

"To throw off the scent maybe?" he said.

The bartender returned with my beer.

"What scent? You'd be out looking for some throat-crushing hooker-killer and you wouldn't know dick about dick if not for my help. *I* did it? Way to break that case wide open, Detective. Good work."

We both drank. A lot.

And then, the awkward, techno music-filled silence.

"Shit," Knox said finally, "I guess that was pretty fucking flimsy. Sorry, Lee."

I shook my head and frowned. "You got one thing right."

"What's that?"

"I'll tell you later." I said, getting up.

"Where you going?" he asked.

"I'll tell you later."

Sure, I'd pissed him off, but what can I say?

The bastard had screwed up my date.

12

I spent half of the next morning on the phone. First, I called Tracy to apologize and explain. She hinted that lunch in Forest Park would make us even.

I told her that sounded nice.

I have never told anyone that anything sounded nice.

The other phone calls didn't fill me with glee, butterflies, or mild nausea. They also weren't particularly helpful, but at least nothing else sounded 'nice.'

Knox was right, but his point was so obvious I wasn't going to admit to him that I hadn't already thought of it: if the killer knows a rare martial art, a super genius detective would, y'know, check out all the places where one might obtain that type of hard to find knowledge. Out of all the schools I called, only one would accept visitors. The others claimed to be closed-door systems, strictly invitation only. I'd deal with them later. I glanced at my appointment book; I had five appointments that afternoon. I scheduled my visit for immediately after lunch.

Hopefully Tracy was as adventurous as I believed her to be.

I met her by the St. Louis Art Museum, on the huge, sloping hill creatively known to locals as… Art Hill. She wore a black tank top, shorts, and tennis shoes. It was the most casual I'd ever seen her. Her hair was tied up in a loose ponytail, and wisps of blue-black flitted around her face with the breeze.

She didn't wear makeup. She didn't need to.

I spread a blanket and we sat overlooking the Grand Basin. Below us, joggers jogged, children played, and executives played hooky. Tracy brought sandwiches from a place across the street from her apartment.

We talked and ate and laughed.

My cheeks actually started to hurt from smiling.

When the food was gone, she looked up at me and smiled shyly before sliding closer on the blanket and lying against me.

I'll admit it, I froze.

I choked.

I damn near soiled myself.

Some people say that dating…or whatever this was… is like riding a bicycle.

Some people are frigging idiots.

She nestled her head into the crook of my arm and closed her eyes with a contented sigh. Looking down, her face dappled with the late summer sunlight, I couldn't breathe. Because I had never seen anything as beautiful as that girl in that moment. And the feel of her in my arms? And the fact that she smelled the way that angels smell, in the best dreams you've ever had?

What else could I do?

Of course I kissed her.

I kissed her until there was no air left in my lungs, and my lips burned and buzzed in protest. I touched her face and studied her while we caught our breath. And when I leaned down to kiss her again the corners of her lips lifted in the slightest of smiles, as if to say, "Yes. Again. *Please.*"

13

We arrived at the Synergy of Heaven studio with two minutes to spare. In truth, I'd nearly forgotten all about the whole thing. As they say, time flies…

The school was located in a big, upscale storefront, with great plate glass windows in the front. A massive Yin and Yang symbol adorned the window, along with some Chinese characters. I scanned the characters, but they didn't seem to make any sense. The characters for 'harmony', 'chaos' and 'peace' were positioned inexplicably next to the characters for 'snow pea', 'pork' and 'fist'.

I opened the door for Tracy and followed her inside.

I did not stare at her ass when she went in.

Much.

I'm a gentleman, after all.

The school looked as if an episode of Kung Fu had exploded in an aerobics studio. Plaster Fu dog statues guarded every doorway. All the walls were decorated in red and gold. A massive stick of incredibly shitty incense burned in front of a tacky plastic altar. A tape of Chinese lute music played over the speakers. A few beginners were on the mat; I think they were trying to practice Pushing Hands, but I couldn't be sure. They may have been performing a dramatization of young girls slap-fighting over who the cutest Backstreet Boy was, I don't know.

An overweight American guy walked out of the back room and headed straight for us. He looked to be about forty-five, with long, braided salt and pepper hair, a goatee, and serious eyes. He wore a black and white silk kung fu uniform and an air of superiority that stunk up the place worse than the shitty incense or his blue light special aftershave.

We shook hands, and he introduced himself as *Sifu* Mort Green. We introduced ourselves. Sifu Mort immediately took a liking to Tracy. He moved as if to kiss her hand, but she managed to pull away in time.

I liked her more and more.

Mort didn't seem to notice. He just turned to me and said, "So, y'all are interested in Tai Chi?"

I nodded. Tracy, I think, was still in shock over the attempted hand molestation.

"What most interests you in Tai Chi, Rand? Mind if I call you Rand?"

I smiled feebly and said, "That's fine. Mostly, sir, I was interested in the martial aspect of Tai Chi."

He laughed and said, "Tai Chi is not about *fighting*, Rand. Tai Chi is about harmony. It's about *synergizing*."

"...Synergizing," I said. The word tasted pointless on my tongue. It made me want to ask for an order of the chaos pork or harmony snowpeas that were advertised on the window.

"That's right. For instance, if you were to push my right arm..." he said, raising his arm to indicate where I should push, "...I would *synergize* your energy."

I pushed his arm lightly. Every muscle in his arm and chest tensed as he turned robotically. I remained attached to him and didn't feel the least bit synergized, but he said, "Well, you get the idea."

A playful gleam sparkled in his eye as he said, "Now you try!"

He shoved.

Hard.

I turned, dissipating his energy... *synergizing* it, if you will. I expected him to at least know how to fall correctly, but his face skipped across the wooden floor like a pebble across a placid pool.

Tracy, the dear, immediately tried to help him up. Mort managed it on his own, though, and mopped his sleeve across his face; it came away bloody. I expected anger from him, but he merely extended his right fist, covered it with his open left hand in the traditional martial salute, and bowed.

"Forgive my arrogance, sir," he said.

I could feel Tracy staring at me, and I felt that old familiar heat in my cheeks.

"Listen... are you the only instructor here?" I said.

"Yes, *Sifu*."

I sighed. "I'm not your master. Is there anybody else in town that you know of, any other teachers, maybe?"

"Cheng Xing is the best, I'm told."

"Yeah, and available through invitation only." I said.

He smiled a pink-toothed smile and said, "Perhaps I can assist. A letter of introduction from me may get you in."

I didn't have anything better going for me, so I waited while he scribbled out a brief letter. He stamped a red ink seal on it and handed it to me.

Mort grinned again and said, "I do know that Sifu Cheng often takes his students to Millar Park for practice. I have gone there to practice sometimes, and his students often gather to watch my form."

Yeah, I bet they do. Wide-eyed with disbelief.

I thanked him for the letter, though, and Tracy and I went out to her car.

I opened the letter and read it. The red seal at the bottom proclaimed 'Happy Choi's meats are best.'

I folded the letter, stuck it in my pocket and looked up to see Mort waving to us from the window. We both smiled and waved, and Tracy quickly drove away.

At the next stop light, Tracy kept staring at me until I said, "What?"

"You… That was amazing."

"No," I said, "amazing is not the word. Sad. Sad would be the word for that."

14

We went back to the park for my car. As much as I hated to leave the magical, candy-colored, teenage wasteland of giddy lust that was my time with Tracy, I had to get back to work. On the drive back to the shop, I turned up the radio really loud and sang badly to whatever was on. I think it was Chicago. The Peter Cetera incarnation. It may even have been "You're the Inspiration."

Clearly, I have neither shame nor musical taste.

The afternoon's clients provided a nice break from reality. Things like asthma and irritable bowel syndrome I could deal with. Hell, even the police stuff wasn't too bad, now that I had a plan. Never mind that my plan was basically to poke around where I didn't belong until somebody poked back. It was something, at least.

As far as Tracy, well, I was at a bit of a loss. I couldn't stick a needle in her, or kick her ass, and really, those are my only comfort zones. I didn't know what to do with anybody who could, at any point, make me bust out in that "Power of Love" song from Karate Kid II.

So I focused on healing.

And did my best not to fixate too much on my dinner with her at eight.

At my place.

Gulp.

The minute Mrs. Sanchez, my last pincushion of the day, was out the door, I ran up the stairs and surveyed the damage: Dishes in the sink, dirty laundry on the floor, and a general unpleasant funk about the place. The place looked like a combination between the average bachelor pad and a Turkish prison cell.

I rummaged through a kitchen drawer for some incense and came up with a single shriveled stick of Nag Champa.

Good enough.

I opened the windows, lit the incense, and got to work straightening the place up.

Amazing how much mess you can cram into a place in just six months.

With the dishes washed, the laundry done, and the cardboard boxes shoved away into a back closet, the place started looking halfway presentable. Didn't smell too bad, either.

I took a quick shower, shaved, and dragged a brush through my hair. My closet was a disorganized mess, but I grabbed a pair of black jeans and a black t-shirt.

Feeling pretty good about things, I checked the time. Everything was set, and it was only quarter till eight.

I was a master of the universe.

Then it hit me…

'Dinner' meant that I was supposed to provide some sort of food, usually of the cooked variety.

Shit.

I ran to the cupboards and scrambled to find something remotely edible.

And the doorbell rang.

I spat out as many curses as my deflated lungs would allow and went to answer it.

I stopped in front of the door, ran my fingers through my hair, wiped the sudden abundance of sweat from my face, and cleared my throat. Then I opened the door.

"Hi." she said with a slight wave, her eyes downcast shyly.

"Er…hi." I said, because I'm smooth like that.

After an awkward minute, I moved my stupid, gawking ass out of the way so she could come in. She wore a black and violet dress that accentuated curves I never knew she had, and that was impressive since I liked to think that I was becoming something of a scholar when it came to her curves. Her jet black hair was swept up and secured with long, deadly looking pins; I made a mental note to keep my hands to myself. I also noted her big, dark eyes, her pale, fine neck, those ever-lovely legs, and her long and delicate fingers.

I cleared my throat again and offered her a drink.

She asked if I had beer. I didn't let on that beer was about the only thing I had.

I took two bottles from the fridge, popped the tops, and explained how I'd completely spaced dinner. While I fumbled the words, she watched with an amused, lopsided grin and finally said, "That's okay. We could order in."

There was something predatory in her eyes that said I wasn't getting off the hook this time. That was okay by me. While I was on the phone, she scanned my bookshelves and ended up at the CD rack.

"...Huh..."

"What?" I said.

"What what?" she said, wide-eyed.

"You made a disappointed 'huh' sound." I said, grinning.

"No, I didn't."

I nodded. "Sure did."

She blushed slightly and said, "It's just...you have really weird taste in music."

"I do?"

She raised an eyebrow and said, "Um, yeah? You have a royal crap-ton of, like, Chinese CDS and then...it's... I mean, classic rock, anyone?"

"What's wrong with that?" I said.

She poked me in the stomach and said, "Live in the now, man! Don't be an old geezer!"

"I told you. I'm older than I look."

She stuck the tip of her tongue out at me and said, "You're not *that* old."

I grinned. "Okay. How old do you *think* I am?"

"Unh-uh. I'm not playing that game," she said.

"Why not?" I said.

"Because I'll guess one way or the other too far and insult the shit out of you. Just tell me."

"Does it matter?" I said. I'd wondered that a lot, myself.

"No," she said, laughing, "Why, what are you....thirty?"

"I'm forty-two." I said.

She laughed again and said, "Bullshit."

I smiled and shrugged.

"You are not," she said, looking to see if I was indeed pulling her leg.

I kept smiling; I could've whipped out my driver's license, but that would've just been tacky.

Her smile faded a little. "Are you?"

"Does it matter?" I said again. It occurred to me then how unfair this was. I should've told her immediately, before any feelings had developed. Of course, I couldn't speak for her, but my feelings developed the day she walked into my shop with her friend. Maybe I should just start shouting out, "I'm forty-two," to everybody who came into the shop. That'd fix 'em.

She stared at me, searching. I was certain, for a moment, that she was going to leave. Instead, she came closer, stood up on her tiptoes, and kissed me. She stopped, stared at me some more, and kissed me again, deeper. Laying her head on my chest, she said, "This is weird."

"It is?" I said.

"No," she said, "not at all. And that makes it weird."

Later, when the pizza arrived, I took a spare blanket from the hall closet and, at Tracy's suggestion, spread it out on the living room floor so that we could have a 'carpet picnic.'

While I got plates for us and another beer for her, she went down to her car and came back up with a massive, sticker-covered CD case.

"What's that for?" I said.

"Culture." she said, unzipping the case and flipping through the clear plastic pages. After much deliberation, she slipped a disc from its sleeve and put it in the stereo.

"This," she said with a flourish, "is Dead Can Dance. Listen, learn, and love."

She closed her eyes with a smile and made a slow, swaying turn in time with the music, gliding up to me like a ghost, wrapping her arms around my neck and looking up with those eyes; she made my chest ache, though not unpleasantly.

My hands found her waist as if by magic and slid down over her hips. Our lips found each other and reunited happily. I bent my knees enough to clasp the backs of her thighs and lift her to me. She kicked her shoes to the floor and wrapped her bare legs around my waist.

Lightheaded as I was, I'm not sure how we ended up against the wall. I was conscious only of the heat of her mouth, the swell of her breasts as her breathing came in shuddering sighs, the pressure of her hips arching against mine.

And then, at the unlikeliest of times, my brain kicked in.

You barely know this girl, it said.

Technically, this was true.

You're practically old enough to be her father, it said.

She doesn't seem to mind, I retorted, and besides, you're only as old as you feel, right?

My brain, ever the smart-ass, said, S*o what are you, then, huh? Ninety?*

What about Miranda? What about Grace?

I mentally told my brain to go right on off and fuck itself.

Luckily, Tracy brought me back to reality before I had to resort to the ole 'I'm rubber and you're glue' defense.

She whispered, "What about the pizza?"

"It can wait, right?" I said.

"Mm-hm," she muttered. "It can *watch* for all I care."

Take *that*, brain.

15

"Is it lame of me to ask what all of this means?" she asked, later.

Pizza in bed at three a.m. with a beautiful naked woman. Does life get better?

I think not.

I'd figured that *I* knew what all of this meant, but I said, "Hm?"

Because I'm clever like that.

She drew her legs up to her chest and rested her chin on her knees. A half-eaten slice of deep dish cheese with black olives dangled from her hand.

"This. Us. *Is* there even an *us*? I mean, was this just for fun or…or what?"

I took a bite of pizza and wiped my mouth with a paper towel.

She said, "Shit. I'm fucking it up, aren't I? I'm totally doing the girl thing. I'm sorry, forget I said anything. It is what it is." She slumped and said, "I just… I don't want you to think I go around doing this sort of thing…"

I leaned over, cupped her chin in my hand, and lifted her face enough to kiss her.

"I don't." I said. "And it wasn't fun."

Her eyes widened.

I stammered, "No! I mean it *was* fun… but I just meant… that it wasn't *just* fun. I like you. A lot."

"You do?"

She smiled.

"You couldn't tell?" I said.

She shrugged and said, "Lots of guys want to fuck me. That

doesn't necessarily mean they like me."

It wasn't a boast.

"*I* like you." I said. When in doubt, repeat yourself.

"Well, I like you, too." She said, tilting her chin up and blowing me a kiss.

I dropped my slice of pizza into the box, tossed the box to the floor, and slid closer. She bit her lip and raised an eyebrow.

"Again?" she said.

I bit her neck in response.

She wrapped her arms around me, tossed her pizza at the box on the floor, and giggled, "I guess you really *do* like me."

In the early morning hours a pale sunrise filtered in through the window painting her sleeping body in shades of peach and pink, casting shadows that shifted with the slow rise and fall of her breath. I sat and watched her. I wanted a cigarette and a strong drink, but I refrained.

Instead, I thought about the mechanics of 'like,' and about the way it becomes…more than 'like'.

After much careful thought, I decided that what we had, whatever it was, was really something. Two adults pouncing on each other like a couple of teenagers in the middle of the night, with pizza-breath, no less, felt like something more than just casual. But then, what did I know?

I thought about Miranda.

And Grace.

And promptly began to really feel like a piece of shit.

I got up, found an old, stale pack of Marlboros in a desk drawer, and went out on the balcony for a cigarette.

I didn't get much sleep that night.

That, in itself, wasn't anything new.

I wasn't sure about Tracy's sleeping schedule, though, and I didn't want to wake her. I got up around seven, ran through a little practice quickly, and showered. I scribbled a note for Tracy and walked down to the market. On the way, I passed HK Trading and barely restrained the urge to stick out my tongue.

I hit a different market, and realized that I didn't know what she would want for breakfast. We'd gotten a meatless pizza; did that mean she was a vegetarian? I tried to think of our previous meals together, but I'd never paid very much attention to the food.

And here I thought I was observant.

This girl had knocked me for a loop. Boy, had she.

"Lee *Laoshi*, you're smiling… I don't think I've ever seen you smile before."

I looked up at Mrs. Yip, the owner of the store, and felt color rush to my face. *Great*, I thought, *I'm walking around like a dopey kid with a crush.*

I asked Mrs. Yip how she and her family were doing and continued shopping while she ranted about her husband. We'd been through this many times before. I knew just when to throw in an 'uh-huh' or a 'you're kidding'. She never seemed to mind. Part of it was that she just wanted to practice her English.

I half-listened and decided to just get a little of everything and hope for the best.

I took my groceries to the counter and waited for Mrs. Yip to give me a total. She looked at the food and looked up at me. Her eyes looked huge behind her thick glasses. Mrs. Yip was used to me only buying a six pack and a packet of chow mein noodles at any given time. I think she was in shock. As she added up the items, I went to the small flower stand by the front window and picked a couple of nice long-stem pink roses. When I laid them upon the counter Mrs. Yip's eyes lit up.

"Oh… Very good, Lee *Laoshi.* Very, very good! No wonder you smile, eh?"

She winked at me as if we shared a secret and finally told me the total. I handed her the money and she said, "You do know what pink rose mean, right?"

"I'm sorry?" I said.

"All flowers have meaning. Pink rose mean perfect happiness."

"Oh. Well, that's nice." I said, helping her bag the groceries. "Thank you."

Again with the *nice.*

I took my bags and told her to have a nice day. She said, "You too, Lee *Laoshi*, and good luck. It is a horrible thing, to have to be alone."

I stopped and turned. "Yes. It is," I said, and left.

I got back to the apartment, set the groceries on the counter, and went to check on Tracy. The bed was empty. The shower was running. Clothes, sheets, mozzarella cheese, and black olives were strewn across the room. So much for the cleaning.

I went to the kitchen and got to work. I had just finished with the pancakes when I heard the bathroom door open. I took a bowl from the cupboard and cracked six eggs into it. I added milk, some grated cheese, a pinch of cayenne pepper, and a few super-secret ingredients. With a whisk from the drawer, I proceeded to beat the shit out of the mixture. I melted some butter in a pan and poured in the egg mixture. These were the world's best scrambled eggs, and this was the first time

I'd made them in years. If nothing else had impressed her, I knew the eggs would make her swoon.

Assuming that she actually ate eggs…

I would've panicked, but she came up behind me then, slid her arms around my waist, and held me tight. I scooped the finished eggs onto a plate and turned off the stove.

"Hey," I said. "Sleep well?"

"Like the dead," she said. "I hope you don't mind that I helped myself to your shower…"

"Not at all." I said.

"I borrowed a t-shirt too."

I turned around to face her. Her hair was damp and brushed back, tucked behind her ears. The black t-shirt looked huge on her, but it was only long enough to cover the tops of her thighs. It was obvious that the shirt was the only thing she was wearing.

Gulp.

"That's fine. It…looks good on you."

She grinned and said, "Thanks."

I gave her a quick kiss. Anything else would've led places I wasn't sure I had the energy for. At least not until after breakfast.

She said, "Ooh, what are we having?"

"Well, what do you like? I've got pancakes, eggs," my heart skipped a beat, "we can make bacon, sausage, toast… I could make French toast…"

"Oh, gosh, I'll eat anything," she said.

Phew.

"Do you need any help?" she said.

"Um…you could put the bread in the toaster," I said.

She went into the living room and put on some bouncy, punky music. She came back, bebopping to the beat, and started making toast.

While she was occupied, I took a knife from the drawer, cut the thorns from the roses, and laid them on the table, beside her plate.

"Coffee, tea, juice, milk?" I said.

"I'd kill a drifter for some coffee." she said.

I paused. "…Alrighty, then."

I made coffee. I wasn't sure if I was any good at making coffee or not. As far as I'm concerned, the nasty burnt bean water always tasted like shit, so I had no real frame of reference. I only ever drank the stuff when exhaustion loomed.

While making the coffee, I heard her gasp. I turned and saw that she'd found the roses.

A few moments later, she tackled me, and we ended up on the kitchen floor. Luckily, I'd cut out the thorns. It turned out that I *did* have some energy.

And the food wasn't too bad reheated, though if this trend kept up, I was going to need to buy a new microwave. Once we were capable of sitting at the table and keeping our hands to ourselves, Tracy said, "So, do you have to stab anybody today?"

"Are you referring to my clients?" I said, after swallowing a bit of bacon.

"Yeah."

"No. I'm free today."

"Sweet. You wanna hang out?"

I almost choked on a bite of pancake. *Hang out?*

"Um…sure." I said.

"If you don't want to, that's okay," she said, though it clearly wasn't okay.

"No, I do. I'd love to."

She beamed. "Excellent."

"So…" I said, "Do you like the eggs?"

She set her fork down on her plate and leveled her gaze at me. She said, "Randall, I have told you at least five times that they are the best scrambled eggs I've ever had. Do not ask me again."

"Okay," I said sheepishly.

We talked for a bit about what we were going to do while we 'hung out.' She asked if I would take her to the movies.

"Like a real date," she said. "Dinner and a movie. No mysterious phone calls that pull you away… no beating up poor, clueless Tai Chi teachers…"

"Yeah, I've been meaning to explain about that," I said.

"Do you have a computer?" she said.

"Yeah, in the office. Why?"

"Then you can explain while I look up movie times."

I led her back to the office and gave her the short version of the story. Though I meant to make myself sound like some cool, exotic expert, it clearly didn't work.

She sat at the computer desk, started typing, and said, "So why do the cops need *your* help with a murder investigation?"

"Well, I told you… it started out that they needed a translator, but then, with the girl who was killed…"

"What's this?" she said, cutting me off. She held up the crime scene photo of Mei Ling that Knox had given me.

"Oh." I said. "That's her…that's the girl."

"What girl?"

"The one who was killed. We've been trying to find out who she is."

Tracy stared at the picture for a long time. "She's dead?" she said.

"Yeah, and she had no identification. The cops ran her prints and couldn't come up with anything. The detective I told you about gave me that photo. I was going to take it around the neighborhood, see if anybody knew her."

Tracy looked up at me, eyes wide, and said, "I know her."

16

Nothing cool or funny or clever to say came to mind, so I stuck with the time-honored, "...What?"

She looked down at the picture again and said, "Yeah. I'm sure of it. It's her."

"You know her?"

"Well, not *know* know, but she came to the club like a week ago. Dressed to the nines, y'know? I'm not the best with faces, but she bought a virgin Piña Colada, an eight dollar drink, with a hundred dollar bill and told me to keep the change... I'd remember anybody that treated me that well."

"You're sure she's the girl in the picture?" I said.

She held it up and said, "Look at her, she's gorgeous. More so in person. And breathing. And not blue."

I picked up the phone and dialed Knox's cell. When he answered, I said, "I think we've got something on your girl."

I asked Tracy for the name and address of the club and relayed it to him, saying we'd meet him there in twenty minutes. I hung up, grabbed Tracy, and kissed her hard on the lips.

On the way to the club, Tracy asked how Mei Ling was killed.

I told her.

"That's why we went to that idiot's school," I said. "Whoever murdered Mei Ling, he knows what he's doing."

"How do you know?" Tracy said.

"Not just anybody can do that... it's not about muscular strength. This guy is adept at one of the internal styles, maybe even Tai Chi Chuan."

"You just lost me." Tracy said.

"In Chinese martial arts," I said, "there are literally thousands of different styles, but they can be divided into two main types – internal and external. External is the designation given to styles like Shaolin, Wing Chun… the stuff an untrained person might generically call 'Kung Fu' or 'Karate'. External styles, to a great degree, rely on outer strength. In a fight, typically the bigger, stronger, faster guy wins.

"Internal styles, on the other hand, cultivate internal energy and whole-body coordination. Tai Chi Chuan is probably the most well-known internal art, but there are others, like Pakua Chuan and Hsing I Chuan. The strikes in internal arts aren't designed to cause surface level damage or even to break bones, necessarily; the kinetic energy is meant to sort of bounce around on the inside, tearing up organs, things like that.

"In Mei Ling's case… what we're talking about is a two hand palm strike to the rib cage. A good external stylist would have no problem breaking ribs or causing organ damage, but the extent of damage to her organs, combined with the relative lack of damage to her body superficially, that's the classic trademark of an internal stylist."

"So you went to the school looking for someone good enough to have killed her."

"Yeah."

"And that dude wasn't it, huh?"

"He could barely stand up on his own without assistance." I said.

"Where are you gonna look next?"

"Well, that's the tricky part. The other teachers that I know of in town won't take outsiders. They teach only to family and to personally chosen students, so it's tough to tell the good guys from the bad guys when they're all basically hiding."

"What kind of bullshit is that?" she said.

I shrugged.

After a minute or so, she said, "What happens if you find the guy?"

"The killer?" I said.

"Yeah," Tracy said, brushing a strand of purple hair from her eyes. "What do you do if you find him?"

"To be honest, I really haven't thought that far ahead."

17

Knox muttered an unsavory word to himself as we watched the security tape. The Outer Limit had cameras over its back door, and, when Mei Ling left, she ran out the back.

We watched it again.

It was her, alright. For all the good that did. Knox swore again; a different word this time, at least.

"You don't seem happy." I said.

"It's just another dead end. I'm glad your little girlfriend spotted her, but this doesn't mean a fucking thing."

"The glass is always half-empty to you, isn't it?" I said. "You know she was here, at least."

"Yeah. Which means exactly dick. She's got no record, we know that already. So we get to see what she was like when she was up and walking around. Whoopee-shit."

"Hey," I said, "every piece of information is one more piece of the puzzle."

"Thank you, Charlie-fucking-Chan," he said.

"You're grumpy." I said. "See if I call you next time I find a witness to one of your damned crimes."

He was not amused.

After Knox took down all of Tracy's information, we left.

When we were outside, I said, "Do you have a pen?"

She checked her purse and found one.

I didn't have a piece of paper, so I scribbled a few notes to myself on the skin of my inner forearm. Just in case.

I looked up from my arm to see Tracy watching me curiously.

"Still want to catch that movie?" I said.

Tracy reminded me that she was still wearing an old pair of my practice pants, cinched and held with safety pins, and my trusty black t-shirt. She asked if we could swing by her place first so she could change.

She lived in a loft in Soulard, ten or fifteen minutes from the club. I parked the car, and we hiked up the four flights of stairs to her apartment. Neither of us huffed or puffed, probably due to all the cardiovascular exercise we'd gotten lately.

She'd painted the huge windows with a translucent paint to mimic stained glass. One scene depicted a group of happy skeletons dancing in a cemetery. Another showed impossibly thin vampires in capes and party masks at some sort of ball. Still another showed a pumpkin patch in a full moon, but all the pumpkins were leering jack-o-lanterns.

She must've seen me staring. She said, "I did those for Halloween a couple years ago, but they turned out so good I decided to keep them."

"They're pretty amazing," I said.

"Thanks," she said.

She flitted off to the bedroom to change, and told me to feel free to look around.

Framed prints of Edward Gorey's Alphabet hung here and there, in no discernible order, along with other prints by Gahan Wilson and Charles Addams.

She had more CD's than most music stores I've been to, and they filled numerous racks throughout the apartment and spilled over onto the nearest available flat surfaces. The dining table and chairs stood out, painted as they were to match the night sky. The stars, arranged into constellations, were done in glow in the dark paint.

I heard a rasping snuffle noise and turned to see a horribly ugly creature staring at me.

"Jesus Christ," I said.

The thing was perched atop a cinder-block-and-two-by-four bookshelf like a wrinkly miniature gargoyle and glared down at me with yellow eyes. Tracy appeared at my side, wearing a black tank top and baggy black cargo pants. I felt a sorrowful twinge that those legs were covered, but I'd get over it.

Eventually.

"It's alright, baby. He's a friend. C'mon," she said, patting her chest. The horrific greyish thing jumped down onto her shoulder and situated itself. It never stopped glaring at me.

"Will you be offended if I ask you what the hell that thing is?" I said.

She gave a playful glare and said, "Randall, this is Titus Andronicus, Tito for short. Tito, baby, forgive Randall, for he knows not what he says."

She kissed the thing on its nose.

Ew.

"Okay, but what *is* it?" I asked.

"Randall! You're going to hurt his feelings. Tito is a cat, silly." I could tell that on some level she was enjoying this.

"Cats are hairy. Where is Tito's hair?" I said.

"He's a sphynx. They're a hairless breed."

"Of course they are." I said.

I normally had no problem with cats, but this thing looked like Satan.

Tracy cocked her head, narrowed her eyes, and said with a grin, "If you want to spend any time with me, you're going to have to get along with Tito… he's my schmoopikens."

"Isn't he just everybody's?" I said, reaching out to pet him.

Tito inclined his head slightly, as if he had deemed me worthy to touch him. I scratched the top of his head lightly; he felt like a warm, dry peach.

Funky.

18

We went to a local pub for dinner. Burgers and beer – maybe not the most romantic of meals, but it was alright. Given our track record with food, maybe romantic wasn't what we needed.

"So, when we last left off, I believe young Randall was learning how to stand around for hours? What happened next?"

"A bunch of stuff that eventually brought us together here. I believe we're supposed to… what was your phrase? 'Live in the now?' So what difference does it make?" I said.

"It makes a difference because we don't really know each other."

"I think we know plenty."

"Ahem, 'every piece of information is another piece of the puzzle'. Sound familiar?"

"What kind of asshole talks like that?" I said, biting into a fry.

"C'mon, man, talk!"

I took a swig of beer and said, "Alright. So the standing practice provides a foundation. When you stand in a posture, over and over, after a while your body learns to relax into it. Once Master Wu was confident that I could stand, he taught me to move. From each standing posture to the next. *Tai Chi Chuan.*"

"Like the guy at the school we visited." she said.

"No, nothing at all like that guy." I said.

"But still, it's like the stuff the old people practice in the park, right?"

"There are a lot of teachers that teach a health exercise they call Tai Chi, but real Tai Chi Chuan is more than a health exercise, it is, first and foremost, a martial art. One of the translations for Tai Chi Chuan is

'Supreme Ultimate Boxing.'"

"The inside kind," she said.

"Internal, yes." I said. "Wu had me practicing the form, the movements all strung together, for four to six hours a day."

"Damn."

I shrugged. "It was fun compared to just standing. After a few months, he started to teach me about the energetic anatomy of the body. The meridians and acupuncture points, the ways that energy moves through the body, that sort of thing, as they related to my practice.

"When I was fifteen, my father died of a heart attack. I didn't really have anywhere to go, so Master Wu invited me to stay with him. From that point on, every moment was a training of some sort. Mornings belonged to Tai Chi Chuan, afternoons were for acupuncture and evenings meant studying Taoist texts and herbalism.

"When I was twenty-three, I was allowed to take over a portion of my teacher's case load. The simple ones, mostly. When I was twenty-five, he told me he had nothing more to teach me. So I moved to the states, opened a practice, and that's that."

I finished my beer and went back to my burger.

Tracy was watching me.

"What?" I said.

"You know what."

"Do we really have to talk about this?" I said. "What about you? Tell me about yourself."

"I'm an open book. I have no secrets." she said. "You, however, are leaving out quite a big chunk of your life. If you don't want to tell me, that's alright, but just say so. Don't insult my intelligence."

She put up a good front, but I could tell that I'd hurt her feelings. And I didn't want to keep things from her. So I put my food down, ordered another beer when the waiter came by, and I told her.

I told her about moving to Seattle and opening a practice, about teaching Tai Chi in the park there, and about meeting and falling in love with one of my students, a Chinese-American woman named Miranda Chan. I told her how, after a long courtship, I married Miranda on a cool September day, and how our daughter, Grace, was born eight years later, two days after our anniversary.

Tracy looked surprised, but she kept listening, so I continued. I wanted a drink, something stronger, or a diversion: a fire alarm, maybe, or a tornado, but nothing came. So I dug my fingers into that old wound and found it still fresh, still ripe with infection, and the words spilled out on their own. I listened passively and studied her eyes for that sickening pity that so many people exhibit, but, in her, there was none. Only concern.

All she said was, "What happened?"

"We were bad parents," I said.

And it was true. Neither of us knew how to relate to the new, innocent, utterly helpless life we'd brought into the world. We loved her, of course, but that's not the point. I loved the goldfish that I had as a kid, the one I starved by forgetting to feed it.

No, we loved her more than anything, and we wanted to do what was best for her. We tried. I read all the books; I bought all the recommended toys and books and mobiles and cds. Miranda nursed, even though it hurt her every time she did it. And Grace grew, in spite of her inept parents.

She was really something.

But my practice was taking off so I was almost never home. I tucked her in at night. That was our time together. A story, a kiss, and that was that: my obligation fulfilled for one more day. I had other things, more important things, to worry about.

And Miranda, she would start mixing a little vodka in with her iced tea around noon, mourning her lost career, her lost life, and end up napping the afternoon away while Grace was at daycare.

When it happened, Grace was four. Miranda "had a headache," and I was at the office. I was supposed to take her to the zoo that day, just the two of us, but I forgot and booked patients by mistake. So Grace played outside, alone, because her parents couldn't be bothered with her.

She'd been gone for hours before either of us even knew. The police did their best, but none of the neighbors saw anything. She could've runaway, and neither Miranda nor I would've blamed her.

A week later a patrolman found something, wrapped in plastic sheeting and wedged between some rocks, down by the harbor. They called me, and I had to identify her body.

The police caught him a few days later. Steven Allan Hayes. A registered sex offender. A monster. He was afraid of being caught again, of going to prison. He said that's why he did what he did.

But he was caught, and he did go to prison. He was there for a week before another inmate beat him to death. After everything he did, the time he spent planning, the execution of his actions, the destruction of something so pure and innocent; it only took a fist hammering his temple, and he was dead in minutes.

He got off so easy.

Tracy had started to cry, and I hated to see it. I hated to have caused it.

But she had to understand this: that on that day in June, Hayes didn't just take Grace's life. Miranda and I went to counseling, but we couldn't ever forgive each other; we couldn't forgive ourselves.

"So I left," I said. And it really had been that simple. I packed my things as Miranda watched. I left her some money. We never said goodbye. I drove, stopping wherever I ended up at night, sleeping in cars or motels, and, each morning, driving again. When I ended up in St. Louis, I hadn't planned to stay. It was to be just another stopping point, until I woke up one morning realizing that I was tired of trying to escape myself. It hadn't worked anyway.

That's why I stayed. And even though I wanted to die, I couldn't even do that right.

So I did the only thing I knew. Found a storefront, opened a practice, and started to live again, moment by moment, hour by hour, and, eventually, day by day.

Tracy had scooted her chair closer to mine; somehow our hands were intertwined.

I wanted to tell her that I would understand if she didn't want to see me anymore, now that she knew the kind of man I really was. I wanted to tell her that she deserved better, that she deserved a real future with someone. I wanted to tell her so many things, but then her arms were around me, holding me, forgiving me, and the only thing I wanted was to be the man she thought I was.

She took me home that night to her apartment, and, in her arms, I pretended to sleep.

19

The next morning, I got an idea. It was so simple, and I don't know why it hadn't occurred to me before.

I hit the east side first, that pervert's oasis in a desert of blight. The surrounding buildings were blasted, abandoned, and overgrown. I spent some time and money going from club to club, drinking nine dollar beers and asking questions. Everyone was helpful, as long as you greased their palms first.

At 'The Sapphire Room', my fifth club of the morning, I met Jade. When I walked in, she was on stage working the pole over like it owed her money. She was small and petite, but muscled like a cat. Her jet black hair was streaked with scarlet and gold. Even in the dim, reddish light of the club, I knew why she chose her stage name – her eyes were an unnatural pale green. Some of the men in the club were so intimidated by her presence that they didn't even sit at the stage… they just wadded their dollar bills into balls and threw them at the stage.

After her set, she gathered her cash from the stage and came down to the bar. She got an ice water from the bartender and leaned in close to me. She smelled like Jasmine.

"Interested in a private dance?" she said.

"Sure." I said.

She smiled, took my hand, and led me to the back of the club. The hallway was lined with doors. The floor was sticky. She opened one of the doors and closed it again quickly; I saw a brief flash of flesh writhing in the darkness.

"Whoops," she said with a singsong quality, "occupado."

We went to another booth, and she gestured for me to enter. It was small, maybe five by five, with black walls and floor and a single metal chair. She closed the door behind her and slid the cheap lock into place. The DJ introduced a Prince song and Jade started to move to the music.

"Gotta pay before you play, baby." she said, extending her open palm.

"How much for the dance?" I said.

"For you, twenty. Or thirty-five for two songs."

I gave her a fifty dollar bill and said, "I'm not actually interested in a dance."

She pocketed the money, but said, "Dancing's all you'll get from me, baby. I ain't a ho."

"I just want to talk."

She slid up next to me and ran her knee up my thigh.

"*Dirty* talk?"

"No. Information. That's all."

She narrowed her eyes and said, "'bout what?"

"I want to know about the massage place across the street."

"Taste of Asia?" she laughed. "Yeah, you get more than talking or dancing for fifty bucks there…"

"What else do you know about it?"

She shrugged. "Used to work there, back when it was Siamese Ally's. Awhile after, ah, ownership changed… I quit."

"Why?"

"Ally was cool. She let the girls do their own thing. You give a guy a massage…if he's cute or you like him, whatever, you maybe give him a little extra. Y'know, only if you want to. No big thing. When it turned into Taste of Asia, well, it was expected. The bosses wanted freebies, too."

I frowned. "Madame Chong?"

She giggled. "That old bat was just a washed up ho. She kept the girls in line. The bosses came in every now and then to check stuff out, make sure things were going how they wanted it. They always came with the new girls, too. Wanted first pick, I guess."

"So you just…quit?" I said.

"Yeah. One of the guys asked me to do some really nasty shit, so I walked. Since they bring in their own girls, they didn't care if I stayed or went. I was old news, so to speak. Plus they're just used to getting their own way… so many of the newbies will do anything, thinking they can fuck their way into the family or something…" she stopped and blushed.

I had a strange feeling that she wasn't one to blush easily. She stood up and smoothed her hands down the front of her short skirt.

"Okay. Song's over. Thanks." she said, moving to unlock the door.

"What family?" I said.

"Nobody. I didn't say nothin'."

"Wu-Jing? The Huang-Feng clan? Eight Tigers..?"

Her eyes widened and she slapped her hand across my mouth. "Quiet!"

"You didn't want to work for the Eight Tigers, so you quit."

She hissed, "Shut up, goddammit. Word gets back that you're asking around about them, we're both fucked."

"Did you know Mei Ling?" I said.

"No. I don't know who you're talking about. I don't know anything." She squirmed to get away, but I held her by the shoulders and kept her still.

"The dead girl. I'm sure everybody's been talking about it." I said. She looked away, so I asked her again. "Did you know her?"

She looked at the floor. "No. But I knew of her." she was whispering now, her voice shaky. "She came in a couple weeks ago, with a batch of newbies. I saw her a few times…always seemed real shy."

I had a thought. Such an uncommon occurrence, and yet here it was, twice in one day. It shocked me.

"The bosses keep a close eye on the girls, right?"

She nodded.

"Do they set up the girls with places to stay?" I asked.

She nodded hesitantly.

Cha-Ching.

20

I met Knox in the lot across from the apartment building. The building was a brown, boxy brick structure built during that phase in the 70's when all the buildings were made to look ultra "modern." Much like the women it housed, it looked far older than it truly was. Various graffiti adorned the walls, and litter and weeds collected along the ground.

"No point in putting up whores in a palace, right?" Knox muttered, pausing to light a cigarette. Then, "You realize we're not gonna find shit here, right?"

"Why do you say that, detective?" I said.

"Whoever offed her, you really think he's gonna leave evidence in her fucking apartment? I mean, that's bad guy 101, for chrissake: ransack the apartment."

I shrugged. He was probably right, of course, but neither of us had any better leads. So we crossed the street and went inside.

The hall was dim and smelled like mildew and piss and god knows what else. We had no idea which apartment had belonged to Mei Ling, so we did what any team of high-powered crime-fighters would do.

But after checking and finding that there were no names listed on the mail boxes, only apartment numbers, we went door to door and knocked. Many of the girls wouldn't speak to us, presumably because Knox looks very much like The Man. Once I got him to back off and let me do the talking (in Mandarin), things started going a little bit smoother. I took Mei Ling's photo from my jacket and started showing it around and before long we were pointed in the right direction.

Toward Apartment 4B.

We trudged up the steps and to her door. It occurred to the detective then that he didn't know how we planned to gain entry. I pointed out a particularly interesting display of urban artwork outside the window at the end of the hall and suggested that he study it closely, for clues.

Then I picked the lock. Ah, sweet youth. You never know what sort of degenerate skills will become handy in life. Hanging with the gangs back in Hong Kong had so far proven a better investment in time than, say, algebra had.

Knox and I both just pretended that Mei Ling had been careless with her locking habits.

The apartment was small and bare, but clean. Knox looked through her bedroom while I stood by. Her closet had a few outfits in it, nothing particularly sleazy, and shoes. Knox knelt and pushed aside a few pairs of expensive-looking shoes; in the back of the closet, wedged into a tight corner, was a black leather case.

He set it on the bed and tried to open the golden clasps. With a sigh, he said, "Too bad her lock carelessness didn't apply to this briefcase..."

I wondered aloud if any clues might be hiding out in the refrigerator. Knox decided to check.

I found a paper clip and used it on the briefcase.

When he came back, he had a small purse. From the kitchen table, he said. He held onto the purse and opened the briefcase.

We both just stared. Any snappy line I might've said was promptly erased by the four-inch deep stacks of twenty dollar bills lining the case.

When we finished staring, Knox carefully unzipped the purse, and emptied it on the bed. There were a few wadded bills, a bit of lint, and a California driver's license for a Mei Ling Zhao from San Francisco.

Age 19.

21

We went to an early dinner, Knox and I, at a steak restaurant just across the river in Illinois. I was not impressed. I'm not a hard-sell, either, but it just honestly wasn't very good. The beer, however, *was* good and made everything else better.

Knox stuffed a bite of sirloin into his mouth and, chewing, said, "'Kay, so what's a nice young girl like our Mei Ling doing here, a thousand miles away from home, in a massage parlor… with a bun in the oven and a suitcase full of cash? Besides getting whacked by some kind of evil Taoist martial arts expert, who ensures that she, and presumably her child, is damned to one or more of the many confusing Chinese hells…"

"Here's something to ponder," I said, "did she bring the cash with her, or did she somehow make the money here?"

He thought about it as he chewed. "Brought it," he grunted.

That was the likely answer, of course, unless she'd stolen it. I offered that up as an option.

"Stolen from who?" he asked, sipping his Bud Lite.

"The more I learn, the more I know that I know nothing." I said.

"You and me both."

A cloud of cigar smoke billowed over my shoulder. I glared at it and tried not to breathe. When it dissipated, I said, "And if she didn't bring it with her, and it's not stolen… how does a nineteen year old girl make that kind of cash?"

Knox grimaced at the pungent smoke and said, "I can tell you how *that* girl could make that kind of cash… blackmail, maybe, or selling inside information about the Eight Tigers…"

"To whom?"

He shrugged.

I rubbed my fingers along my temples and rolled my shoulders to shrug off some of the tension that had settled there. We switched to other topics, things we knew a bit more about. He asked how I got into acupuncture, and I gave him a brief version of the same story I'd told Tracy, minus the bits about my family.

I learned that he had a first name – John – and that he was married to his high school sweetheart, Marta. Aside from that, I didn't learn much more than what I already knew: Knox was alright. When we ran out of things to say and cigar smoke to breathe, I picked up the tab and we split.

It was quarter to seven. He wanted to poke at a few leads before heading home, and I had my own things to do. Before he left, John Knox said, "Just so you know, I appreciate everything you've done... but, uh, the department wouldn't. Keep your nose clean, eh?"

I told him I'd try.

22

I went home in the morning and checked my appointments for the week. It didn't take long to call and cancel them all. Afterwards, I made my travel arrangements. My flight left at eleven thirty-five p.m. I went upstairs and threw some clothes into a duffle bag. The ease and speed with which I packed left me sad. Too few entanglements, too little to anchor to. On the other hand, the ease and speed with which I'd attached myself to Tracy was troubling, too. Was I really so desperate for human contact? Or was *she* the x-factor? Was it something inherent in who she was that was so irreplaceable to me?

All I knew was that when I was with her, I wasn't wishing I was anywhere else. I didn't wish it was tomorrow, or next week, or next month; I wasn't pissing away the moments of my life.

I was alive, and happy. Actually happy.

And yet, here I was… sitting with a stuffed gym bag, planning to go away. And for what?

I didn't know what I thought I'd find, I just knew I had to look.

I showed up at the club at nine-thirty. I hadn't really looked around the place before, but The Outer Limit sort of reminded me of Tracy's place. Not in décor, maybe, but in its feel. It was a weird amalgam of brick, hardwood, velvet, and neon. Panels of stained glass hung over the bar and the bottles of liquor were illuminated from beneath by an eerie green light.

I saw Tracy the minute I walked in. She was serving a purple foo-foo drink to a preppie-looking kid who had the honor of bearing the shittiest looking $200 haircut I'd ever seen.

Tracy, of course, was luminous.

I could tell just by body language that the kid was laying it on thick with her. She watched him with a kind of detached amusement and smiled. I headed over and leaned on the bar.

Her eyes lit up.

"Hi there. What can I get you?" she said, clearly in professional mode.

"A beer," I said, "and maybe your phone number?"

"Comin' right up, *sir.*"

She grabbed a Heineken from the cooler and set it down. Then she took a pen and scribbled her home and cell phone numbers on a cocktail napkin. This was helpful, considering we'd exchanged bodily fluids but not contact information.

"Son of a bitch." the kid next to me said.

I turned and grinned. The preppie kid sneered.

Tracy leaned over the bar and said, "I know I'm not supposed to do this, but I can't resist," before kissing me.

The kid got up and walked off, cursing.

If Tracy noticed, it didn't show.

She said, "This is a nice surprise. I know it sounds really dumb and girly, but I've missed you."

"Doesn't sound dumb at all." I said.

She grinned and said, "Did you miss me?"

I nodded.

"Say the words then, tough guy."

I smiled and said, "I missed you. Very much."

"Yay! That makes me happy."

I drank some beer and said, "Unfortunately, I have another surprise that's maybe not so happy."

Her smile faded. "Is everything alright?"

"Yeah. It's just…well, something came up, and I'm going to be out of town for a few days."

She cocked her head and said, "Oh."

"I'll be back as soon as possible."

She nodded and said, "When do you leave?"

"In about an hour."

She looked away from me. When she finally spoke, she said, "You can call me… if you want to. Only if you want to, though."

I held up the napkin and said, "I will."

"I didn't mean to push. The other night, I mean."

"You didn't. You deserved to know."

"Okay." She said. She didn't look like she believed me. "Take care of yourself, alright?"

"You too." I said.

She checked to make sure her boss wasn't around, and gave me another short kiss goodbye.

I got to the airport, bought a cheesy-looking kung fu magazine from the gift shop, and picked up my boarding pass. I was reading an article about an obscure Wu Tang sword routine when a voice over the loudspeaker called out, "Flight 2987 – non-stop to San Francisco – is now boarding at gate 8A."

It was time to go.

23

With the time change, I arrived at San Francisco International airport at 12:55 a.m. I picked up my rental car - a Yugo of all things - and set out for the hotel.

I found myself at the Hilton at 2:30 in the morning.

I'm not too great with directions.

I stumbled into my room, admired its elegance for all of ten seconds, and passed out. It was ten when I cracked open one blurry eye to look at the clock. The room *was* nice. It took me a couple minutes to find the bathroom. I took a long hot shower and began to start to sort of feel human. I wasn't feeling up to practicing the full form, so I did some Silk Reeling exercises, a set of slow, full-body movements used to develop the sort of spiraling energies used in Tai Chi Chuan. They were enough to loosen up the muscles and get some blood flowing.

The first bit of detective work on the agenda was finding breakfast, but I wanted to call Tracy. She answered on the third ring with a throaty hello.

"Hi," I said. "I didn't mean to wake you…I forgot about the time difference."

Her voice brightened. "Hey!" she said, "You got in okay?"

"Yeah."

"I'm such a 'tard. I realized after you left that I don't even know where you are."

Uh-oh. This had to come up sooner or later.

"…San Francisco," I said.

After a moment, she said, "Randall, what are you doing in San Francisco?"

"Well," I said, "there are some really great herb shops in Chinatown, not to mention the amount of…"

"You're still poking around about that dead girl, aren't you?"

Busted.

"…Um…Yeah."

"Isn't that something for the police to be doing?"

"Nobody besides me and Knox gives a shit, Tracy."

"What if you get in trouble or something?"

"I'm not going to get in trouble. I'm just going to see what I can find out, nothing crazy. And I really am going to stop off at some of those herb shops…see if I can find some really potent Horny Goat Weed for when I get back to you."

She giggled. "I'll stock up on the Gatorade, then."

"Buy stock."

"Alright. Keep me posted on whatever you find out, and be careful," she said with a yawn.

"I will. Get some sleep."

"'Kay. Bye."

"Bye."

I planned to drive around for a bit looking for some decent local food, but the traffic and my lack of direction-sense got on my nerves, and I ended up giving in to my raw hunger.

Denny's.

One bad case of heartburn later, I checked my arm - just below the faded notes I'd written outside of Tracy's club, I'd copied Mei Ling's address from her license - and decided to just walk to her apartment. She'd lived a couple miles away in the midst of Ashbury Heights. I found the place and walked up to the front door. She'd lived on the ground floor of a building that was once a large house, but had been cut into three moderate sized apartments.

I knocked on the door, just in case. No one answered.

I checked the mailbox. Massive stacks of junk mail.

I walked around the building.

Bingo.

Mei Ling had a back porch.

And a back door.

It didn't look like anyone was around, so I took a credit card from my wallet and jimmied the door in under a minute.

I went inside and closed the door quickly. The place looked like any other young woman's apartment. Fruit (now rotting) and diet soda in the fridge. About a hundred pairs of shoes in the closet. Surprisingly upscale wardrobe.

Family photos in frames throughout the place. Frowny-faced mother and a strict-looking father. Mei Ling, standing in front of them, smiling demurely.

Another one showed her arm in arm with a guy. They were on a beach. They looked happy. I took it and a few others and stuck them in my pocket.

I looked around some more, but the only thing that jumped out at me was that the place looked as if she could come home at any moment. Her closet was full. She'd never put a stop on her mail. My chest ached a little. It might have been breakfast, but I didn't think so.

I was pondering the situation when I went to the back door and found it blocked by a very large, very muscular Chinese man in an expensive suit.

Well, poop.

24

He wasn't a cop; I knew that much for certain. This was a good thing. It meant that I could hurt him if necessary.

"Can I help you?" I said, summoning as much righteous indignation as I could manage, considering I was clearly breaking and entering.

The voice that came out of the giant, muscled human wall did not fit his appearance – polite, refined, with a strong British accent. "You are trespassing on Miss Zhao's property."

"I'm a friend of Mei Ling's." I said.

He shook his head. "I'm afraid not, sir. Please come with me."

"Where to?" I asked.

He stepped aside slightly and gestured to a black Jaguar parked in the rear alley. A big part of my brain was arguing over whether to fight or flee, but a calm little voice in my head suggested just going with him. After all, it's not like I'd learned much of anything useful so far.

On the other hand, Oddjob here could just be taking me out to a landfill to whack me.

Ah well, what the hell.

I let him escort me to the car. He gently helped me into the back seat and slid in beside me. The man in the driver's seat, the only other occupant in the car, was dark-skinned and dressed in an immaculate, dark violet silk suit. His braided hair hung loose around his shoulders. He wore black sunglasses that obscured his eyes.

"He come peacefully, then?" the driver said. His accent sounded almost Spanish.

"Yes." Oddjob said.

The driver smiled, showing brilliant canines, and said, "Drat."

25

We drove.

My hosts were not very talkative. Any question I asked was ignored, so I decided to save my breath. I was starting to wonder how long it was going to take the authorities to find my corpse when we pulled into an underground parking garage.

I didn't know where in the city we were, but the area, above ground at least, was very upscale. Before we got out of the car, the driver turned to me and said, "You going to behave?"

I nodded.

He nodded.

We understood each other.

We took an elevator up, and they escorted me discreetly through the opulent lobby to another private elevator in a back hallway. The driver pulled a key card from his pocket and slid it into a slot in the elevator's console. We rode this elevator all the way to the top - the thirty-first floor, the penthouse.

It was beyond belief. Greenish-black marble floors, polished teak walls, hidden, ambient lighting, and a *waterfall.* A freaking waterfall.

And that was just the entryway.

They led me to a large, high-ceilinged studio. The first thing I noticed was the couch.

To be honest, the *very* first thing I noticed was the nude redhead *on* the couch.

A young Chinese man stood at an easel, painting her.

I didn't care much for his color choices.

When we entered the room, neither the artist nor the subject appeared to notice.

We waited.

Finally, the artist laid down his brush and gestured to the model. The woman stood and walked from the room with such grace and poise one could almost forget that she was bare-ass naked in front of a bunch of strangers.

"What is your name?" he said, turning to face me. I recognized him as the guy on the beach from Mei Ling's photo.

"Randall Lee." I said. At this point, I didn't see much point in lying.

"Why did you break into Mei Ling's apartment?"

"I just wanted to find out what happened to her," I said.

The man blinked. When he spoke, he said, "Mr. Lee, I am typically a patient man but as of late my patience is wearing thin. I will ask you this one time – do you know where she is?"

Uh-oh. I really felt like squirming under the pressure, but I kept cool.

"Yes," I said.

It stunned him.

I said, "You're her boyfriend?"

The driver grabbed my elbow and said, "You don't ask questions, he ask questions."

But the artist ignored him. He stepped closer to me and said, "She's my fiancée. Where is she?"

I felt bad for the guy, but I wasn't sure yet if he was the kill-the-messenger type.

"St. Louis," I said.

He was still thinking about that when the driver said, "If you know she in St. Louis, why you say you want to know what happen to her?"

Shit.

Well, they say the truth will set you free, so I decided to give it a try. If it didn't work, I always had explosive, desperate violence as a backup plan.

"She was murdered," I said. "I came here to find out why."

The room became very still. Mei Ling's fiancée went to the couch and sat. He slumped slowly and laid his head in his hands.

The driver said, "You are not a cop."

"No."

"Then why do you do this thing?"

I wasn't sure how to answer, so I said, "Because nobody else will."

26

The artist was Tony Lau. He was the only son of Jimmy Yi Lau, boss of the Eight Tigers Society. The Eight Tigers ran most of the rackets throughout San Francisco – heroin, money laundering, pornography, prostitution, extortion, even pirated movies.

The 'Taste of Asia' parlors belonged to Jimmy Yi Lau.

Over an exquisite lunch in the apartment, I found out that Tony was actually getting some attention for his art.

Ah, what the hell do I know?

I learned that Oddjob's actual name was Lawrence, and that the driver was called Daniel.

That was about it.

Tony Lau claimed that Mei Ling spent the night at his apartment a little over two weeks ago. He said Daniel had driven her home. It was the last he'd seen or heard of her. I remembered what Tracy told me and thought it unlikely that Mei Ling had been abducted. Still, one does not go from the top of the food chain to the bottom in two weeks. In any case, I believed Tony's story. He'd managed a stoic front since hearing the news, but it was obvious he was upset.

He must've believed me too. I remained breathing, and he gave me his business card and told me to contact him if I found out anything. I stood to leave. Daniel offered to drive me back to my hotel. I decided to take him up on the offer, since I didn't know where in the hell I was.

Before I left, I had to ask one question. "Did you know that she was pregnant?"

Nothing in the man's face changed. Without a word, he stood and left the table. Daniel took me by the elbow, a little roughly, and guided me from the apartment. During the drive back to the hotel, neither Daniel nor I spoke. When he parked at the curb, he said, "It's a hell of a thing, you know. She was… a good girl."

I hadn't gotten into the details with them about how and where her body had been found. I figured Tony Lau had enough to deal with.

I left the car, got up to my room, and sat down for a good long think about everything.

And promptly fell asleep.

I got up around seven in the evening and practiced for a while. When I was finished, I took a shower and looked at the room service menu.

I checked the minibar. Six bucks for a domestic beer (not counting the ten dollar "restocking fee.")

Damn.

All of this activity covered up nicely for the fact that I didn't know what the hell else to do here. I thought about calling Knox and asking for some helpful detecting tips, but I didn't think he'd be amused. I wanted to call Tracy, to hear her voice, but I didn't. I am a male, and we are such stupid creatures sometimes.

I took out the pictures I'd snagged from Mei Ling's apartment and looked at them. My mind kept seeing the image of her on the slab in the morgue.

Several things occurred to me:

One – any leads I *wanted* to follow out here were likely to get me into trouble. Big trouble. I'd gained some small amount of trust from Tony Lau; it wouldn't be a great idea to go poking around at his dad and his business.

Two – Maybe Mei Ling's murder was some kind of revenge hit from another Triad. If so, then what? Triads, as a rule, handle Triad business.

Three - the recurring thought that I was totally inept at this, as I was with most things in life, and that I should just order that roast beef sandwich I'd been eyeballing on the room service menu, buy a sixteen dollar beer, and hop the first available flight home.

Three was sounding better and better.

27

I woke up in the morning, after a depressing night of staring at shitty infomercials, and felt awful. I was wasting my time here. Time and a lot of money. And to think, I had clients back home, possibly in pain, because I was off playing Sam-freaking-Spade.

On top of the feelings of failure, woe, and disappointment, I felt lonelier than I ever had in my life.

Specifically, I missed Tracy. And I don't mean that in the way people usually do. This wasn't a fleeting feeling or a casual twinge. It wasn't a John Hughes marathon type of emotion.

This was pain.

This was a drowning man's longing for oxygen.

I needed to hear that I wasn't a failure. That I was important, even in some small way, to somebody other than a dead Chinese girl I'd never met.

I knew I could just pick up the phone and call Tracy, and I knew that I probably would, but it would only make things infinitely worse because it just drove the point home that I was here and she was there. I couldn't smell her hair or kiss her neck. I could hear her laugh, but I wouldn't see the way her eyes gleamed.

In short, my sappy ass had it bad.

I pulled the phone book out of the drawer and looked up a few numbers. I wanted to call to check on a few flimsy leads but my heart just wasn't in it. I set the phone back in its cradle and had another sixteen dollar beer.

When I picked up the phone again, it was to arrange for my flight home.

I would be back in St. Louis at 8:35 p.m. that night. Unable to resist the opportunity for masochism, I immediately called and got Tracy's machine. I left her the time when I'd be in, and said that I'd try back later.

After showering and packing, I went down to the lobby and checked out. I had the bellboy hold onto my luggage in the check room, though. I figured I could screw around sightseeing for a bit until I had to get to the airport.

I spent a good part of the day just wandering around, lost. I went to Chinatown and glared at each person as if I knew exactly what they were hiding; sadly no one threw themselves at my feet to confess.

Some of the sights and sounds and smells reminded me of the festivals when I was growing up. It would be easy to pretend that I was back in Hong Kong. Everything stood out more, seemed more real than real. I wanted to go around touching everything. I didn't, though. That would've been weird and creepy.

It's a strange sensation, to be homesick for two places at once.

I learned one valuable lesson, though. One of the best ways to cure any feelings of depression or inadequacy is to somehow trigger the survival response: Adrenaline- nature's first anti-mope drug.

In my case, the 'trigger' was a group of well-dressed thug types I caught following me through Portsmouth Square. Considering my mental state, they might've been tracking me for awhile. Of course, there was always the possibility that I was being paranoid…

So I strolled along, looking at shops, and turned down the first alleyway I saw. They followed. Five guys: three Chinese and two American, wearing Armani suits. The alley was a dead end, thanks to a parked produce truck at the other end. Chickens in crates squawked at us and each other. I turned from the chickens and met my shadows.

"Eight Tigers, I presume?" I said.

A few of the guys exchanged surprised looks. A big American kid stepped forward; his nose was crooked from numerous unset breaks. He stabbed his index finger at my sternum and said, "You been pokin' your nose where it don't belong, man."

I laughed and said, "Oh, come on. That's a bad guy 101 line… surely you can do better than that?"

He ground his jaws together and stabbed harder with his finger. "Fuck you!"

More originality.

I took the offending finger and bent it backward with a crunch until it touched his wrist. He screamed.

One of the Chinese guys started reaching in his jacket. I kept hold of the American's broken finger and rammed him in the chest with my shoulder. It accomplished two things: for one, it deflated his lungs and shut him up. It also sent him flying into the Chinese guy, knocking him on his ass.

A kid to my left lunged in with a knife. I yanked the American back by his now very broken finger and threw him into the two other guys. My own little Three Stooges routine.

I leaned back in time to avoid the incoming knife and slapped the kid's elbow with my left hand, and his forearm with my right. It felt effortless, but with my full weight behind the strikes, his arm bones shattered like carnival glass.

The big American was up on his feet again, hugging his broken finger close to his chest. He came in with a wild, looping hook punch from his good hand. I caught him with open palm strikes to the elbow and nose simultaneously. He decided to lie down.

One of the two remaining guys issued some kind of war cry and dove at me.

I guided him by and kicked him in the back of the skull as he passed. He skidded across the pavement with his face.

The last kid tried to run, but I snagged the back of his jacket and threw him to the ground. I grabbed him by the face and said, "Go tell Jimmy that he's not fooling anybody. I know what he did, and when I can prove it, he's gonna go away for a long, long time."

Okay, so that was a bit of a Good Guy 101 line, but I was so happy to actually be the good guy that I wasn't going to give myself too much shit about it.

The kid nodded, wide-eyed and I let him go.

We both left the rest to squirm and cry on the ground, and I went back to the hotel for my bag. I had a plane to catch, after all.

28

The flight was terrible. We hit some turbulence from a thunderstorm, and the kid in the seat next to me spent half the time tossing his cookies. A little acupuncture would've done the trick, but the kid's mom wasn't about to let me stab her son with needles, no matter how much I tried to convince her.

What a beautiful ending to a lovely trip. Upon arrival, no one leapt into my arms. No one showered me with kisses.

Tracy hadn't come. And to top it all off, the airline lost my bag.

I walked to the long-term parking lot, picked up my car, and went home. The apartment was smaller and dingier than I remembered it being. Cold shadows huddled in the spaces untouched by piss-yellow streetlight. I took a beer from the fridge and went to the bedroom. I turned on the TV as a diversion, but there was nothing on but more infomercials. I was not in the mood for any bouncy exercise pitch men, so I just turned the damned thing off. The silence and emptiness were worse.

I went into the living room, and turned on the stereo. The music I heard was not mine, but it was familiar. One of Tracy's CD's. She must've left it. I turned it up and went back to bed. After I finished my beer, I turned off the lights and stared up at the cracks in the ceiling.

29

The next morning, I walked down to the park and practiced a little. When I was finished, I called Knox on my cell; he'd left a few messages on my machine while I was gone.

"Where you been, Lee?"

"Meditation retreat. What's new?"

"Lots. I spent a good portion of my weekend sifting through financial statements and a shitload of other paperwork. Taste of Asia, as we know, is run by Lau Enterprises. Lau Enterprises is, of course, the business front for Jimmy Yi Lau, head of the Eight Tigers and his son, you ready for this…"

"Was engaged to Mei Ling Zhao," I said.

"How the fuck'd you know that?" he said, sounding deflated.

"Ancient Chinese secret," I said. "Does Lau Enterprises have any other interests in this city?"

"We're looking into it."

"You and the mouse in your pocket?"

"Pretty much. You got anything else you want to tell me?"

"Nothing solid."

"At this point I'll take liquid or gas."

"No, that's pretty much all I know for sure," I said.

The line went silent.

I could hear the gears in his mind turning. They could use some oil.

After a minute, he said, "This is getting considerably more fucked up. You know that, right?"

"Mm-hm."

"If any other flashes of insight come to you in your meditation, pick up the goddamned phone, alright? I'm the cop and you're the civilian. Keep that in mind."

"Just doing my civic duty, officer. Keep me posted."

We hung up.

None of my clients knew I was back yet, but that was just as well.

I thought about calling Tracy, or even just stopping by the bar, but I didn't.

Again, male pride.

Instead I just walked back home.

To pout. All by myself.

I saw her black cavalier parked out front from a mile away. It was easy to recognize from the roughly ten thousand bumper stickers on the back. The faded, neon pink Vintage Vinyl, the orange and black Nine Inch Nails logo, the Misfits… a collection of bands and stores and sayings that reminded me of just how old I really was.

I opened the door to the stairwell that led up to my apartment and saw her at the top of the stairs, by my door. She was leaving a note, from the looks of it. When the door closed, she turned and saw me.

I met her halfway, on the stairs. Her hands cupped the sides of my face; her lips smashed into mine with almost enough force to shatter my teeth and knock us both down the stairs. I guessed that she'd missed me too. I lifted her and carried her up the stairs. At the door, I fumbled with the lock while she made soft sounds against my neck that caused my brain to boil in its own juices.

We made it inside, but only just.

Boy, was it good to be home.

30

She hadn't eaten, and by nine-thirty I had a bit of an appetite, myself.

We ordered pizza again. It seemed the safest choice. Through some universal anomaly, we both found ourselves unable to stay away from each other. In public, things could get ugly. In the aftermath of our lovemaking (there was no 'glow'… just a lot of gasping and sweat and, well, bruises), I saw that she'd dyed her hair. Parts of it, anyway. Her normally inky, purplish black hair was now accentuated with intermittent streaks of platinum blonde and pink.

"Do you like it?" she asked.

I nodded. It was different, but it suited her. She could probably staple dead marmosets to her scalp and still be sexy as hell.

"I stupidly got it done Friday night, knowing that I was spending the rest of the weekend with my parents."

"I take it they don't like it?"

"My mom says I look like a hooker."

"Thanks, mom."

"I know, right? Anyway, that's why I didn't know you were coming in…I hadn't been home. Sorry."

"I figured maybe the quarterback of the football team swept you off your feet or something, and you realized that you didn't have to be with an old fogey like me."

"Okay, first thing? Ew. Vomit. Secondly, old fogey, my ass. Though I did have an interesting conversation with my parents about you…"

"Oh?" I said. My voice actually cracked.

"Yeah. They were all happy at first, when I told them that I'd met someone and that I liked that someone very much… My mom said she thought that I was coming out."

"Coming out of what?" I said, genius that I am.

"The closet, Randall. My mom thought I was a lesbian. And preferred that possibility, actually."

"Oh."

Master of conversation, that's me.

"I told them everything. And I ended up having to remind them that I'm twenty-six years old and that I'm not retarded…"

I watched her. This was bothering her. I figured she'd work it out, or not, but I clearly had nothing witty to say, so I stayed quiet.

"My mom, in turn, reminded me that she's forty-seven. I got a whole lecture on wants and needs and how I'm going to want to get married and have kids and blah, blah, blah."

"Do you?" I said.

She looked up at me and shrugged. "I don't know what I want, Randall. Mostly, I think I just want to be happy, and you make me happy."

"Then why do you look so sad?"

"Because none of this should fucking matter, and I hate that it does. I mean, I look at you and everything makes sense, but when I'm alone…I have these stupid thoughts. Like, that you were learning to drive when I was *born*. You know?"

I nodded.

There wasn't anything to say. There was nothing that either of us could do to change this. I wanted more than anything for us to just let all this go, but the truth was that her mother's ideas were nothing new to me; I'd thought similar things each time Tracy and I saw each other. What was I doing? What was I taking, stealing, from her? There was so much of life that she could be experiencing, but she was hanging around with a schlub like me.

And then there was marriage.

And the issue of children.

Christ.

In the end, it was something too big to deal with. We ended up watching The Maltese Falcon on channel nine and eating our pizza in relative silence. She fell asleep in my arms.

For now, this was enough.

31

Morning came and with it, breakfast – hot coffee and cold pizza. Tracy, being environmentally conscious, decided to conserve water by inviting me in to shower with her; I put aside my typical modesty and acquiesced.

This was the fate of the planet we were talking about, after all.

The heaviness of the previous evening was forgotten, or so it seemed. For the moment, we were content merely to fill each moment with each other.

If there is a deeper purpose to life, I have yet to find it.

When at last we dressed, t-shirts and sweatpants were the order of the day for both of us. Mine was the standard plain black. Tracy wore a brilliant yellow Descendents concert shirt with a stick figure drawing on it and the words, "I don't want to grow up." It fit her, in more ways than one.

"Do you have appointments today, or are you playing hooky and doing the amateur sleuth stuff?" she said, slipping on her t-shirt. Watching the cloth descend over her abdomen, I felt the same sadness that I always felt every time she got dressed.

"Neither," I said. "I'm spending the day with you, if you'll have me."

"Whatever shall we do?" she said with a grin.

"Anything you like."

"Can we go to the art museum and stare at all the neo- post-modernistic- alt- impressionist- destructo- metal pieces?" she said, falling back onto the bed.

"If we must," I said.

"Can we get sushi for lunch?" she said, rolling over onto her stomach and leaning her head on her hands. She looked like a punk Gidget.

"Sure."

"Will you kiss me even with unagi and wasabi breath?"

"Definitely."

"Can we go to Six Flags? Will you win me a big, gigantic, useless, probably made-in-Taiwan stuffed animal?"

"Even if it takes me all day," I said.

"Yay! You, sir, are the best boyfriend ever!" she said, sliding up onto her knees and grinning as she bounced on the mattress.

I was slightly dumbstruck at the idea of being someone's 'boyfriend.'

32

At some point in conversation, I'd made the mistake of mentioning to her that I'd been slacking in the practice department, so she insisted that I do the form. She wanted to see it, she said.

It was a picture perfect October day outside, so we walked a few blocks to Millar Park. There, amidst the fallen leaves and skeletal trees, I assumed the beginning posture.

"You sure about this? The whole thing takes a long time…you'll be bored out of your mind."

"I'll deal. Do it," she said.

I sighed and became still. As I began the form, I let myself focus only upon the movements. It wasn't easy, even with the years of practice. I felt like a nervous kid around Tracy, and I was terrified of screwing up. It was stupid, I know. I managed to make it through without accidentally tripping myself in slow motion, and was surprised to see that not only Tracy was watching. A small group of young Chinese men and women stood back, seemingly assessing my skill.

When I finished, Tracy applauded.

One of the group, a scrawny kid who looked to be in his early twenties, approached me and said, "Your Yang style is very good."

"Thank you," I said.

"Who is your teacher?"

"Sifu Wu Cai."

He nodded and said, "Would you like to push hands with us?"

I started to apologize and say that we had to leave, but Tracy said that she'd like to see the practice. The kid stepped forward into a bow stance and raised his right arm. I mirrored his stance and placed the palm of my hand against his forearm. This was *Tui Shou*, 'Pushing Hands,' a two person practice that allowed each practitioner to gauge the others balance, as well as their ability to diffuse and deflect - as well as issue - attacks.

I pushed into his center, he effortlessly rolled back, guiding my energy aside and counter-attacking with his own push. I redirected his energy and pushed again, lower. The kid was good. There was nothing stiff or wooden to his movements, and I was really pushing him. He didn't anticipate my movements; he waited, listening and interpreting each strike anew. After a few seconds, we shifted into the two-handed practice. Before long, we were free fighting, moving from technique to technique, alternately attacking and diffusing each other's attacks. His classmates showed no emotion, they only watched with detached interest.

While I was stupidly distracted watching the others, the kid pressed his fingertip into the soft tissue of my wrist, at an acupuncture point called *jingqiu,* and issued *fa-jin,* the explosive, intrinsic energy used only during combat, when you're really out to hurt somebody.

The power of the strike numbed my arm and made breathing difficult. He was already moving in with a follow up hit, though, so I couldn't just stand there.

I coiled my arm around his and shifted backward, pulling him forward into a palm strike to the face. He moved to counter, but, with my weight sunk into my rear leg, I kicked him in his right hip with my left heel. He was spun like a top into my waiting arms, which snaked around his throat and head; I applied the choke, and within seconds the boy was out.

I dropped him and looked to the others. Nobody else seemed anxious to get frisky, so I shook out my arm and tried to rub feeling back into it.

Tracy stared at me like I'd grown a second head. What had probably looked perfectly civilized to her had turned ugly in less than an instant, and chances were that she hadn't even seen the kid attack me.

Before I could explain myself, an ancient looking Chinese man knelt at the boy's side and jabbed him in the chest until he regained consciousness. While the boy staggered to his feet, the old man faced me and scowled.

He wore a tan windbreaker and a pair of blue jeans that had been pulled up almost to sternum height. A green stocking cap sat in a lumpy cone upon his head, and tufts of his grey eyebrows peeked out from beneath it like a couple of chilly caterpillars.

"You deserved that," he said. "Sloppy. Very sloppy."

"And him?" I said, gesturing to the boy.

"He's a freaking idiot."

"His Tai Chi Chuan is very good," I said.

The old man waved his hand before his nose, as if he smelled something foul, and said, "His Tai Chi is donkey balls. His Tai Chi does not deserve to smell my shit!"

I didn't know what to say to that. Tracy looked at the hunched old man with an expression of curious disgust.

"Would you do me this great honor, sir?" I said, raising my arm to push hands with him.

He slapped my arm down and shouted, "You Americans all move like goddamned Frankenstein's monster…imagine the arrogance of some bignose such as you aspiring to the supreme ultimate… Bah. You aren't worth my time, shithead."

With that, he turned and walked away to his apartment on the far side of the street. His students followed. Tracy watched them go before saying, "Who the hell was that guy?"

"Master Cheng Xing."

"The guy you wanted to check out? Well, he didn't have to be a dick."

"When you're as good as him, you can be however you want to be."

"What are you talking about? He's a total feeb. He can't even stand up straight… I bet you could totally kick his ass."

"If Master Cheng had wanted a fight, I wouldn't be standing here now. Appearances, especially in Tai Chi, can be deceiving. Don't forget that."

She seemed unconvinced.

I rubbed my wrist again and suggested that we go. I wasn't going to wait around in case Master Cheng changed his mind.

33

During lunch at a beautiful sushi place on Delmar, Tracy asked about the latest developments in the case. I told her about Tony Lau. She knew the name.

"He's an awesome painter," she said. "He's going to be huge."

"Really?" I said.

She nodded enthusiastically.

"They got a few of his pieces in the contemporary galleries at the Art Museum. Really cool stuff. God, that's so sad that she was his fiancée."

I agreed that it was and had a glass of sake.

"You really think his dad did it?" she said.

"Well, I think his dad arranged it."

"Why would he do that?"

"Maybe she stole the money from him… maybe she was blackmailing him… I don't know." I looked over at the sushi chef, watching him work. He deftly sliced a thin piece of raw tuna.

"If you don't know, then how can you be sure it's him?" Tracy said.

"Well…he sent those guys after me in San Francisco."

"Yeah, but you said those guys were nancy-boys."

"So?"

"So you said the guy that killed Mei Ling was like a kung fu master or something. If the Eight Tigers did it, and they knew that you knew, wouldn't they send that dude to do you in?"

"Unless that 'dude' is from St Louis," I said.

"You mean like that old Cheng guy."

"Somebody like that, yeah."

"What does he have to do with anything?" Tracy said, picking up a piece of spider roll. She picked out a bit of the soft shell crab and popped it into her mouth.

"Mei Ling was killed here. Maybe her murderer was a local, too? And if he's a local, I thought Cheng would probably know any decent martial artists in town."

Tracy frowned. "Doesn't that kinda blow your other theory, though? I mean, unless Lau went through the trouble of finding and paying the guy all the way from San Fran or something… I dunno, I just don't see how all of this fits together."

"Join the club, dear," I said. I had hoped that talking through things with Tracy would help sort them out in my own mind. It hadn't worked.

After lunch, we hit the Art Museum. The closest I'd ever been to the place was my picnic with Tracy, when we'd first met. On the way, in my car, we found some small musical common ground – David Bowie. We both agreed that he was – ahem – 'The Bomb.'

The museum was alive in a way that most artsy places I'd been to were not. There was nothing somber or even especially quiet about it. Everyone seemed respectful, but there was a genuine feeling of fun to the place.

Even amongst the neo-post-modernistic-alt-impressionist-destructo-metal pieces.

I stared up at the formless scrap metal and broken glass and attempted to meaningfully ponder it, but I just didn't get it.

I felt Tracy looking at me. When I turned, she was grinning conspiratorially.

"Before you even ask, it doesn't have to *mean* anything, y'know. None of this does. That's the problem with people… they think too much. Just let it all go. Think back to when you were a kid. You can remember that far back, can't you?"

"Hey, now," I said.

She wrapped her arm around my waist and slid in close.

"When you were little, really little, remember how things looked? How the textures were? The way you just wanted to reach out and touch everything? Go back to that… and look at this again. Look at everything that way. Don't try to fit it into your preconceived notions, don't try to give it a meaning or figure it out… just *look* at it, feel its texture in your mind."

For all the simplicity of the idea, it worked. The useless piece of shit

I'd been staring at became something I wanted to climb. A marvel of angles and lights and shadows.

The transformation was shocking. I remembered my teacher's words, "Stop thinking you know so much and see the world like a baby sees it. When you know it all, there's nothing more to learn, nothing more to see. For a child, the world is open, miraculous."

I leaned down and kissed Tracy on the forehead.

"Thank you," I said.

Even a dinosaur can learn new tricks.

We spent a good part of the afternoon and early evening wandering the galleries. We spent a long time in the Asian collection, and I explained some of the religious symbolism to Tracy. She seemed genuinely interested, and it kept me from feeling like too much of an idiot.

The contemporary gallery, as promised, featured a few of Tony Lau's paintings. I couldn't tell you what it looked like. I was too fixated on an information placard on the wall.

I excused myself from Tracy long enough to head outside and make the call.

Knox answered on the first ring.

"You find out anything else about Lau Enterprises?" I said.

"A bit. They've been scooping up bargain basement real estate around the bad parts of town, renovating it and selling for extravagant prices. Some stuff they're keeping. Seems they're intent on creating a real Chinatown again… why?"

"You think the Eight Tigers are moving more business into the city?"

"It's possible. You find anything out?"

"Lau Enterprises is sponsoring an exhibit at the art museum."

"No shit? Of junior's stuff, I presume."

"Yeah," I said.

"Interesting."

Yeah. Real interesting.

34

We went to Tracy's apartment after the museum.

She offered to cook. I offered to eat. It was a match made in heaven. Except, of course, for the mutant cat-thing that glared at me the whole time, but I was even getting used to that.

"Hello again, Tito…" I said, reaching out to pet him. He got up and walked away, staring disdainfully at me over his shriveled, wrinkly shoulder. She turned on MTV and got to work. It just so happened that we were lucky enough to catch the fifteen minutes of actual music videos on MTV.

She made vegetable and herb samosas with raita and matar paneer. With the spicy Indian food, we drank a dark amber beer. It was, as Tracy said, "The Yum."

"I was almost going to be a chef," she told me over dinner. "Spent a year in cooking school and everything."

"What changed your mind?" I said.

She dipped one of the vegetable dumplings in creamy yogurt sauce and said, "Patience. I don't have enough. And cooking, real cooking... the gourmet shit… it just gets sort of pointless. You spend so much time preparing some foo-foo dish, just so some schmoe can scarf it down in twenty minutes. Not to get overly crude or anything, but no matter how good the food is, or how long it took to make, it's going to end up in a toilet somewhere, y'know?"

"You ever hear of the sand paintings that the Tibetan Buddhist monks do? Some of those mandalas take weeks to make, and when the painting's all done, they destroy it."

"What kind of pointless shit is that?"

"It's not pointless. It's a lesson: Nothing lasts forever. All things are fleeting."

"Right, well, no shit. Why dwell on it? Why not just enjoy things while they last?"

"That's exactly the point. For a great chef, the joy *is* the preparation. For the monks, it is in the creation of the sand painting, not in wondering how long it will last. In China, they use the word Kung-fu to mean a kind of expertise that surpasses surface beauty. Confucius once said, 'To study and at times practice what one has learned, is that not a pleasure?'"

Tracy said, "Ah, so."

"In graphic art, each painting or drawing is better than the one that preceded it; hopefully… this is Kung-fu. We imbue each thing we do with a bit of ourselves, and in all that we do we unfold a bit more, like a flower blossoming."

Tracy tilted her head and smiled. "So really, nothing is pointless?"

I drank some beer and said, "Oh, sure. Some things are. Boy bands, reality television, fast food, Ashton Kutcher movies… that sort of thing."

35

In the morning, I got dressed and kissed Tracy goodbye as she slept. If all went well, I would stop in to see her at the bar later. I went back to my apartment and changed clothes. The Midwestern autumn was finally in full gear, so I dressed in thick sweatpants, a black cotton t-shirt, a thick grey sweatshirt, and a pair of alpaca socks.

I went back to Millar Park for my morning practice. I practiced Zhan Zhuang for twenty minutes, in a posture known as the three circle stance. When I was finished, I didn't need the sweatshirt anymore; my body felt swollen and humming with energy. I began to practice the form.

Master Cheng Xing and a few of his students were gathering. The students were warming up with some five animal movements; I felt Master Cheng was watching me. When I completed the first section, he came over and said, "Wu Cai is your master?"

"Yes, sir," I said.

He nodded curtly and said, "Your technique is not horrible, but like most American shitheads, you are in too much of a hurry."

I bowed my head slightly.

"It is not your fault that you were not born Chinese, but if you truly wish to learn this art you will have to try much harder. If Wu was willing to teach you, you must be hard-working… perhaps you can transcend your hereditary disadvantage."

"Thank you, master," I said.

"I said perhaps, asshole," With his accent, the last word came out 'ass-hoe'.

"Will you help me then, master?" I said.

He scowled and said, "Impatient! Impertinent! Not to mention ugly… I will teach you when you can knock me on my old wrinkled ass, eh, big-nose. What do you think of that?"

He zipped up his windbreaker and stomped back to his students.

I thought about taking him the letter of introduction from the Synergy of Heaven School, but realized that could only get me killed.

36

I took Tony Lau's card from my wallet when I got back to the apartment and called him. The voice that answered wasn't Tony's; by the accent, I realized it was Daniel. For most of the conversation, I was talking to myself. He answered only when necessary to ask his own questions or clarify a piece of information.

I mentioned the upcoming exhibit and asked if Daniel would be accompanying Tony to the show.

He said he would.

I said I'd see him there.

"Indeed," he said, and hung up.

Clearly, Daniel was my kind of conversationalist. Of course, I'd never heard him fumble anything, or say anything stupid or inappropriate, so I still had that going for me.

I sat on my couch and wondered. I wondered about the art show at the end of the month. I wondered about whether or not Lau senior was going to make an appearance. I wondered what I'd say to him if he did. I wondered what was in the fridge, but was too tired to get up to find out. With my eyes closed, I wondered what Tracy would be wearing to work tonight, and if I would be able to coax her out of whatever it was once she was off the clock. With that wondrous train of thought in my head, I drifted off into a lovely mid-morning nap.

37

That night, Tracy wore thigh-high fishnets, a black and violet leather skirt, and a tight black corset.

As for the other wonder, well, a gentleman would never say.

38

My cell phone rang.

When I opened my eyes, I realized that I'd been pinned to the bed by a small, sleeping, gargoyle-looking cat. As I fumbled for the phone on the nightstand, Tito woke with a start and bolted, leaving thin, bloody furrows in my chest.

Thanks, Tito.

I flipped open the phone and got up to look for something to staunch the bleeding. I listened to the voice on the phone, threw in an occasional 'uh-huh', and walked into Tracy's open living room. She was up by one of the Halloween themed windows, at an easel, painting. She wore only an oversized Morrissey concert t-shirt, and the sight of her legs nearly made me swoon.

Or maybe it was the blood loss.

Probably, it was her legs.

I took a paper towel from the kitchen and used it to dab at my wounds. Then I hung up the phone and kissed her neck.

"Good morning, sailor," she said.

"You want to take a ride with me?" I said.

"Where to?"

"Police station."

"Why?"

"There's been another murder, but this time they have a suspect in custody."

"Ooh, do I get to see a for real dead body?"

"Probably not."

"Do I get to question the suspect and shine bright lights in his face? You can be good cop and I'll be bad cop!"

"Um…no."

"Well, hell. You're no fun."

We got dressed. Tracy in a pair of tight, faded jeans and another oversized concert shirt - this one was The Cure. I threw on some loose cotton pants and a grey t-shirt that I'd tossed in the back seat for just such an eventuality.

In the dingy waiting room of the police station we sat on green vinyl chairs and waited for Detective Knox. The black and white TV in the corner played an old re-run of Love Connection. Chuck Woolery was doing his infamous two-and-two thing when Knox finally showed up.

He looked drawn and tired. His normally immaculate appearance was uncharacteristically unruly – hair mussed, face unshaven, eyes red and bleary.

He nodded to me and said, "Who's this?"

I said, "Tracy Sandoval, from the club, the security video, remember?"

He ran a hand through his hair and muttered, "Right, sorry."

"So, what's going on?" I said.

He led us back through a dimly lit hallway and opened a grey door. Inside, the room wasn't much bigger than a closet. One wall featured a window looking out into an interrogation room. I'd seen enough movies to know it was one-way glass. Knox said to Tracy, "You can hang tight here. Anybody asks, you're a potential witness."

She nodded.

Knox left the room and gestured for me to follow.

I did.

We went next door, to the interrogation room.

He offered me a seat. I took it. He pulled a digital recorder from his pocket and set it on the table. He got up and walked out. I blew a kiss to the mirror that was not a mirror on the wall.

A few minutes later, Knox and a few uniformed officers brought in a young Chinese man. He looked familiar. Knox took the seat to my right while the uniforms pushed the suspect into the chair to my left.

The kid looked scared shitless. His pale, splotchy face was slick with the sick-smelling sweat of the unjust; his wide eyes were bloodshot and darted from me to the detective and back every three of four seconds.

Knox leaned back in his seat and slipped a cigarette into the corner of his mouth. As he lit it, he said, "Talk."

The kid immediately stuttered, "I…do...no…speak….English."

Knox looked to me.

I asked the kid if he spoke Mandarin. He shook his head.

I asked if he spoke Cantonese. He hesitated.

Knox threw a manila folder on the table and spilled its contents. At first, my mind couldn't translate the images in the photographs into recognizable shapes. The forms were familiar but wrong. Spread open, strewn, dark with blood. At first, that's all I could see – blood. So much blood.

"Ask him about her," Knox said. "Ask why he did it."

In Cantonese, I said, "Why did you kill this girl?"

The kid shook his head violently, throwing droplets of sweat like a dog. He said, "No, no, no," over and over.

"DNA evidence at the scene, buddy-boy." Knox said.

I looked at another photo, one of the girl's face. It was unrecognizable. The eyes were swollen shut, the nose was smashed. The girl's teeth had cut through her lips before cracking and splintering under some horrific force. Her hair was saturated with blood, but I saw one strand that had somehow escaped the flow.

"Do you have an I.D?" I said to Knox.

"No. This fucker smashed her teeth and cut off her fingertips. We've got forensics guys working on her, but they're not too hopeful."

"I think I might know who she is," I said.

He looked over at me and took a deep drag on his cigarette. "Of course you do. Care to share?"

"I think she was a dancer at The Sapphire Room, in Centreville. Her stage name was Jade. I think she was killed for talking to me."

Knox thought for a minute and said, "Body was found wrapped in plastic in a ditch in Centreville."

I looked away from the pictures before they made me sick. My chest was heavy, my mind fuzzy. I felt like I should force myself to look, like I had to shove my nose in yet another life erased because of my fuck-ups, but I couldn't do it. Just one more weak moment, one more failure.

To the kid, I said, "Are you Eight Tigers?"

He slid back in his chair, stood up, and said, "I want my lawyer." Knox told me to translate, but I was stuck staring at the kid's clothes. I hadn't paid any attention to them before. Acid washed jeans. Bruce Lee t-shirt. Jean jacket, complete with patches.

Kangaroo high tops.

I said, "How's your friend?"

The kid froze and stared at me.

"You know," I said, "your friend, Scarface? How's his hand? His teeth?"

Whatever color was left in the kid's face drained and he repeated his request for a lawyer.

Knox hit me in the shoulder and said, "Translate."

I sang a happy composition of my own, a medley of 'It's a small world' and The Police's "Synchronicity."

39

When we couldn't get anything else from the kid, Knox offered to buy Tracy and me some breakfast at a nearby diner. The waitress looked like Meatloaf after a particularly vicious knife fight, and she sounded like Fran Drescher after gargling with acid, but at least she was rude and mean enough that I didn't feel bad for making the comparisons.

Knox ordered ham and eggs, I ordered biscuits and gravy, Tracy got the apple Belgian waffle. Unfortunately, the plates that came to the table looked more or less identical, and didn't resemble any of the things we'd ordered.

I started to protest, but Knox just shook his head.

"Trust me, it's better if you just smile and nod and eat whatever they bring you. They got Tums at the counter. Besides, half the force eats here, and we haven't lost anybody yet."

"I don't like you," I said.

Throughout the "meal", the three of us talked about the case.

Finding a public defender that spoke Cantonese was going to take a little time and until then, we at least knew where the little shit would be.

I told Knox that I didn't think he did it.

He and Tracy both asked why I would think that, considering all the evidence to the contrary.

"He's nothing, a follower. That Scarface kid…he's the boss of that pathetic little crew, and he seems just tough enough to take on an unarmed woman that's half his size."

"And the DNA evidence?"

"I wouldn't be surprised if everyone in the gang took a turn on her, but that's a whole lot different from bashing her skull in."

Tracy set her fork of steaming goo down and grimaced.

"Sorry," I said.

"So we're looking for the rest of this gang, and especially the leader," Knox said.

I nodded.

"Any ideas?"

"You're the detective, detect something," I said.

"Lately, I'm thinking both of us missed our true callings… "

"Ah, Johnny boy, there's plenty of time to be a fry cook after you retire," I said.

Knox gave me the finger.

Tracy perked up and said, "Do you have one of those books of suspects? Y'know, like they always do on TV?"

"A photo lineup? Yeah."

"Maybe Scarface is in that?" she said.

Knox shook his head and shoveled some slop into his mouth. He seemed unfazed by all of it. I could not make an attempt to taste the stuff.

"No," Knox said, "but I'm checking hospital records…if he was as busted up as you say, Lee, then he's bound to have left some kind of paperwork."

I nodded and stared at my plate. I could've sworn I saw something move. When I was certain it was nothing more than a trick of the light, I said, "And, if nothing else, there's always Plan B."

"What's Plan B?" Tracy said.

"Use the minnow to catch the shark."

"Jesus, you watch too much fucking TV," Knox laughed.

"Doesn't mean it wouldn't work," I said.

"Doesn't mean it would," Knox said.

"Doesn't sound very ethical, or legal," Tracy said.

"That's why you should leave it to me." I said.

40

When Knox had to get back to work and be all police-y, Tracy and I went and had a real breakfast at my apartment. Including my special scrambled eggs. After breakfast, we showered and dressed and lounged on the couch together to watch TV. Sometime during The Price is Right, we both fell asleep. I woke up before Tracy, and managed to wriggle off of the couch. It was four-thirty, but the sky was already a dusky grey. I yawned and grabbed a beer or three from the fridge.

While she slept, I practiced a bit. It helped loosen up the crick in my neck and the overall stiffness that comes from an afternoon of couch-sleeping, but my mind wouldn't shut up and play nice. Instead, it kept running its mouth off about every aspect of the increasingly fucked up case and my increasingly fucked up life. I kept seeing images of Jade, if it *was* Jade, juxtaposed with the rest of the dead I'd seen in my lifetime.

Mei Ling.

Madame Chong.

Jade.

My little girl.

And nobody cared. Maybe they'd heard about them on the evening news and they'd shake their heads sadly and say, "Pass the mashed potatoes, please," and then get on with their lives. Because sometimes somebody falls through the cracks and gets ground up in the machine, and the other sheep just lower their heads and keep on grazing. These things happen, they say. Some of them probably deserved what they got, they say.

These lives meant nothing to anybody now, except me.

And none of them had a chance, or a choice, and there would

never be any "justice." There wasn't anything anybody could do to make things right, not for them. And if there could not be justice, then by god there could at least be vengeance. Knox couldn't do it. He could ensure a nice cozy cell for as long as it took for Lau or whatever other Triad fuck ordered this to get them out.

I hadn't noticed at first, but rather than the slow, even pace that I usually kept while practicing the form, I'd sped up, performing each movement as they were intended to be performed in combat – at full speed, and with the explosive release of *fa-jin,* the whip-like power that made the movements deadly. My muscles remained relaxed, but I felt my blood and *chi* race.

It felt good.

Primal.

Vengeful.

And I knew then the answer to Tracy's question: I knew what I would do if I ever found the killer.

When the form was complete, I was covered in sweat and out of breath. I was sore.

Tracy was watching, wide-eyed, from the couch.

I felt hot from the exercise and embarrassment, but I summoned up a smile for her and suggested dinner. Once she was convinced I wasn't having some sort of wild seizure, she agreed.

"Maybe I could finally take you on that tried-and-true dinner-and-a-movie date," I said.

She shrugged and said, "So far, the movie thing's been a jinx."

"Third time's gotta be a charm, right?"

I got cleaned up, and we decided to try this new Italian place down the street from Tracy's apartment.

We went downstairs and out to the street. Before reaching my car, I felt a pang of guilt; I'd been neglecting my patients. Since returning from San Francisco, I hadn't so much as stepped foot in the clinic. I probably had a shitload of messages.

I stopped and dug my keys out of my pocket.

"What's the matter?" Tracy said.

"I have to check something in the shop. It'll only take a second."

"'Kay."

I slid the key into the lock and turned it. The door swung open. I stepped forward, into the doorway.

Several things happened simultaneously, or so it seemed. My foot encountered a slight, springy resistance. Before I consciously registered the sensation, I retracted my foot quickly and twisted my waist, striking

Tracy in the chest with my shoulder and knocking her back and off her feet. There was a sound like thunder, and then I was weightless. The sky spun, and the world seemed muffled. Pain crept in from every direction like a pack of jackals and smothered everything else.

41

It seemed to be only moments later that I regained consciousness, but I knew that couldn't be. Thinking was *really* hard. I realized that this must be what it felt like to be George W. Bush. The thought made me giggle, but that hurt, so I stopped.

I looked around, but I knew first by smell where I was; that antiseptic pissy smell only belonged in two places, and I wasn't nearly old enough yet for one of them. I felt around for the call button and, upon finding it, hit it with all my strength.

Which wasn't saying much.

Fifteen seconds or three hours later, I wasn't sure which, a hefty blonde in support stockings was shining a miniature sun directly into my brain, via my eyeball, and asking me how I felt. I wanted to hit her with a witty one-liner, but for the first time I realized that the inside of my mouth tasted like the floor of an adult bookstore. I felt pretty certain I was going to vomit, and that was no fun, but a wave of determination drove me to aim for her sensible shoes.

It's good to have goals in life.

42

When I came around again, it was because the world was a dizzying wheel of spiky unpleasantness, and I wanted to get off. Opening my eyes didn't help any in itself, though the sight of a familiar face made things somewhat more bearable.

"We're never going to get to go to the movies, you realize that?"

With my mouth's status having moved from adult bookstore floor to the relatively more pleasant truck stop bathroom floor, I managed to croak out her name.

"It's alright," she said, "don't try to talk."

Tracy's hair was pulled back in a ponytail. She had a nasty scrape on her forehead and a band aid on one cheek, but otherwise looked alright.

I swallowed, a Herculean task, and said, "Wanna fool around instead?"

She laughed and reached out to touch my face, but hesitated and grimaced.

Christ, I must've looked a mess.

I wanted to feel her fingertips, however much it hurt.

She settled for my hand, and took it tenderly.

"What…happened?" I said.

"They strung a tripwire to your door. It detonated a home-made concussion grenade."

The voice was deeper and definitely not Tracy's, but my foggy brain took a minute to place it.

Knox's scruffy mug came into focus over Tracy's shoulder.

Huh, I thought, he *can* grow facial hair…

To Tracy I said, "Are you alright?"

"A little bruised, but yeah." she said. "…You took the brunt of it."

"…Am I okay?" I asked.

Knox said, "No, you've got a concussion…"

"The bomb did its job then. Just like it says on the label."

"Nah. Wasn't the grenade that gave you the concussion. That honor goes to your car."

"My car?" My throat was so dry it ached, but I wanted to know what was up before the white coats came with their torture carts.

"Yeah. After you shoved the lady out of the way – a very noble and quick-witted gesture, by the way…even if you did get a bit rough – the force of the blast blew you through the passenger-side window of your car, which is why you might feel somewhat less than a hundred percent at the moment. For the record, in addition to the head trauma you've got four snapped ribs and a busted collarbone."

"How's the car?" I quipped.

It was good to know I could still quip.

"Fucked," he said.

"Dammit," I said.

I loved that car.

43

I hate Jell-O.

It wasn't always that way, but spend enough time in a hospital, and it's bound to happen. Over the two weeks following my 'accident', I grew to really despise the stuff. I wasn't too fond of "Misty" either, the SS Nazi heifer whose shoes I'd yakked upon.

But hey, I did make it to her shoes, at least, which is nice.

What Knox neglected to mention was the approximately ten billion shallow cuts I'd received on my face and arms and the two or three deep ones - one of which was on my neck - that required a daily cleaning and dressing change.

From Misty.

With some sort of sulfuric acid-like substance and something that felt suspiciously like a wire brush. She always felt the need to tell me how lucky I was that the neck wound wasn't an inch lower, where it would've opened my carotid artery.

Between Misty and the Jell-O, I was about ready to open it myself.

Tracy came by every day, lucky for me, and Knox stopped in every few days. There was no real news on the case. The kid they'd had in custody - turns out his name was Kip Yam - was free; with nothing to hold him on, they had to let him go. Knox thought for sure the DNA evidence would be enough to keep him, but it turned out that the sample had been somehow tainted and was inadmissible.

Figures.

That was the bad news.

The good news was that things were not as bad as they could be. The concussion grenade in my shop wasn't meant to be a concussion grenade after all.

Whoever had built the damned thing had tried to make a claymore mine.

"See," Knox said, "the bomber packed the thing tight with scrap metal, ball bearings, all kinds of shit… problem was, the casing was this thin, shitty aluminum. Now, I'm no explosive expert, but one of the bomb squad guys explained to me that when a bomb explodes, the force travels out the path of least resistance…"

"Makes sense," I said.

"Now, the bomber wanted the path of least resistance to be…well…you, basically. But when he built the casing, he double wrapped and reinforced everything except where the trigger fell, on the bottom. When the thing blew, most of the frag material, the metal and shit, went almost straight down into the floor. You caught mostly shockwave."

"So I've got a totaled car and a big hole in my floor. Awesome," I said.

"Beats a big hole in your head or chest."

"To be fair, I've never had a big hole in my head or chest, so I cannot say. I know for a fact, though, that the other things suck quite a lot."

He stared at me and grinned. "They 'suck', huh?"

I shrugged. "Perils of dating a youngster."

"Worth the risk, though, eh?"

"Yeah, she's the bomb. Now go find out who blew me up before I have to get all jiggy up on a mofo f'shizzle, a'ight?"

"You don't even know what you're saying, do you?"

"No, now get lost. I don't want you in here when Misty comes to give me my sponge bath."

44

The worst part of the whole thing, besides the Jell-O, Misty, and the stomach-wracking nausea, was the way that sometimes, when doing the simplest and most inane things, the whole world would seem to flip and knock me right on my ass (incidentally, one of the other sites of those deep cuts I mentioned – apparently my ass got hung up on the broken car window. Joy.)

A big part of Tai Chi Chuan is balance. When stepping, one does not commit weight to a foot until it is on secure ground, much like the way a cat steps… it was this sensitivity and balance that allowed me to detect the tripwire in time to knock Tracy aside. Right now, though, thanks to the brain-scrambling, my balance was screwed. It was like being drunk without the pleasant side effects.

I was told that the sensation would go away in time. Whether it took days, weeks, or months, no one could say. That was unacceptable. I'd been an invalid for long enough. When Tracy came for her visit, I took a sheet of paper from a hospital notepad and scribbled out a page of Chinese characters.

"What's this?" She said.

"Shopping list. There's a tiny shop right off Olive and 82nd…near the park. The sign isn't in English, but you'll find it. The windows are all covered in brown paper. Give the list to the guy there and tell him *Lee Laoshi* needs his help."

"Who?"

"*Lee Laoshi*," I said again slower, "Teacher Lee. Me."

"Oh. Groovy. Alright," she folded the list, slipped it in her jeans pocket, and leaned over me. I got an excellent view of her cleavage.

"You're sexy when you talk that oriental talk," she drawled. Then she kissed me.

It hurt a little, but in a good way.

45

"I'll give you this, potato-head, you did it. You knock me flat on my ass. No wonder you can't walk, your balls are the size of an elephant's. And sending a young girl like that, have you no shame?"

The old man sat on a stool by my hospital bed. His hands looked gnarled and twisted, but looks could be deceiving; the deftness with which he handled the thin steel needles showed more of his true nature, though he was less than gentle with each insertion.

I figured that part was on purpose.

It was worth it, though. The treatment was unlike anything I'd ever done or seen. Like any true master, he was capable of taking the extremely complex and making it simple. Simple enough for a potato-head like me, anyway.

Looking down his nose at me, he inserted another needle into a point in my ear lobe.

"Now," Master Cheng said, "I thought I'd seen the last of you months ago, but you keep showing up… what are you some kind of stalker?"

His eyes widened suddenly and he said, "You gay for me, Lee?"

"I need help, Master."

"No shit! Look at you," he said, flicking one of the needles protruding from my arm.

"I'm looking for a killer." I said once I was done wincing.

"What for?"

"He's hurt a lot of people. At least three women are dead because of him. I thought you could help me find him."

"What do I look like, Lee, Barnaby-freaking-Jones?"

From her seat on the other side of the bed, Tracy said, "Wait a minute. Randall, I thought…"

"That I suspected Master Cheng?"

"Well…yeah," she said.

"I know of much better things to do with young ladies than kill them," he said, wiggling his bushy white eyebrows.

"Oh, puke," Tracy said.

"Master Cheng is one of the reasons I decided to stay in St. Louis," I said. "My teacher always admired and respected him. He said Master Cheng was the finest doctor he'd ever known."

"Damn right," Cheng muttered.

"He's always turned me away as a student, but I thought for sure he would lend his expertise to a police investigation."

"I hate cops," he said.

"At least you didn't let me sit here and suffer," I said.

He stared at me with disdain. To Tracy he said, "You know what passes for Kung fu these days?"

She smiled and shook her head.

"Mush-head numbskull kids sit around mashing buttons. Memorizing combinations for their video games. No one seeks anymore. No one strives. Far easier to go to Wal-Mart and buy a gun. Any dipshit can pull a trigger."

He ran a hand over his mostly bald head and slumped in the chair.

"What a world," he said. "The few who want to learn, learn shit. Tai Chi has it the worst… bunch of sissy *Gwailo* in cheap silk, dancing around in slow motion, waving their arms. They have the gall to call *that* Tai Chi Chuan?

"Believe or don't, young lady, but I am not a young man. When I am gone, there will be no one left with my skill. This one, for all his big-nose American stupidness, has some small Kung fu."

He turned to me and, twisting a needle, said, "Perhaps when you are well you may yet learn something."

"Does that mean you will teach me?" I said.

"It means that a pathetic sad old man is desperate enough to put his last bit of faith in a half-crippled American dumb ass."

Tracy looked at me as if I were insane for smiling.

46

Irony is a bitch.

Here I was, a guy who's spent a good portion of his life peddling 'alternative' healing and natural cures, practically begging a doctor to give me something with a bit more kick than extra strength Tylenol. Apparently nobody told the quack that I was a mass of broken bones, deep tissue bruises, and ten billion lacerations. Not to mention the concussion, that joy of joys.

But Mengele told me to alternate hot and cold compresses.

Why I oughta…

On the bright side, arms slings are sexy. Tracy says so anyway, and that's good enough for me.

And though I didn't get to puke on Misty's shoes again, I did give her a long distance one-finger salute from the car before we left. I also shouted out things she could do with her damned Jell-O that shocked even Tracy.

We went back to her place since mine was partially blown up and could easily become more blown up if any ne'er-do-wells were so inclined.

I'd never been happier to see a shriveled, naked cat-thing in my life. I'd actually missed the weird little bastard. Ole Tito must've felt the same, because as soon as Tracy got me situated comfortably on her couch, he planted himself on my lap and immediately started to purr. Tracy cooed at the cuteness of it all, and one could almost hear Ebony and Ivory playing in the distance… Until the little shit jumped right onto my (still very tender) ribs and we both learned just how high a human being can levitate with the proper motivation. Tracy said she was pretty sure one of the doormen from the bar could get me some Vicodin, but I opted for a more time-tested, natural remedy – Whisky, and lots of it.

Knox called and told Tracy that a car would patrol the area from time to time in case any of those ne'er-do-wells decided to try again. This was pretty comforting to me, because at the time I would've lost a bout to Misty's Jell-O, let alone some mad Triad bomber or our infamous Dim Mak killer.

So we rented a truckload of movies and spent a lot of time together on the couch watching them and, occasionally, making out like rave kids. A perfect combination of casual hang-out, slumber party, romantic getaway, and excruciating, mind-numbing pain. Still, it was the most fun I'd had in a while, what with getting blown through my car and all.

I went to see it in the police impound lot. I had to say goodbye. Looking at the twisted wreckage, I had to admit that I was pretty impressed with myself for surviving the whole ordeal, but still… I loved that car.

It was going to take a lot of getting used to, being a pedestrian.

47

The old man took a pair of reading glasses from the pocket of his flannel shirt and slid them on, blinking with magnified eyes as he got used to the change in vision. He leaned forward and peered at the photos laid out on the table, clucking and shaking his head occasionally. I looked at them too. The photos had been taken after Mei Ling's body had laid long enough for the blood to pool from her tissues. Her skin, in the photos, was no longer blue but a pale olive. The only obvious discoloration on her body was in the area from the tops of her breasts to her ribs – the areas she'd been struck.

It looked almost as if someone had dipped mittens in black paint and tried to feel her up.

When Knox said something about the dark bruising, Master Cheng said, "Poison blood collect there."

Knox waited for a minute to see if the old man was going to explain further, but he didn't. Shaking his head, the cop went out to get more coffee.

Master Cheng perused the rest of the photos and grunted. Then, sitting back in his standard issue uncomfortable police department metal chair, he folded his hands over his round belly and closed his eyes. Within seconds, he snored softly.

When Knox returned with coffee (and a tea for Cheng), he looked at the old man and said, "Jesus."

With a dry lip smack, Master Cheng said, "Flattery will get you nowhere, Detective."

His eyes were still closed, his posture remained the same, and his breathing was slow and even.

Knox leaned on the table and whispered to me, "Find anything out?"

I shrugged.

"Two different styles," Cheng said, still seemingly asleep.

"I'm sorry?" Knox said.

The old man opened his eyes and said, "Do not be. Like your lumpy-headed friend, you cannot help that you were born into a hairy, brutish, ape-like American body. To the list of your nation's failings shall I add hard of hearing? I said these were two different styles."

I frowned and looked down at the pictures.

"What do you mean, master?" I said.

"I mean just what I say."

I picked up several of the photos and studied them.

"Are you saying they fought?" I said.

"Who?" Knox said.

"The girl and her murderer. Pay attention," Master Cheng said.

Knox took the photos from me and flipped through them.

"The full story is there for one with eyes to see. Look at the girl's hands. Carefully. Are they the hands of a young girl?"

"Her hands look delicate, Master," I said.

"Look at her knuckles – she has undergone conditioning training," Cheng said.

I looked at the photo. How Master Cheng could tell anything about her hands from these pictures, without a magnifying glass at least, was beyond me.

"Her build, the condition of her hands, the injuries she sustained… I would guess that the girl practiced some type of Shaolin martial arts. Her killer, if my intuition is correct, is a practitioner of Chen style Tai Chi Chuan."

"How could you know that?" I said.

"I cannot *know* it, but the bruising along the insides of her arms, especially in the areas of the *Chize* and *Kongzui* points, bring to mind certain tactics I've known some Chen practitioners to use."

I looked at the photos and for the first time caught the faint, brownish, smudge-like bruises in the crook of her right elbow and forearm.

"Additionally, though we cannot tell from these photos, I would not be surprised to find similar bruising on her hand, in the *Taiyuan*. If this is the case, the utilization of the *An* strike as a deathblow was, in actuality, a mercy."

"What are you guys saying? Lee, you're the translator. Translate,"

Knox said.

"Ah, it's acupuncturist talk, mostly," I said, which was only a whitish lie. "The fight was brutal enough that killing her with such a swift blow was a kindness."

"Brutal? She's got barely a mark on her…"

"The killer is sloppy. Too skilled to be an American, surely, but still an amateur. If he were expert, she would have no mark on her at all. Only her organs would show the extent of the damage," Master Cheng said.

"So any idea how we catch this guy?" Knox said.

Master Cheng stood and slipped on his windbreaker.

"Not my department. You are the cop," he said, standing.

"Yeah, that's what you two keep telling me. Whoa, pal, where are you going?" Knox said. "I still have a lot of questions."

The old man shuffled out of the room and said, "I have no more answers for you. I must take a piss and then it's home for a nap. Tomorrow, Lee. Six o'clock."

With that, he left.

Barnaby-freaking-Jones, indeed.

48

"Stop, stop, stop!"

I froze, holding the stance, expecting some sort of correction to my form. Instead, he gestured to a chair.

"Sit, dummy. Your footwork is fine…perhaps even good. It's when you move that is shit."

With the grey skies threatening to unleash sheets of rain and ice, Master Cheng had decided to hold our first class in his living room. Though the room was small and filled with clutter – stacks of old newspapers, TV guides, and dog-eared issues of Prevention magazine covered every available semi-flat surface – Master said this was ideal. Tai Chi Chuan, he said, should be practiced not only in wide open spaces but in small, cramped spaces, hills, anyplace with uncertain terrain. The key, he said, was being fluid and adaptive.

Part of my adapting included practicing one-handed. Though my injuries were mostly healed - miraculously so according to my doctors - I still had to keep my arm in a sling to immobilize my collar bone. I would occasionally forget myself and start to use the arm - proof, Master Cheng said, of my lack of mindfulness – but pain is an excellent teacher.

When I sat in the easy chair, its plastic cover crackling a protest beneath me, I was glad for the break. My hips and lower back ached in ways they hadn't since I was a child. Master Cheng's training involved lower stances and smaller movements; he said my large frame style was fine for "children and geezers."

Master sat across from me and sipped Coke from a McDonald's cup.

"When you practice, you visualize your opponent," he said, wiping his chin with his sleeve.

"Yes," I said. It was a classical training method that taught the mind to move the *chi* through the proper meridians and to the proper body parts for each combat application.

He nodded and said, "Watch. This is my Tai Chi face."

Without any change in expression, he stared at me blankly for probably thirty seconds.

"This, dummy, is your Tai Chi face."

He immediately grimaced, eyes glaring, teeth clenched, and held his breath until his face was red.

He said, "I presume much, but hope that you see the difference."

I nodded and kept my chin down, hoping to hide the grin that threatened to overtake my face each time I remembered "my Tai Chi face."

"When you are visualizing the opponent," Cheng said, "your mistake is to imagine *fighting*."

This puzzled me a bit. It must've showed, because the old man stood and assumed a stance; I knew from his position that he meant for us to push hands.

I stood, mirrored his stance, and placed my forearm against his. As we began to move, his push neutralized by me, my push neutralized by him, he said, "Do we fight now?"

"No," I said. Pushing hands was primarily an exercise to develop sensitivity and *nian jing* or 'sticking energy'. Only by relaxing completely can one interpret the incoming push and properly yield to it; fighting or struggling is counterproductive.

"Find my center, boy… c'mon, get me!"

When I pushed against him, it felt like pushing against a revolving door. It was surprising, because practicing with Master Cheng's student had been like trying to push against smoke. Perhaps the master was getting too old and inflexible to follow his own teachings.

Out of respect, I did not want to exploit the weakness, but I knew that if I didn't really go after him that could be seen as an insult to his skill. So, after neutralizing his push I slowly found his center of gravity, his root, and trapped it; I pushed in until he could not yield any more. At the last possible second, before pinning his arm to his chest, I felt his weight – the revolving door I'd managed to lock into place – dissipate.

I managed to avoid hitting the coffee table with my face, but that meant that instead my full weight fell on my shoulder, sending neon-bright mushroom clouds of pain from my collar bone to my brain. I rolled over, panting from the effort of it, and looked up at the old man.

He still stood in the same place, his feet never having moved, and giggled.

"See? This is the game of Tai Chi Chuan… pushing me is like pushing a beach ball in the water. Just when you think you've sunk it, it just rolls out from under you."

I nodded and staggered to my feet, half of my body numb with pain.

"In defense, you must be like the beach ball, you see? In attack, you must be like the whip. A whip, you understand?"

He mimicked snapping a whip with one hand.

I nodded.

"A whip is loose, fluid… a rigid whip is nothing but a club! Clubs bend and break; the whip entangles, it flows around, and at the last second, it snaps against its target and transfers the built up force. This…" He performed a movement called 'Brush Knee and Twist Step' slowly, calmly. "…is the whip. *This…*" He did the technique again, but wearing the grimace he'd worn earlier. "…is a club."

The pieces came together in my mind and I finally understood. Or, at least, I thought I did.

"When you practice, visualizing an opponent is good. Your attitude, though, must not be one of fighting…it must be one of mischief. Your goal is not to strike or break or maim or kill. Your goal is to tag and trap and lure… to play with them as a cat plays with a mouse."

"I understand, Master, but…"

He smiled and said, "But you know in your head what each movement is really for, yes?"

"Yes," I said. Most of the postures in the form illustrated techniques that, when done correctly, were not only lethal, but brutally so.

"This is not your concern. Your concern is to practice correctly, in the spirit of play. When we play, we are as children. We relax, we smile, we enjoy. When we fight, there is tension. Tension is not Tai Chi Chuan.

"When I practice 'Brush Knee', all that I am is 'Brush Knee'. This is *Wei Wu Wei,* to do without doing. When I am 'Brush Knee' or 'White Crane Spreading Wings' or any other movement, I am like a child. The person who steps outside of nature's harmony to strike me will find that I am as formless and soft as a cloud. I only move – no attack or defense – only move; if they are broken or injured within my movement, well, they had no business being there. A person who jumps in the ocean should not be surprised to get wet, yes? This is his problem, not mine. I will not fret about this; all that I do is in the spirit of play."

It had been a long time since I had practiced just for the joy of it, since I had kept a spirit of play. Too often, my shadow opponent took on a face.

Too often, my practice *was* stiff.

It had been a few years since I'd truly practiced Tai Chi Chuan; all this time, I'd been fantasizing about a revenge I could never have.

49

When the day's lesson was finished I walked across the street, through the cold rain, and unlocked Tracy's car. She'd handed me the keys when she'd stumbled in, bleary-eyed from work, at five in the morning. Before falling into bed and passing out, she told me to wake her by two o'clock so we would have enough time to eat and shop before we had to get ready.

With all the excitement, I'd nearly forgotten – Tony Lau's exhibit.

On the way home, I took a brief detour to drive past my place. The police tape was gone, but the doors and my shop window were still boarded up. The landlord still hadn't given me a time or date for the repairs. I thought about relocating, but I'd just started building a client base and moving now wouldn't be great for business.

Of course, one had to be open for business to have a business, so there I was back to square one. Depressing. Really damned depressing.

I was too sore to practice and it was too early in the day to get drunk, even for me, so I did the only other thing I could think of to shake the blues – I went back to Tracy's.

After a shower and a turkey and swiss on wheat, I crept into the dark bedroom and slid into bed next to her. I laid there and felt her beside me - the soft curve of her chest, rising and falling, in a thin cotton tank top. The long, elegant line of her legs. The heat of her breath.

Somewhere in the midst of that perfection, I slept.

50

Parking was hell, but we still made it in time to meet Knox and his wife, Marta, at the entrance to the museum at quarter to eight. Marta was cute. Short blonde hair, green eyes, tasteful red gown that still managed to show off some cleavage and leg, both of which were very worthy of display. Everyone was introduced to everyone and we all went inside.

The museum was specially decorated for the exhibit. Long silk banners emblazoned with Chinese calligraphy and I Ching trigrams hung from the ceiling in the sculpture hall. Classical Chinese music played, and waitresses dressed in silk brocade *cheongsams* wandered the hall, offering champagne and appetizers. Tracy and I grabbed some champagne and I picked up a program from a table by the door.

'Changes – Elements of the I Ching' it read.

Apparently, each of Lau's sixty-four paintings depicted a different hexagram from the book of changes. The pamphlet gave a short bio of the artist, conveniently leaving out anything about the family business, of course.

"Holy shit," Tracy said, smiling slowly.

"What?" I said following her line of vision to a small dj booth set inconspicuously in the corner and the bored kid working it.

"Chucky. He used to dj at the bar," she said, heading in his direction. I followed; in the long black evening gown she wore, being behind her was an enviable position.

"Yo, Chuck," she said as we approached. A few older, artsy types in the vicinity cast snotty glances our way – apparently they didn't think enthusiasm or excitement belonged in a museum – but Tracy never noticed and, thanks to my rough-and-tough demeanor, the uptight busybodies decided it was best for them to mind their own damned business.

"Bunny? Christ, what brings you here?" The kid said. I felt no warm fuzzies for 'Chucky' right from the start. Maybe it was the shaved head, or the neck tattoo half hidden by his collar, but I like to think it was his eyes that clinched it. To be more specific, they were all over my girl, and in a mighty familiar way.

"...'Bunny'?" I said. If luck was with me, that didn't come out half as snotty as it sounded in my head. Tracy gave me a look. Whoops, no such luck. Her tight-lipped smile spoke volumes.

"Randall, this is my *friend* Chucky. Chucky, this is Randall."

Chucky grinned and threw his hand my way. I shook the thing with just the right amount of firmness and for the right amount of time. Big hands on that kid; long fingers.

Tracy nodded to me, clearly happy that I was playing nice.

Screw that. I was pretty proud of myself for not immediately chiming in with, "Yeah, I'm Randall...Tracy's *boyfriend."*

"So, what brings you here?" Chucky said, turning back to Tracy. Clearly he was done with me. I slid a half step closer to Tracy, keeping well within the kid's peripheral vision. Childish?

Sure.

Was I going to keep it up?

Damn skippy.

"Ah, the artist is a friend of Randall's," she said.

To the kid's credit, he didn't say 'who?' like I would have in his place.

What he did say was, "Wicked. Guy does cool stuff. I mean, y'know, I prefer our work..."

He smiled. Perfect teeth. Tracy looked down at her champagne as if it suddenly had colonies of sea monkeys in it. Her cheeks had a healthy tinge of pink to them.

"What work would that be?" I said. To the untrained ear, you really couldn't tell my teeth were clenched or anything. Tracy still meditated on the tiny bubbles; Chucky said, "Oh, we worked on a painting a while back."

I gave the appearance of detached interest, I hope, as I said, "Really? Sounds great."

"Oh yeah, man, Bunny's the best model I've ever worked with."

The sound I made resembled a "Hm" but really meant "I want to feel your corneas squish between my fingers."

Our eyes met, he and I, and there was no mistaking it – we understood each other just fine.

"So how did you manage to land this gig, Chucky?" Tracy said brightly.

Before Chucky could turn, I said, "This little nickname…Bunny…What's that all about? Where'd that come from?"

Tracy's hand was on my elbow. She said, "We're losing John and Marta…Randall?"

Still looking at me, Chucky laughed and said, "Remember that old commercial with the bunny? 'It keeps going…and going…and going…'? That's my Bunny."

Even though she was doing her best to hide it, Tracy was red with embarrassment and anger.

"God damn it, Chuck," she hissed.

"What?" he said, playing totally innocent.

She turned and walked away, toward the ladies room; the sound of her heels on the marble floor echoed like thunder.

I glanced at Chucky. He grinned and spread his hands and said, "Women, huh, man? No hard feelings or anything, by the way… I mean that's all ancient history."

Putting on my most charming smile, I said, "Hey, sure! No problem. But if you ever call her Bunny again, I will tear off your genitals with my bare hands and stuff them down your throat, alright Chucky-ole-pal?"

The grin slid off Chucky's face and dribbled away; I held up my glass in a silent toast and left to find Tracy.

Knox and his wife were on their way into Lau's gallery. I knew John didn't give a damn about the paintings, but he wanted a chance to have a friendly chat with Lau senior.

I didn't plan on being so friendly. I don't take kindly to organized attacks, especially the kind that explode. First, though, I had Tracy to think about. When she emerged from the ladies room, she was perfectly composed but the look she gave me was serious and hurt and angry. Before I had a chance to say anything, she said, "…Don't look at me like that. I didn't tell you because I knew how you'd be about it. It was a long time ago, and it wasn't anything serious."

"Okay."

"I hate when you get all jealous and shit. I don't need you puffing your chest out at every guy who looks my way, you know. How would you like that shit?"

"Well…If you puffed your chest out at every guy that looked my way, they wouldn't be looking my way for long," I said.

It didn't even rank a smile.

"How long did it take before you threatened to beat him up?" She said.

I noticed just how fizzy my champagne was; I could see the attraction in just staring at it.

She sighed wearily. "I am going to go look at the exhibit and then I'm going home. I've got a fucking headache."

She pushed past me and went into the gallery.

I finished my champagne.

A distinguished looking Chinese man in a very expensive suit entered the museum.

Judging by his escort – eight young, well-muscled guys in similar suits – I figured this was Jimmy Yi Lau, just the guy to take out my frustrations on. Unfortunately for me, his guards led him through a side gallery before I got anywhere close to him. With things going as they were, I decided to hit the gallery and find Knox. I figured that, if nothing else, I could count on him not to piss on my already crappy evening.

The exhibit gallery was packed with the city's pseudo elite; the opening night reception was strictly invitation only. I was certain the mayor was there, and probably some other prominent local folks, but I wouldn't know them if I saw them. Out of the throng, I saw Tony Lau and Daniel, Knox and his wife, Jimmy Lau's entourage, and, in a far corner, Tracy with an older couple. She was smiling, at least, and seemed to be having a good time.

I noticed the first painting, the hexagram *Khien.* Done in the style of Chinese calligraphy, the image depicted two dragons, one black and silver and the other white and gold, entangled in the throes of battle. That, or they were fucking.

"Pretentious and fruity, with hints of elderberry and peach, wouldn't you say?"

I turned, acknowledged Knox's presence, and said, "You find anything out?"

"Yeah. That I hate this kind of shit."

"Have you no appreciation for culture, detective?"

"Sure I do… I heard there are girls in Hong Kong that can do this really cool trick with a ping pong ball…"

"Filthy *Gwailo.*"

"Count on it. You see big daddy Lau?"

"Yeah, him and his goon squad," I said.

"I take it you two didn't get to chat?"

"Not even close," I said.

He nodded. "Me either. Can't imagine why a businessman would need an armed escort to go to an art museum."

"They're armed? How can you tell?"

"Well, those bulges by the armpit? On each guy? Either those are shoulder holsters, or Lau needs to change the name of his gang from Eight Tigers to The Abnormal Chest Tumor Boys."

I stared at him for a second before saying, "How many glasses of champagne have you had?"

"Three, why?"

"Abnormal Chest Tumor Boys? Really?"

"What, I thought it was funny," he said.

"Should you even be drinking? We got our prime suspect here, and you're getting sauced."

"Like I need an intervention from *you* of all people. Look, if I need to jump in and arrest Lau, I will, but that's not going to happen, Lee. Not here. Too public, too much shit going on. We're not going to get the guy to slip up here. So we just do what we can."

"Alright, fine. Have another drink, I'll tell Marta she's driving."

"You got some kind of a master plan, Mr. Comedy?"

"Don't I always?"

"No, not really," he said.

"Well, then there's not really any point in starting now," I said.

I decided to fall back on what little plan I did have: wander around, keep my ears open, occasionally make an ass of myself and see where that takes me. In other words, pretty much the same stuff I always did.

I saw Daniel alone, admiring a painting called '*Pi* – In search of beauty'. Unlike the first, this one was a large canvas covered in thick, chunky layers of paint. Remembering Tracy's lesson of art appreciation, the picture – seemingly a portrait in earth tones – reminded me of melted crayons.

"Kinda makes you want to reach out and touch it, doesn't it? Just to feel that texture…" I said. Not the most elegant of openings, I know, but I had to say something.

"I have touched it," he said.

My mind scrambled for something to say, but I was born lacking the fundamental ability to small-talk. Luckily, Daniel said, "Have you learned anything new?"

I sat beside him on a wooden bench in front of the painting.

"A great many things," I said.

"Oh?"

"Yeah… uh… some things your boss may not want to hear, actually."

He didn't acknowledge that I'd said anything, though I knew he'd heard.

"Several things seem to indicate that Jimmy Lau is responsible for Mei Ling's death."

He kept on with the silence.

"I know this makes things…difficult, to say the least, but…"

"This is not possible," he said.

"Look, I know it's a shock, but…"

"This is not possible. Leave it be."

"Daniel, I need to…"

He stood abruptly and shouted, "Leave it be, god damn you."

I sat there and watched him storm off. After he'd left, and after the majority of the other patrons had gone back to ogling the artwork instead of me, one of the waitresses came to recover Daniel's abandoned glass.

As she did, I said, "Pardon me, Miss… Could I ask you a question?"

"Certainly, sir."

"Do I smell?"

"Pardon?"

"Am I offensive to you in some way? Be honest."

"…No…sir…"

"Ah, good. Just been that sort of evening. Thanks."

I caught sight of Jimmy Lau and his boys on the other side of the gallery and decided that, if nothing else, I could use my powers of irritation for good instead of evil. On the way across the room, however, I was intercepted. I didn't mind terribly because it was a beautiful woman who hijacked me.

Either all had been forgiven, or Tracy was an excellent actress. She was all smiles and fondness and warm cuddles as she led me over to the older couple I'd seen her with earlier.

"Randall, this is Lawrence and Genevieve," she said.

As neither of them extended a hand, I didn't offer mine. Instead I smiled and nodded, a skill I was quickly becoming adept at. Another skill I'd become adept at, just that evening, was that of rolling with the punches, so to speak. I barely flinched at all when Tracy said, "Dad, mom, this is Dr. Randall Lee, the man I told you about."

I flagged down another waitress and asked if they'd stocked any scotch for the occasion. She shook her head apologetically.

One thing can be said about my luck – at least it's consistent.

51

Tracy's parents seemed like decent people.

Lifetime members of the art museum, devoted teachers, involved parents, committed Catholics…

And then there was me: the lecherous old scumbag out to deflower their beautiful, virginal angel. Reality was looking out for Mr. and Mrs. Sandoval that night – Neither Chucky nor I shattered their illusions.

Though my brain repressed the memory of most of that conversation, I retained bits about my practice, how I'd helped Tracy, and my strange collaboration with the local police. Sensing an opportunity to exit, however inelegant, I said, "Hey, speaking of that - I don't know if Tracy told you or not, but I'm actually here tonight because the sponsor of the event is a high level gangster that might have had his son's fiancé killed. So I'm going to go see what's up with that. You guys have a great night; it was really nice to meet you both."

All three Sandovals looked at me like I'd just pulled down my pants and chased them around the room, but I wasn't about to miss another chance at Jimmy Lau. The big boss was schmoozing with some yuppies near the painting of the hexagram *Sung* – Conflict, while his guards stood around being inconspicuously menacing. I wondered for a minute how to approach him, but the whole scene – a murderer enjoying his drink and conversing about culture and business while a young girl and her unborn child lay rotting in a box somewhere – enraged me so much that I stopped thinking and just acted.

Thinking too much had never done me much good anyway, honestly.

I strolled right up like I owned the damned place and made it within ten feet of the man before the biggest and most muscular

Chinese man I'd ever seen stepped in front of me and slapped his meaty palm on my chest. "This portion of the gallery is off limits at the moment, sir. Feel free to come back in ten to fifteen minutes. Sorry for the inconvenience."

A polite thug. Must be a new model.

"Tell you what, Bolo, take your hand off me before I snap it off and shove it up your ass. Sound good? I need a word with your boss."

The flat palm on my chest curled slowly into a fist, crumpling my shirt with it. He pulled me in close. It's hard to feel manly when your feet are an inch off the ground, but I held my own.

"Mr. Lau is not interested in talking with you at the moment, sir. Please take your business elsewhere."

The other guards were staring, I noticed. So were the yuppies and Lau.

Cool, an audience.

"I apologize," I said, "but I just wanted to make sure I hadn't hurt the other guys too bad. I know there's not a lot of desk jobs in the Triads, and I'd hate to think I ruined their careers as professional muscle…"

Lau grinned and excused himself from his upwardly mobile company to come closer.

"Samson," he said, "let him go. It's alright."

I looked up at the beefy guy holding me and said, "Your name's Samson? Really? Cuz I was only screwing around with the Bolo Yeung joke…"

Samson didn't think I was funny. Either that or they sneer and growl as a sign of approval on whatever mutant-steroid-freak planet he came from. He dropped me. I smoothed out my shirt with whatever dignity I could muster (think Sean Connery after a good ass kicking).

Lau extended a hand and introduced himself. I shook it, though he disgusted me, and said, "I'm the guy from San Francisco, but I'm sure you knew that already."

If he did, he didn't let it show. In fact, his expression remained a warm neutral the whole time. I bet he'd be a bitch to play poker with.

"Well, Mr. guy from San Francisco, what is it that I can do for you?"

"For starters," I said, "why'd you send your boys to rough me up?"

His eyes lit up as if he'd just recognized an old friend. "You must be Mr. Lee! Shall we go for a walk?"

"If it's all the same to you, I'd kinda prefer staying in a visible, public place."

"Afraid?"

"Smart." Okay, that was probably a lie.

He laughed and clapped me on the shoulder. His guards still glared menacingly. I tried to muster up a doe-eyed mew for them, but it just wasn't in me. Lau called over a waitress and said, "A drink for my friend, anything he wants."

She looked at me and I said, "You got any scotch?"

I didn't have high hopes.

"Single malt, sir?" She said.

"Uh…yeah. Sure," I said.

She nodded and hurried away to fetch my drink.

Thugs always have the best fringe benefits.

"Mr. Lee, I am afraid we may have started off on the wrong foot," Lau said. "My people informed me that you were asking questions about Ms. Zhao, and I told them to bring you in. I am committed to finding the man who killed her, Mr. Lee."

"Yeah? You and O.J. put together a task force?"

"Mei Ling was like a daughter to me, Mr. Lee."

"Why not have the cops bring me in, then?"

He sipped his drink and said, "American police have never done anything but cause me problems. One cannot be Chinese and successful, it seems, without being accused of being a criminal."

"You trying to tell me that you aren't one?"

I thought for sure that if I chipped away at him, I could break that nice-guy façade, but he just kept on acting like my favorite uncle.

"I am a businessman, Mr. Lee. Import/export, shipping, that sort of thing. Boring, tedious business, I'm afraid, but lucrative. People are not interested in the truth, though. It's much more interesting for them to say I am a gangster, you know."

"Eight Tigers, Lau? You trying to say you're not the boss?" I said.

"I don't deny it at all," he said.

That threw my line of questioning. I was all ready to shout out Aha! and lay out the evidence Knox had found linking him to the Eight Tigers, but now there was no need. Instead, I went with a time-tested follow-up question.

"What?"

"Tell me, Mr. Lee, do you know how the Triads came into being?"

He waited. I tried to think of something clever, but I had nothing.

"No?" He said, "During the Qing Dynasty, when the Manchu ruled China, a group of patriots formed an underground organization called *Tian Di Hui*."

"The Heaven and Earth Society," I said. I figured I could at least seem like I knew a little bit of what was going on. The waitress returned with my drink. I sipped it. Nice. Maybe I was working for the wrong side.

"Correct. The term 'Triad' came from the Society's use of a triangle to represent the balance of heaven, earth, and man. Their purpose was to return China to Han rule… just as your founding fathers sought to expel the British."

"The founding fathers never dealt much with prostitution, drug trafficking, or assassination… to my knowledge, at least."

"Now, now, Mr. Lee… the Triads have a long history of providing to the people the things they desire. Sometimes the desires of the people fall outside the law, true, but whose law? Under communist rule, the Triads smuggle Christian bibles, Buddhist sutras, and other religious items to the people. During the Cultural Revolution, it was the Triads who were entrusted to keep the old ways safe from those who would destroy them. On a more personal note, the Eight Tigers Society has bought out low-rent housing in several major cities, including St. Louis, and renovated entire neighborhoods for the immigrants seeking to start prosperous new lives in this country. If doing these things for my people makes me a criminal then so be it."

"Gosh, sir, I guess you're right…you're not a scumbag, you're a cultural hero. That's why you run a string of massage parlors, right?"

Gotcha, I thought.

"Again, I do not deny it. Are you familiar with the One-Child policy of the People's Republic of China, Mr. Lee?"

"Yes," I said.

"Then you know that life is not easy for young girls in China. Some do not make it past their first day of life… Many families cannot afford to have daughters, you see. It is a harsh reality of the world. We do our part, bringing some of the unwanted here to this country where they have a chance at something."

"The life of a whore is hardly a chance."

"It is unfortunate, but we must require a service from the girls we assist. This is true, but it is hardly the terrible fate you suggest. Two years of guaranteed work. In return, they receive a home. When their two years are up, they may do whatever they wish. I see that this disgusts you, Mr. Lee, but what do *you* do for them? Many of these girls do not speak English, they have no education, they have no skills. They do what they have to, to survive. And I do what I can to help them, to make their lives better."

"So you're a saint," I said.

He laughed and said, "No, Mr. Lee, not a saint. Neither am I the monster you believe me to be. If I were, would we be having this discussion?"

"We wouldn't be talking at all if your boys were better with their bomb-building, would we?"

At this, finally, he frowned. "I do not follow," he said.

"Ah, now we're getting somewhere. Does the name Kip Yam mean anything to you?"

He shook his head. "Should it?"

"Well, maybe you don't micromanage to that level, but he's one of your local boys here. Cops held him in connection to the murder of a stripper, one of your former employees."

He still acted cool, but I could tell I'd finally weaseled my way in.

"A *local*, you say?"

"Yep," I said.

"He claimed to be Eight Tigers?"

"Yep."

He slammed the last bit of his drink and flagged down the waitress for another.

"I do not have any men in this area, Mr. Lee."

"Bullshit."

"Though my business is none of yours, Lee, I am in a good mood tonight so I will humor you for a bit longer… I have no men in this city. To be frank, it's not worth my time. Chicago, yes. New York, yes. Vegas, New Orleans, Atlantic City, and, of course, San Francisco. Not St. Louis. My deputies from Chicago come down every few months to ensure that our interests here are doing well, but there is no need for a permanent presence. If someone here told you they were Eight Tigers, they lied to you."

He reached into his jacket pocket and produced a small gold case. Flicking it open, he took a business card and handed it to me. "It's been a pleasure to speak with you, Mr. Lee, and if I can be of any assistance with the matter of Ms. Zhao, let me know. For now, though, I would like to enjoy a relaxing evening around my son's beautiful work, if you don't mind."

I pocketed the card, shook his hand again, and bid him a good evening.

Lau and his boys left to wander amongst the paintings; I stood around and drank. Lately, it seemed to be about the only thing I did well.

52

"What'd you get?" Knox said.

"Free scotch," I said, holding up the glass.

Knox frowned and rubbed the imaginary stubble on his chin. Marta was off powdering her nose, Tracy was still with her folks, and us boys had a moment alone to talk about the train wreck that was this case.

"Lau says the Eight Tigers isn't involved," I said, finishing my scotch. I flagged down a familiar waitress and told her to bring me another – on Mr. Lau's orders. She nodded and hurried off.

"Of course he fucking says that…what'd you think, under your justice-seeking glare he'd just up and confess?"

"He sounded convincing," I said.

Knox sighed heavily. "Do you honestly think a guy could make it up the ranks to be the big boss without being a cold-blooded fucking snake? C'mon, Randall, think for a minute. What did he say when you mentioned the suitcase of cash?"

Shit.

"I…forgot to bring that up."

Knox leaned back against the wall and lightly banged his head into the marble.

"What, I'm sorry…it slipped my mind," I said.

"That's it, I'm un-deputizing you."

"You can't un-deputize somebody…is that even a word?"

"Yeah, it's a word, alright. And I can. It slipped your mind, Randall? What the fuck, man?"

"Y'know what? Next time, *you* interrogate the Triad boss, alright?

You need somebody stuck with needles or, like, a tongue diagnosis - I'm your man. But it's not like you were scrambling over to pump Lau for info. I had the shot, I took it. I didn't know what I was doing, obviously. Sorry… shit."

Knox sighed again. The waitress returned with my drink. Before she could walk off, I caught her elbow and held her in place long enough to drain my glass.

"Another, please? Thanks. Lau says it's cool. Really."

She frowned but left, staring at the glass as she walked away.

"You talk with Junior yet?" Knox said.

"Nah, haven't seen him, but he's the man of the hour and all…he's prolly schmoozing."

Knox started to say something, but Marta returned and leaned on him, saying, "Can we go soon? These shoes are killing my feet."

"Soon, babe," he said, kissing her nose.

I glanced over and caught sight of Jimmy Lau walking alongside his son. The older man had his arm around the young man's shoulders and reached across to ruffle his hair with the other hand – the portrait of fatherly pride. The elder Lau must've told his guards to give him some space; only the massive Samson fell within my line of sight, and he didn't seem to be paying any attention to the boss.

I watched for a second longer and saw the huge guard standing there, just staring at his own hand. The room, for me, took on a sort of electrical silence, a super-heightened version of reality I'd only experienced twice before: on the day my daughter was found, and the day I nearly blew up. I pushed past Knox, scanning the room quickly for anything that seemed out of sorts before looking back at Jimmy and Tony Lau. Whatever had keyed up my spidey senses hadn't yet alerted anyone else. I glanced back at Samson to see that he still stared blankly at his palm. At this distance, I could see the dark spots on the man's hand, but I couldn't make out what they were.

A moment later, Samson began to gush all over the floor.

The flow of dark, inky blood started from his nose, but quickly spread until it leaked from the corners of his eyes, ears, and mouth as well. No one else noticed for a minute, the guards were so adept at blending with the scenery that the other patrons no longer noticed them at all, until I shoved my way through the crowd, calling out to Knox as I went.

Someone screamed at the sight; Samson slumped to his knees before flopping over onto his side. Jimmy Lau saw me, a look of worry crossing his usually neutral features.

I arrived to the spot where Samson laid and knelt down beside him. The man's eyes rolled around nonsensically in his head, and his body began to seize, the huge planks of muscle stiffening and shaking. The heels of his dress shoes tap danced on the marble floor, the clicks echoing in the now-quiet museum as onlookers gathered to watch him bleed.

I pressed my fingers to his neck, feeling for a pulse. What I felt was too fast and too hard. The guy's heart was ready to burst. I grabbed his shirt and ripped it open, looking for some sign of the trauma. Samson blindly clawed at my arms, his mouth working frantically. The only sound was the wet rasp of a drowning man. More of the blackish fluid spilled from his mouth and spattered my shirt. When he squeezed my forearms, his fingertips erupted, spraying thick, black poison blood from the nail beds.

A woman near me screamed, and I turned to see that quite a crowd was forming around us. The screamer was my favorite waitress. I stood, grabbed her shoulders, and spun her around so I could see her hair. It was wrapped in a complicated imitation Chinese bun, and held into place with bobby pins.

Jackpot.

I grabbed a handful of the pins and yanked, accidentally pulling out a few chunks of hair with them. I'd apologize later.

Kneeling back down, I bent the pins in half.

"Holy Christ, what the fuck happened?"

I glanced over my shoulder at Knox and said, "Bad shit. Stay with Lau and watch him."

Samson made more gurgling sounds. I turned his head and shoved my fingers into his mouth; the excess blood had already begun to congeal, choking him. I cleared his airway and kept his head turned so that the fluid could drain out. I ripped his sleeves to expose his arms, located several points, and began to shove the pins into them. Several of the onlookers groaned at the sight, but that was to be expected; I swore to myself that I'd always keep a pack of acupuncture needles in my pocket from that moment on.

The points I'd stuck oozed black. I turned several of the pins counterclockwise and then felt for his pulse again. It was still too fast, but it had already begun to slow somewhat. I wasn't expecting the guy to make a complete recovery, to recover at all in fact, but I had to try. If nothing else, I hoped he could tell us who'd done this to him, assuming he knew.

I looked back at Knox. He had Jimmy and Tony Lau with him,

and the three of them stared down at Samson and me. Jimmy looked visibly shaken; his skin was grey, one hand pressed to his chest, the other holding a small silver pistol. I looked down to check my makeshift needles again, but did a quick double-take at Lau. He seemed to age before my eyes. His skin had become papery and ashen; he gasped and fell.

"Shit!" I said, scrambling over to his side. "I said watch him, Knox, dammit."

"I *was* watching him. What the fuck was I watching *for?*"

"Secure all the exits. Don't let anybody leave."

"How the fuck am I supposed to do that?"

"Call for backup or something, I don't know. Do your cop shit."

"Fuck," he muttered, running for the entrance.

I felt for a pulse, but there was nothing there.

"Dad? Dad? C'mon, dad…" Tony crouched down next to his father and took his hands. I took a deep breath and let it out before standing and scanning the room again.

"You!" Tony screamed to me, "You're supposed to be a doctor - help him."

"I'm sorry…I can't. He's gone," I said.

"Try CPR or something, c'mon…"

"He's gone, Tony. I'm very sorry, but there's nothing I can do."

Lau slumped down by his father and wept. I pushed past the crowd and ran out to the parking lot. Nothing moved. No squealing tires. Nobody hauling ass out of the lot.

Because the killer knew he didn't have to.

He'd won again.

53

After Samson was taken by ambulance to the hospital and Mr. Lau's body was taken to the morgue, after police interviews and statements and searches of the building and everything else, I met Tracy at her car and together we drove toward home. The car ride was an exercise in uncomfortable silences until she said, "Randall, what happened to that man… the big guy?"

I thought over my answer carefully before saying, "You know how acupuncture works?"

"…Well, you told me the whole thing about balancing yin and yang, and something about heat and dampness or something… mostly I was looking at your eyes, so I just did a lot of nodding and smiling."

Nice to know I wasn't the only one.

"Just as the body has veins and arteries that carry blood to all of the organs, the body has energetic veins and arteries, called meridians, that provide each part of the body with the energy it needs to do its work. Imbalanced or stagnant energy, among other things, can be corrected by using needles to break up blockages, increase or decrease the energy in an area, whatever's needed. Follow so far?"

"I think so."

"Okay. So when the old masters, thousands of years ago, were developing and cataloguing the various points along the meridians, they would *buy* prisoners from the jails to experiment on. This was a very different time, you understand… this was an acceptable practice then. The masters would stimulate a point, over and over, and observe and document the effects, good and bad. In this way, healers had a standardized reference work for the first time. The masters were primarily concerned with healing and so they did not publish all of their research; some of the material was too dangerous, too damaging in the wrong hands. In some of the internal martial arts, though, there are specific strikes to acupuncture points that can cause incredible harm to the body… they're hidden inside the forms to keep them from the uninitiated, but they're still there."

"So the same points you use to heal people can also kill people?" Tracy said.

I nodded.

"Think of modern medicine… if a person is anemic, their body needs iron, sometimes in large doses. If you give that same dosage of iron to a healthy person, you can kill them. In a way, that's the sort of thing I'm talking about. The man you saw tonight, Samson, was a very healthy, athletic guy. The man who attacked him used a very secret technique to hyper-stimulate the bone marrow."

I felt Tracy staring at me. At last, she said, "Huh?"

"Okay, imagine a factory that manufactures blood. Let's say that on a normal day, the workers are able to turn out 1,000 units. Now imagine somebody comes in and laces the workers' coffee with crack cocaine… that day, the factory turns out 10,000 units. Suddenly, there's no place to put any of it. Do you get what I'm saying?"

"So this killer guy caused so much blood that it just started leaking out of him?"

"The goal was to drown him in his own fluids, yes."

I looked over at her. Her eyes were wide, and she said, "That's pretty fucking harsh."

I nodded.

She said, "So what'd you do to him?"

"Corrected the problem…told his body to knock it off, basically. The problem is, even though his body's equilibrium is reestablished, the rest of that blood has to be drained…it's sort of a full body congestive heart failure."

"Damn. Somebody really wanted him dead that bad?"

"No, somebody really wanted to create a big neon sign saying, 'Look over here, you stupid fuckers,' and it worked. A big flashy, oozing neon sign of death to get everyone's attention while he quickly and quietly killed Jimmy Lau."

"There was nothing you could do for him?"

"No. The killer took no chances with Lau… he used a point that can make the heart instantly falter and stop. Even if he'd been in a hospital surrounded by the best doctors in the world, the disruption to the energetic system could not be repaired."

"*Shit.*"

"Yeah."

"So where does this leave things with the case?"

"Fubar," I said. "I was positive that Lau orchestrated the whole thing."

Tracy nervously chewed at a nail. "Hm. Guess not, huh?"

"Guess not."

"You think this is some kind of big vendetta against the family?"

"To be honest, I don't know what to think about any of it anymore."

I was watching the scenery move by outside the windows and listening to the silence when a sudden thought hit me like a fist to the top of the head. I picked up my phone and dialed Knox.

"Yeah," he said.

"Hey, you got statements from Lau, right?"

"Hard to do now, he's a bit stiff…"

"*Tony* Lau."

"Oh, yeah. Why?"

"Where's he staying?" I said.

"What's it to you?"

"Get men over there."

"You think I didn't already think of that?"

"Where is he, John?"

"Ritz-Carlton, room 290. Don't make me remind you that you're a civili--"

"Thank you." I hung up and turned to Tracy. She was already taking the nearest highway exit.

"On it," she said. "Just tell me where we're headed."

I love that girl.

54

I saw the squad cars on the street and told Tracy to park well away from them. I felt too tired and too irritated to deal with delays from cops, however well-meaning they were. We parked in the hotel lot and got out.

"Stay here," I said.

Tracy raised an eyebrow and put her hands on her hips. "Uh, fuck you," she said.

"This could be really dangerous," I said.

"Might not be," she said.

"I might not be able to protect you," I said.

"Randall? I'm a woman, I have boobs, and I'm a bartender…I've kinda had to learn to handle myself."

I didn't want to waste any more time arguing. We went in, collected what Tracy called "a cubic ass-ton of dirty looks," and made it into an elevator before any hotel personnel could throw us out. When the doors opened on Tony's floor, I found myself looking into a familiar pair of black sunglasses.

"You," Daniel said.

"Me," I said. "Hello, Daniel."

There was no expression on his face; another bastard who'd make a good poker player.

With no telegraphing at all, he dropped into some kind of one-armed handstand-thing.

I didn't get to see much more than that because the heel of one of his expensive dress shoes caught me in the side of the jaw, loosening a few teeth and knocking me into the back wall of the mirrored elevator hard enough to crack the glass. I heard Tracy scream; my brain went through a quick damage assessment and decided I was more or less alright.

I shook off the hit and faced my assailant. Daniel grabbed Tracy as she tried to punch and kick him, and pushed her out of the elevator. Then the doors closed, leaving us alone. He sank down into a low, rhythmic, moving stance. For a moment I thought maybe he just wanted to dance. It was then that his accent finally clicked.

"Brazilian," I said.

He didn't answer. Instead, he dropped low and skittered along the floor like some kind of lethal crab. Even in an extra spacious luxury elevator like this, there was nowhere to go.

The skitter became a spin, and he drove his shin into my left ankle. With all of my weight transferred into my right leg, the kick did nothing but provide me with the momentum needed for a left Lotus kick into the bridge of his nose. His sunglasses snapped in half and dangled from his ears for a moment before falling to the floor. The man beneath them was not so easily broken. Blood lined his flared nostrils, but that was the only sign I'd hit him at all. His eyes, steel blue and wicked, bored through me with an undisguised hatred; the rest of his features betrayed no emotion.

I heard the faint *dings* as the elevator passed each floor on its descent.

Eighteen floors – this could take a while.

He leapt forward like a leopard, throwing his front fist and knee at me simultaneously. I sidestepped and brought my hand down on his fist, trapping it to his knee, as I brought up my left knee – a posture in the form called 'Golden Rooster Stands on One Leg' – into his stomach.

Though I knew that it had to hurt, he made no sound. Instead, he wrapped his calves around my standing leg, locking his ankles together, and hooked his arms around my back, seeking to smother me to avoid another hit. With *Fa-jin*, I shook from the waist like a wet dog and the internal force behind the movement dislodged Daniel from my body and threw him into the elevator wall. I heard a satisfying crunch as another of the mirrored panels shattered. At least I wasn't going to get stuck with the full bill when this thing was done.

Assuming I lived, of course.

Daniel's eye was bleeding now, a thin trail that, in the elevator's lighting, looked like a black tear. He kicked off his shoes; not the smartest move, I thought, considering he was barefoot and there was glass on the carpeted floor.

"Hey…" I said. The rest of the sentence was intended to be some kind of entreaty to just give up and tell me where the rest of his crew was, where Mei Ling's killer was.

Instead, all that came out was, "Ow."

I blinked away the pain and blood that blurred my vision and tried not to look too surprised at the burning wet line that had appeared on my cheek. Especially considering I'd dodged the crescent kick Daniel had thrown at my face.

Then I noticed the long, mirrored sliver of glass held adeptly between his toes.

"Oh, what the..?" I managed before I had to go on the defensive again. I shrugged off my sling; it was really starting to cramp my style. A whirlwind of spinning kicks headed my way; first low, then head-level, then low again. It was unpredictable, erratic, hard-as-hell to get away from.

But then, that was the point, of course.

I got tagged a few times – the left forearm, the right bicep, the left thigh – each time cursing to myself. The injuries hurt more than they should, and they dripped…never a good sign. I was losing blood. I was running out of appendages to defend myself with.

He swiped at my face, his fingers pulled back, manicured nails aimed at my eyes. I ducked it, and put my index finger on the back of his hand. When he pulled back his arm, I stuck to him, following the movement and redirecting it. I trapped his arm to his chest and drove a *fa-jin* palm strike through his hand and into his solar plexus. Daniel rolled with the strike and used the folding motion of his torso to drive his forehead through the bridge of my nose.

I invented several new curse words.

My leg buckled as he shin-kicked the side of my thigh. He swiped again with his other hand; I raised an arm to deflect the attack, but the arm collapsed upon impact.

I was getting weak from the cuts. My vision swam.

Before Daniel could move in for the kill, though, there was a *ding* and the doors slid open. I can only imagine the expressions on the faces of the wealthy patrons as they looked into our little war zone and said, "…Uh…We'll catch the next one…"

Y'see, I didn't look.

Daniel did.

I took the opportunity to stomp on his instep, hard, and I sank into his ribs with the technique *Ji* or 'Press'. It compressed his lungs, knocked the air out of him and put his head through one of the only remaining unbroken panels of mirror on the wall.

Cheap? Sure, but what do you call slicing somebody up with your feet? Besides, as my teacher always said, history really is written by the victors so don't be afraid to fight dirty when necessary.

Later, I planned to make up a story that would make me sound really tough and cool to Tracy. For now, though, I gripped a *Chin Na* pressure point on the back of his tricep and forced him to the floor.

When the elevator doors opened again - this time looking out into the main lobby - a horde of police were waiting, weapons drawn. Tracy was with them. So was Knox.

I stood there, holding Daniel and bleeding profusely, for a moment. Once I'd caught my breath, I said, "Book 'em, Danno."

Just before collapsing.

So much for looking cool in front of Tracy.

55

Hospitals make me grumpy. Especially when I need stitches. Especially when the person responsible for me needing stitches shares a room with me.

"I don't like you," I said to Daniel.

"Told you already," Knox said, "he checked out… he's clean."

"Boys are dumb," Tracy said. "You two couldn't just talk it out?"

"He fucking hit me before I could say anything," I said.

"You hit me when I was not looking," Daniel said.

"Well? You're in the middle of a fight. Pay attention," I said.

The Brazilian just laid there in his bed, looking smug. He already had another pair of sunglasses on. For some reason, this made me irrationally angry.

"All just a misunderstanding," John said. I could tell he was enjoying this. "Daniel here thought you were the one who killed Lau."

What?

"If *I* was the killer," I said, "why would I have bothered trying to save Samson?"

"Diversion," Daniel said.

"Yeah, well, if I wanted to kill your boss, I could have done it in San Francisco," I said.

"Perhaps," Daniel said.

"Why'd you fight back, Lee, if you knew he wasn't the killer?" Knox said.

"I didn't know for sure. And Mr. Flippy-kick here didn't give me much of a choice. Besides, the fact that he knows Capoeira doesn't mean he couldn't know Tai Chi too. Actually, I just kinda figured he was covering up for his boss. I thought maybe Tony might know who the real killer was."

"I would not waste time with that geezer's art," was all Daniel said.

"Have I mentioned how much I do not like you?" I said.

56

With the numerous wounds on both of us, the doc – who I knew on a first name basis from my last stay – insisted that we both stay overnight for observation. This thrilled neither Daniel nor I, but being forced to lie around and watch TV wasn't a horrible thing, especially after taking a beating. I needed a couple stitches, a re-set nose, and a few bags of the red stuff to top me off. Daniel had a pair of broken sunglasses, a few deep tissue bruises, and a cracked rib.

Whoopidee-doo.

Tracy left to feed Tito and take a long hot bath. I told her I was sad that I wouldn't be there.

Lau came to visit Daniel late in the evening and pulled the blue plastic curtain, separating them from me; I could see their silhouettes projected along the plastic partition, and heard whispers, but none of this taught me anything. I flipped on the TV and caught an episode of E's True Hollywood Story. This didn't teach me anything either.

When Lau left, at the end of visiting hours, it was just me and Daniel, a deck of cards borrowed from the nurses' station, and whatever change we had in our pockets. With our dining tables slid together between our beds, we had a halfway decent playing surface.

I was rusty at Pai Gow Poker, but Daniel knew enough to refresh my memory; it wasn't like we were really interested in playing anyway. I looked at my cards and said, "So…Capoeira. How'd that come about?"

"How did I learn, you mean?"

I nodded.

He played his hand, a three-of-a-kind, and said, "My grandfather was a *Mestre* in Sao Paulo. I paid attention. You?"

"I took an eight week Tai Chi class at the Y," I said.

The barest hint of a smile played at the corners of his mouth.

"You playing?" He said.

I laid down my cards, a hand I like to call five-of-an-individual – also known as Crap, and he scooped up the pot of seventy-five cents.

"I read somewhere that Capoeira-guys…"

"Capoeiristas," he said.

"Right…" I said, "…that those guys used to use straight razors held in their feet. Never heard of using pieces of broken mirror, though."

"Necessity, they say, is the mother of invention."

"Oh, so you felt threatened by my… what was it? My 'geezer art?'"

He did that slight smile again and said, "Perhaps. Or perhaps it was my belief that you were Mr. Lau's killer that filled me with unnecessary fear."

He dealt a new hand; I relished the fact that he was askeered of me.

"At the gallery you told me to back off. Why?" I said.

He peered at his cards and said, "Because Mr. Lau was innocent."

"Yeah, but how'd you know that?"

He said nothing, but threw a handful of pennies into the pot. We played cards; conversation was getting us nowhere.

On the bright side, I ended up a sweet forty-two cents richer.

57

By nine-thirty in the morning I was out of the ass-less paper gown and into a new pair of jeans, thanks to Tracy. Daniel and I went our separate ways, with the agreement that we would meet again under more pleasant circumstances.

My arms hurt. A lot.

My face hurt more.

We went down to Delmar; Tracy drove. After perusing a few bookstores, we had lunch at one of the many sidewalk café-type joints that lined the street. It was a beautiful day; seventy-two and clear on a late-October day in St. Louis is not unheard of, but it usually signaled the last gasps of good weather for the year. Things would get ugly fast, so we decided to make the best of it.

I ordered a cheeseburger and steak fries. Tracy did the same. We both drank beer; I'd spent less than a day in the hospital, but I still felt the urge to rebel, to disobey, to be bad. I'd likely order some obscene chocolate cheesecake at the end of the meal, and that would really show 'em.

I ate carefully. As much as I hated it, I felt loosely sewn together and didn't want to risk jarring any of my stitches by moving stupid. I caught Tracy wincing as she watched me.

"You doin' okay?" She said.

I thought about asking her to cut up my food in little pieces for me, but that was just excessive. I nodded instead.

"Randall…why are you doing this?"

I looked up at her. I didn't like the concern in her eyes, but the rest – the wisps of black and pink and blonde that framed her face, the orange and yellow leaves on the tree behind her, the way her perfume mingled with the dying leaves – those things were just perfect.

"Because… I am hungry?" I said.

"You know what I mean. Do you even know why you're doing this? When do you give it up? When do you call it quits and stop getting hurt and just leave it to Knox and the people who do this stuff for a living?"

"Didn't anybody ever tell you that quitters never win and winners never quit?" I said.

I wasn't getting off that easy.

"You didn't even know this girl, Randall. You didn't know any of these people, not really. Why risk getting blown up? Or cut up? Or killed?"

I wiped my mouth, smeared a bit of A-1 sauce into the cut on my cheek, and tried not to pass out. When the crisis had passed, I said, "Okay, in fairness, I got cut up by one of the supposed good guys. As for the rest, what can I say? I'm a big fan of truth, justice, and the American way."

Tracy dug around in her purse – a black tin lunchbox shaped like a grumpy Japanese cartoon character called Batz-maru – and found a pack of clove cigarettes. She lit one, took a drag, and rubbed her forehead as she exhaled. I heard her mumble, "…are you doing it for them or is this all just about you?"

"What's that supposed to mean?"

"Just what I said. She's gone, y'know. There's nothing you can do about it. And the worst thing, the part that really eats at you, is that somewhere, deep down, you know that none of it was your fault."

I took a sip of beer. It tasted like ash in my mouth. I set the bottle down and watched an ant crawling on the sidewalk.

"…Like you said, I didn't even know her," I said.

Tracy set her cigarette down in the ash tray and said, "Randall, sweetie, I'm not talking about Mei Ling Zhao and you know it."

I ate a fry.

"When you told me, you made it out as though everything was your fault."

"Yeah."

"It wasn't, though," she said.

"No. It was Miranda, too. She and I grew up the same. Get a job, get married, start a family… that's what you're supposed to do. Nobody tells you what you're supposed to do then, though, do they? Miranda tried, but she didn't know how to be a wife. She didn't know how to be a mom. It's easy to point fingers, but what was I doing? Working. That was what I knew how to do."

"You did all that you could." Tracy said.

"No, I knew I was blowing it, even then. When Miranda was pregnant, I read all the books I could. When Grace was born, I was the one who fed her, changed her diapers, the whole deal. When she got older, though, and not everything could be solved by shoving a bottle in her mouth or putting her to bed, that's when I got lost. I always thought I would figure it out, that we both would, in time. We didn't get a chance, though."

Her hand was on mine, and I didn't take it as a comfort. It felt like something heavy, something holding me down.

"Listen to me, Randall - it's not your fault. Sometimes bad things happen and we can't control that," she said. And in her eyes, the look, the pity.

"You don't know… I should have been there. That *is* my fault. What's the point of being a father if you can't protect your child? I wasn't fucking there. *By choice.* I couldn't deal, so I hid in an office… I got paid and I worked by the book and I ignored them. Both of them.

"That's why she was taken, that's why he… did what he did to her. Because I fucking failed. Don't you see that? And that fuck, that piece of inhuman shit, took a shot to the temple and went to sleep. After all the things he put her through… What were her last hours like, Tracy? How long do you think she fucking cried for me… to help her… and I wasn't there? And he just gets to go to sleep?"

I knew I was yelling. It was Tracy's eyes, brimming with tears, that made me stop. I didn't give a damn about everybody else looking at us. Screw them.

"You…wanted him to suffer," she said.

"I wanted him to pay," I said, quietly.

"He got off lucky," she said. She wouldn't look at me.

"You're damn right he did."

When she did look at me, the force of her gaze was unnerving. "So this is how you make amends? By finding *this* guy? Then what, Randall? You gonna kill him? You gonna make him suffer? Make him pay for the actions of a dead man?"

She was right. I knew she was right.

But that didn't stop me from being an idiot.

"Please don't lay the whole 'don't stoop to their level' crap on me, Tracy. Just because you took a psychology class once, that doesn't mean you actually fucking know anything. Don't pretend to understand this, okay? Because you can't, and you don't want to. Who have you lost, huh? Nobody. You're just a fucking kid."

She was hurt, I could tell; a part of me was even glad for it. The tears flowed freely from her eyes, but she smiled. It wasn't a pretty smile.

"You're right, I don't know anything. I'm just a kid? Well I know this – you can't live with this hate, Randall. It will kill you. Because in the end, it doesn't change the fact that your daughter is dead. Or that her murderer is dead. It's over, don't you see? Stop carrying this around with you, goddammit. Let it go."

"Easy for you to say," I said.

"She's gone, Randall. And you know what? She's okay. I don't know if you believe in an afterlife, or if you don't believe in anything at all, but either way, Randall, she's okay. He can't hurt her anymore. And she wouldn't want you carrying this burden. Not for her."

For a minute, I thought she was going to leave. To her credit, she didn't. However pathetic and unworthy the old bastard in front of her was, she wasn't ready to give up on him yet. Maybe somebody had told her the quitters never win thing…

After a while, she said, "Could I see her?"

"Grace?" I said. The question took me off guard.

"Yes," she said.

"I don't- "

"You don't carry any pictures of her in your wallet?" she said.

"No," I said.

"Why not?"

I sighed, picked up her cigarette, took a drag off it, and said, "For the same reason I don't keep my acupuncture needles in my underwear."

She frowned.

"It would hurt," I said. "Bad joke."

She patted my hand on the table.

"I'd like to see her someday," she said.

I nodded. "Me too," I said.

58

That night I stayed in my apartment. The super had finally replaced the front door. My shop window was still a big, graffiti-marred piece of plywood, though. Ah, well… Rome wasn't built in a day (probably due to slack-jawed dipshits like my super).

Things with Tracy could've been better, but we would survive. For two independent people always up in each other's business, I was surprised we'd gotten along as well as we had.

I climbed the stairs with nagging protest from my stitched up leg, and unlocked the door to my apartment. I pushed it open a half inch and peered inside. I checked floor level and around the knob, no tripwires. I gave the door a shove and covered my head with my arms.

Nothing. No explosions, no surprises. Just a drab, empty apartment.

I stood up and brushed myself off, wondering if I looked as foolish as I felt, and went inside. The hiss and clank of the radiator seemed loud in the stillness of the place. I walked into the kitchen, my footsteps echoing in my ears. The fridge held a half-empty six pack of Tsing Tao, some pizza that had long ago gone gently into that good night, and a shifty looking bottle of no-name ketchup.

It occurred to me that, on a long shot, my would-be assassins could have possibly corrupted my water supply, so I cracked open a beer. I took a sip; it was cold and bitey and better than ninety-five percent of the rest of my life at the moment. I swallowed half of the bottle in one go, grabbed the cardboard carrier with its two lonely brothers, and took it with me into the living room.

An ironic name – living room – for such a cold, empty place. I set my beers down and flipped on the stereo. All across the radio dial, nothing but crap. I checked the CD player and found it occupied by a disk of Tracy's. I turned it on and sat and drank. When the first bottle was finished, I drank the second. The third was gone before I even realized it was the third. I went back to the fridge and double-checked it for more beer. Then I checked the cabinets for any liquor, but I was dry.

With the music on and the alcohol gone I sat on my worn couch and watched the lights from passing traffic paint the room in shadows and shades of blue and yellow. After awhile, even that slowed and more or less stopped. And there I was in darkness, clutching the useless, empty glass bottle and listening to unfamiliar familiar music.

And when it was finished, and the vacuum was too intense, I closed my eyes and let the emptiness carry me away.

59

I woke in a deep blackness; the only way I knew my eyes were open at all was the blinking red light of the answering machine across the way. I fumbled around for a lamp or a light switch, but I only succeeded in knocking one of the empty Tsing Tao bottles to the floor where it shattered into a billion slivers, all of them hungry for a taste of my foot.

Knowing this, I perched on the edge of the couch and leapt in the direction of the red light. It seemed like a good idea at the time. It wasn't.

I flew over the bits of glass, resisting the urge to stick out my tongue as I flew by overhead, and nailed my forehead on the doorway that separated the kitchen from the living room. I fell backward, marveling at the bright starbursts that flashed before my eyes, and must've flailed my arms in an attempt to catch myself. I pulled the answering machine off the end table and both of us hit the hardwood floor with a thump. As the machine hit, it jarred something and I heard the tape rewinding. As the message began to play, I heard, "Hey? Hello? Asshole! Hello? Say something. I know you're there, you pick up the phone. Hello?"

It listed the date of the message, three days ago, and then it clicked.

I groaned and slid up onto my elbows. It felt great; a few stitches pulled and there was a warm dampness on my tricep. I sighed. Being alone really wasn't my thing anymore, not that I'd ever been very good at it. The answering machine played its next message. I listened for a moment without realizing that the language being spoken was Cantonese.

"*Dr. Lee,*" the voice said, "*life is a gift most precious. You have many patients who rely upon your expertise. Do not disappoint them. You have friends who care about you, the Sandoval girl, for instance. Enjoy your life. Mind your own affairs and stay out of ours. This is the only way to ensure a long and fruitful existence.*"

The machine listed the date – two days ago.

Huh.

The night Jimmy Yi Lau was murdered.

I listened to the message again – it was received at one-fourteen a.m.

The most polite death threat I'd ever heard came in while I was at the hospital getting stitched up. I started thinking about that evening. I got up and turned on the lights – it was only nine fifteen in the evening. I was back in the living room when the phone rang. I jumped – literally- and got a triangle of green glass in my left heel.

After swearing for a while, I answered the phone.

It was Tracy.

"Uh… there's a message here…I think…for you?"

She played it over the phone. Same voice, same Cantonese, similar message.

"What's it mean?" She said.

"It means they know me, they know you, and if I don't get out of their business, somebody's getting killed. Call Knox and tell him about the tape. Give it to the cops as evidence. And get over here."

"…You want me to stay with you?"

"I do."

"What about Tito?"

"We'll get him. For now, though, just throw some stuff in a bag and get out of there."

"Alright. Randall...?"

"Yeah?"

"Is this for real? I mean, are they serious?"

"Yes," I said. I hung up and pulled the blinds on the windows.

In the bathroom, I put bandages on my heel and my forehead. If Tracy asked, I'd just have to tell her some Triad thugs accosted me outside. I swept up the evidence in the living room and tossed the glass in the trash.

At her fastest, Tracy would take at least twenty minutes to get to the apartment. I grabbed my coat and went downstairs. A quick trip to the store would keep Tracy from ever knowing about the horror that was my refrigerator.

60

A block down from my apartment, it began to rain. Cold as it was, the rain soon became sleet. I hurt in a multitude of places, most recently my foot, and I did not have an umbrella. So, in the spirit of living dangerously, I ducked into HK Trading. The old man who'd called me a "Gwailo motherfuck" was not working, apparently. Instead, a young girl smiled and greeted me. The old guy's grand-daughter, maybe?

Whoever she was, she was an improvement, both in customer service and appearance.

I strolled past the video section; cantopop crooned on the stereo. It took me a minute, but I identified the song as a Cantonese version of 'End of the Road' by Boyz II Men. It was the most bizarre thing I'd heard in quite some time, and I wished Tracy was with me.

Remembering that I'd have her as a houseguest, I didn't go straight to the pre-made noodle aisle. I picked out some fresh vegetables, a couple bottles of plum wine, a few sauces, and some fresh shrimp. A few ideas swirled through my mind and struggled to become full-fledged recipes. The rub was that I wouldn't know if they'd succeeded until I'd chopped and steamed and marinated and stir-fried. I wouldn't know until I, or – heaven forbid – Tracy, tasted the concoction. How nerve-wracking.

I went back over to the videos, thinking that I might find something subtitled for Tracy, and had crouched down to read the back of a wild-looking kung fu/horror epic when the bell over the front door jingled and a chorus of voices shouted out greetings to the cute clerk girl. They varied in levels of obscenity and sexual content.

The girl didn't say much of anything. I couldn't see the front of the store, but I could imagine her trying to fade into the back wall like a chameleon.

From the sound of the guys, it hadn't worked.

Despite the outcome of my last attempt at heroics in the store, I couldn't not help the girl out. When I emerged from the video racks, it took my brain less than a second to recognize the crew of thugs hanging around the cash register. Same thugs, different day.

The kid who wanted so badly to be Scarface was leaning on the counter, practically humping the thing, twirling a lock of the clerk's hair between his fingers. The girl looked down at the floor with such dedication that I almost believed it would open up for her and provide a sanctuary.

The other goons were focused on their boss and the clerk, but Kip Yam glanced away for a moment at me. He did a double take. The color drained from his pasty features just like in the cartoons, and he said, "*...Bok Yea.*"

Yeah. "Fuck."

61

I was ten feet closer to the group before the rest of the group reacted to their buddy's curse. When Scarface saw me, he too spat out some curses as he reached into his dingy jean jacket. I let him pull the pistol before I moved, but as soon as the black metal cleared the denim I seized his wrist and twisted it, driving his elbow up until it pointed at the ceiling. The gun discharged once, into the floor, before his hand convulsed and he dropped it. I turned at the waist and put every ounce of energy I could muster through my fist and into his floating ribs. He folded from the blow, bounced off the counter, and fell through a wire rack of shrimp flavored chips. I didn't expect that he'd get back up any time soon.

Yam hauled ass for the door. I couldn't stop him; two of Scarface's boys tried to outflank me. As the one to my left threw a jab, I parried it and used the momentum to simultaneously palm strike him in the chest and carry my right hand – curled into a "fish hook," a way of striking with the back of the wrist – into the other guy's throat before he could take a shot at me.

A third kid jumped in with a jab to my face before his buddies hit the ground. He had good form, didn't telegraph, and knew not to throw his shoulder.

But I managed to catch his wrist. He shifted his weight to his rear foot for a kick; I felt it.

When his foot left the floor, I sank into the posture called *Needle at the Bottom of the Sea*, pulling his wrist down, almost to the floor, disrupting his balance and making it impossible for him to kick. Predictably, he tried to lean back and regain his balance. I followed him up with the technique *Fan through Back* – while holding his wrist, I pulled him in close and simultaneously struck him in the face with the knife edge of my hand.

The girl huddled in the corner with her hands drawn up to her mouth.

I said, "I'll be back. Call the police."

I ran outside and was met with several gunshots. I managed to duck back inside before I got shot. I'd have to remember to ask Knox to teach me that hop- around- corners- and- stick- to- walls- while- searching- a- strange- location thing that all the cops do on TV. Since I didn't know how to do that, I grabbed the back of Scarface's jacket – I was pretty amazed that he was trying to get up already - and threw him through the door. Lucky for him, his buddy was a crappy shot. I heard two dry clicks and then Yam said, "*Tiu nia ma chow hai.*"

What a potty-mouth.

The empty gun clattered to the street and Yam's footfalls echoed off into the night.

I pursued, kicking the dazed Scarface, still struggling to sit up, as I passed. I rounded the corner and saw that I was only about a hundred feet behind Yam. He kept looking back at me as he ran, and that slowed him down. It also kept him from noticing the oncoming car until it was too late to move out of the way. He hit the left front quarter panel, flew over the hood, and landed on his head on the other side.

The driver slammed on his brakes; I tackled Yam before he made it to his feet again and pinned him in a tight *Chin Na* shoulder lock. The clerk must've done as I'd told her. I heard the sirens. I remembered the bandage on my forehead and was glad.

I wouldn't have to lie to Tracy about that Triad run-in after all.

62

John arrived about ten minutes after the patrol cars did. "Heard the address on the scanner and I just had this funny feeling you had something to do with it," he said after telling the officers on the scene to un-cuff me.

I rubbed my wrists, got out of the police cruiser, and said, "Hey man, I was just shopping. I didn't intend to partake in any disorderly conduct…"

"Yeah, well, maybe you need to start shopping at some of the chain stores," he said.

"I like to support the mom and pop joints," I said.

He glanced over at the store, with its mutilated display racks and bullet holes, looked back at me, and said, "Obviously."

"Hey, go ask the clerk, she'll tell you – I'm the good guy here," I said.

Knox leaned on the side of the cruiser. "I did ask her. She doesn't speak English."

I leaned as well. "You'll just have to take my word for it then, won't you?" I said.

He rubbed his temples and said, "You want a ride back home?"

"I think I can walk the block and a half, but thanks."

"Got a call from your girlfriend. I think maybe you'd be better off taking the ride," he said.

"She told you about the message."

"Yep."

I nodded and agreed to the ride.

63

We picked Tracy up at my place and drove to IHOP, the closest place that was still open, for coffee. The ne'er-do-wells were packed up in a couple of squad cars and safely on their way to the station for processing, and Knox decided to let them sit and sweat for a bit before getting down to business. This suited me just fine; I was starving. Our waitress, a helpful bottle-blonde named Pammy, had just brought my stuffed French toast when I made the mistake of looking up at Tracy. She had dark circles under her eyes. They were emphasized by smears of mascara that told me she'd been crying. She looked as though she could start again at any moment.

"You okay?" I said, smooth as ever.

"I don't know. I've never gotten a death threat before, Randall."

Knox and I both simultaneously said, "Don't worry, we'll find them."

Clearly, we'd both been studying our Good Guy handbooks. Extra cool points went to Knox, though; he didn't have strawberry sauce on his chin when he said it.

"How can you be sure?" She said, "I mean, it's not like you guys have a ton of leads or anything."

Her tone implied that we were a couple of bumbling Inspector Clouseau types.

"Au contraire, madam," I said, "we are practically bathing in clues... or we will be soon, anyway. The jerks I roughed up? Somebody's going to talk. *And*, if Samson manages to recover, he can give a description of the killer."

Knox cleared his throat. I looked over at him. He shook his head slightly.

"What?" I said.

"Samson hung on till early yesterday, but he never regained consciousness."

Tracy's eyes widened. "He… died?"

Knox nodded slowly.

I took another bite of French toast and tried not to think about it.

Knox smoked.

Tracy was on the verge of freaking out.

Knox was in mid-drag when he grunted, jerked his chin in a reverse nod, and elbowed me in the ribs.

"That reminds me," he said, "I'd been meaning to tell you, I finally wrestled a report from the investigations guys…the CSI types."

"On Mei Ling?" I said.

"Yeah."

"Glad it was a priority for them…"

He shrugged and said, "Actually they did alright. It interested them. It just took some time to figure some stuff out… there's some weird shit. Like, check this out – the ink used to write all those curses and stuff? They found blood in it. Yeah, blood and some herbs and some type of mercury."

"Cinnabar," I said.

"Huh?" Knox said, eyes narrowing.

"Mercury Sulfide…It's Cinnabar. Taoists used to use it in different immortality potions; it's poisonous. It's in the ink, along with the blood and herbs, to increase the strength of the curse."

"Why is it that every time I find something out, you already know it?"

I shrugged.

"Well I'm getting real goddamned tired of it. What else do you know about the scene that you haven't told me?"

When I was done chewing and swallowing, I said, "Nothing, really. I told you that the whole thing was set up as a sort of perversion of a Taoist burial ceremony, sort of like how Satanists invert crosses and pentagrams. The main difference here is that any pothead teenager can listen to heavy metal records and scribble out that crap but it takes someone with a background in Taoism to pull off something like this. What I can't figure out is the why… Taoists are usually pretty detached. I just don't see what could've brought on this much hate."

"Hell, I dunno." Knox said, "I'm still trying to figure out the Monopoly money at the scene."

I winced.

"What?" He said.

I glanced over at Tracy. She looked tired and hungry. I offered her some of my French toast. She declined.

"Do you really want to know?" I said to Knox.

"Yes, I goddamn well want to know. I said I'm trying to figure it out, didn't I?"

"I just didn't want you to get mad at me when I tell you."

"Why would I do that?" Knox said.

"You just said you were tired of me knowing things you don't," I said.

He exhaled smoke through his nose and stared at me.

"Alright, alright…" I said, "It goes along with the rest of the ceremony. It's an insult. You know what hell bank notes are?"

He stamped out his cigarette in the ashtray and sighed. "Why don't you tell me," he said.

"You go to any Chinese store around here, you'll find bundles of hell bank notes. It's paper money that you burn at Chinese funerals. Supposedly, the fire conveys the energy of the money to the deceased so they have money in the afterlife. You can even buy paper TVs now, and houses… anything you can think of."

"So the dead person can be comfortable in hell?" Knox said.

"Well… in the afterlife. The word hell probably came from the Christian missionaries, but it stuck. We're not talking brimstone and lakes of fire, here… "

"So the killer, as an insult, left stacks of fake money instead of these afterlife things… so she'd be broke on the other side?"

"Right."

"So…" Knox started, but his cell phone rang and interrupted him.

He took it from his belt and answered.

"Yeah," he said.

He listened; from the tight line of his mouth and the furrow of his brow, I could tell the news wasn't good.

"Yeah," he said again, hung up, and stood.

"What's up?" I said.

"Gotta go."

"Alright, let's go."

"No. You two are staying," he said.

I stopped and said, "You drove. We have no way home."

Knox lit a cigarette and said, "Take a cab. Or better yet, don't. Stay put."

Tracy looked at me, I looked back. I turned to Knox and said, "What the hell, John? You wanted to know what I knew, I told you. Your turn. What's going on?"

Knox threw some cash on the table, enough to cover the bill plus tip, and said, "A hit. On our boys."

Tracy said, "What?"

"Look, I gotta go. You two want to tag along, I guess that's fine, but you gotta stay in the car. There's gonna be a shitload of coverage – cops and press – in the area, and the last thing we need is you guys on the front page of the friggin' Post Dispatch, alright?"

Tracy and I stood and put on our coats.

64

The scene was less than five miles from the police station. We turned right on Dr Martin Luther King Drive and the sky flashed red and blue from the myriad visibar lights. The street was blocked off now and closed to traffic, but Knox pulled in beside another unmarked car and got out.

I saw wisps of smoke in the near distance and smelled the hot metal through the air vents. A few firefighters milled about; some of them talked with police. The way everyone moved, the looks on their faces, told me everything I needed to know – the slow, methodical way they approached the scene meant death. Any survivors would have been rushed away already. This was the clean-up crew, searching for the how's and why's.

We did as we were told and stayed put. Tracy slept, huddled in the back seat.

I watched the reporters from the local stations collecting a "no comment" from every cop they encountered. I'd nodded off by the time Knox returned.

"C'mon," he said, gesturing for me to get out.

"What about us being front page news and all that?" I said.

"We'll sneak in the back way," he said.

I leaned over the seat to wake Tracy and Knox said, "You should let her sleep. She should be alright out here."

Considering that whatever had happened occurred a few miles from the police station, I didn't feel comfortable with those shoulds. I woke her and together the three of us wove between a tangle of buildings and emerged from an alleyway and into the crime scene. A uniformed officer nodded to Knox, lifted the yellow police tape and helped us through.

The entire area was maybe sixty feet of street, obscured as much as possible from the public view. I saw masses of twisted, smoking metal. Broken glass littered the ground and caught bits of flashing light, reflecting it; reminding me of the way moonlight bounced off the ocean waves.

"The SUV's slid into position there," Knox said, pointing. At the far end of the enclosure, I saw three black Cadillac Escalades blocking the street.

"The gunmen hid in these alleys and hit them here. If you look, you can see that they picked staggered alleys to avoid a crossfire."

We walked into the street, glass crunching underfoot, to the first patrol car.

"Officer Cox drove this one. He was transporting Scarface and Kip Yam. Shooters on the driver's side here hosed the length of the car. Early guesstimates, based on number and pattern of shots as well as caliber, suggest that the shooters used MAC-10s."

"So they're dead?" Tracy said.

"Yeah. Very much so. Officer Murphy, with the rest of the Chinese grocery thugs, tried to turn around. Dispatch caught part of his call for backup. Then, according to a witness, another black escalade pulled in here," Knox said, point to the other end of the street, "gunned down Officer Murphy's vehicle, picked up the other drivers and gunmen, and fled the scene."

"Did anyone survive?" I said.

"Yeah. One of the unidentified kids in the back of Murphy's car. Little shit hid under his dead friends. Took one slug in the gut, but he's still kicking… for now, anyway."

I felt Tracy close to me. She seemed so small. I put my arm around her to ease her shivering. She had never been this close to this kind of carnage before. I knew I hadn't. There was an immediacy to the violence that echoed through the place; I was happy to feel her next to me.

Knox's cell rang again. He answered. From where we stood a few feet away, I heard an anguished cry from the other end of the line. "…Baby…Yes, baby, of course it's me," Knox said. He turned away from us and walked a little ways away. "No. No, I'm fine. I swear to you, alright? Turn off the TV and go back to bed. I'll be home soon. Yes. Soon, I promise."

He glanced over his shoulder and looked at me. I tried to look like someone who had never eavesdropped in his life. He hung up the phone and said, "Story's on the news… couple cops dead, my precinct… she got scared."

"Sure," I said.

He cleared his throat and wiped his eyes and looked around at the wreckage like he'd never seen it before.

"Shit." he said, "I brought you out here like you'd have some kind of insight into this… but it's just all fucked, isn't it?"

65

The sky was the color of maraschino cherries when I called to make our reservations. Tracy was asleep against me; John drove. At Tracy's, the good detective was kind enough to check the place before we went in. I'd never seen him draw his gun before.

When he was satisfied that the place was clean, we went in, and Tracy grabbed some clothes, her CD's and a fleshy, clawed ball of hatred for mankind. I stood around, fully prepared to kung-fu something, if necessary.

We left, and John drove us to the Ritz.

I steeled myself for the barrage of dirty looks we were likely to get. I'd received glares from people there while dressed in a tuxedo. Considering the way I looked now, I'd be lucky if the hotel staff didn't just shoot me. We went inside, bidding John Knox a good morning, and attempted to saunter up to the front desk in a prosperous manner. When the concierge was finished staring down his long, skinny nose at us, I smiled and said, "Reservation for Charles. Nick and Nora Charles."

With key in hand, we rode the elevator to our floor. It was a much more pleasant experience than my previous elevator trip. I looked at Tracy. She looked at me.

We knew there would be no resisting it. On our floor, every step made it clearer and clearer. With our door unlocked, we entered our suite. I locked the door behind us. Tracy let Tito out of the duffel bag he'd been hiding in. And at last we gave in - we were both asleep before we could even get under the covers.

66

I developed some rudimentary form of what humans call consciousness around ten a.m. In the blissful void of sleep I became aware of a recurring smooth raking sound. My mind conjured nonsensical images of ninja, clad only in strawberry stuffed French toast triangles. One of them was on the balcony, suction-cupping one of those circular glass cutters, the kind that show up in every spy movie, to the sliding door; my dream self cowered in the corner, cursing myself for not considering pastry-covered assassins when choosing a luxury suite.

When I found myself awake, I was sitting upright in the plush bed. Tito sat in front of the doors looking out onto the balcony. He reached up a bony paw, dragged his claws down the glass and croaked out a pathetic meow.

I thought about letting him out, but if he enjoyed perching on the tops of buildings as much as I knew his stone ancestors did, Tracy would never forgive me.

The Ritz, strictly speaking, did not allow cats.

This didn't bother me for two reasons: Tito did not shed, and I still wasn't convinced he actually was a cat. I rolled off the bed, walked to the balcony doors, and crouched down by the cutest of my nemeses. The little guy purred and rubbed against my knee so ferociously that he ended up sliding off my knee and flopping onto my foot. I scooped up the warm sack of purring flesh and went to the couch. Tito and I flipped channels for a bit, but hotel TV pretty much sucked as a rule. So I picked up the phone and ordered some room service. After hanging up with the overly friendly attendant, I called my apartment and checked my messages.

"Hey, Assho'," I heard, "You puss out already? Or maybe you think you already know everything, eh? I call to say that I don't need such bullshit. You come tomorrow or not at all. Eh, Lee? And call me back, shithead!"

Master Cheng's English was never exactly great, but it degenerated into incoherent curses and gibberish when he got really irritated.

What I think it really came down to, though, was that he missed me. I called him, apologized profusely, and confirmed our class in the morning. Before hanging up, he said, "Bring chocolate, you pissy dick-hole of shit-man."

Like I said, he missed me.

I called room 290. The exhibit was not yet over, but I didn't know if Lau was still in town. With all the recent shenanigans, I'd forgotten to ask Knox.

Daniel answered on the third ring.

I offered to buy dinner.

He said, "Pay for the sunglasses you broke and you're on."

"I suppose you're going to tell me those were fifty dollar sunglasses," I said.

"Try *two hundred and fifty,*" he said.

He was clearly still sore over the forty two cents I'd masterfully swindled from him. I gave in to his ransom and told him the time and place for dinner. He accepted. And when he hung up, we both still knew who the better card player was.

67

I ran through some warm up exercises – stretching, some stance training, and the Silk Reeling exercises – and took a quick shower. Since everything I did lately was an exercise in pain, I did not enjoy the shower as much as I should've.

When I heard the polite knock at the door, I immediately thought of the pastry assassins again. I checked the peephole. With the suit the guy was wearing, I knew I wouldn't have to worry about any fancy footwork – unless he didn't mind blowing out his pants and making his escape with his ass hanging out. Anything he could throw at me with his hands didn't bother me. All I had to do was keep close in case he had a weapon.

Paranoid?

Me?

Never.

I opened the door and let him inside. I knew right away that the kid wasn't an evildoer – to him, I wasn't being defensive; I was just invading his personal space. I tipped him a little extra and locked the door behind him. The food looked pretty awesome. Poison crossed my mind, but I pushed that thought aside. At some point, cautious crosses the line into ridiculous.

I went into the bedroom and got Tracy up. She mumbled an impressive train of incoherencies that stretched from the bed to the bathroom. I heard the shower turn on.

I covered the food and checked the TV again. It was the same old assemblage of golf, bowling, infomercials, and soap operas. Tracy emerged, swimming in a huge, fluffy terrycloth robe. I pulled the silver cover from the food with a flourish. Tracy sat in one of the expensive-looking chairs and pulled her legs up under her. She leaned over, picked a piece of bacon from one of the platters, and nibbled at it.

"I feel like such shit," she said.

I had a piece of sourdough toast.

"The last few days have been a lot to handle," I said. She made a sort of nervous laughing sigh and said, "You think?"

"It will get better," I said.

Tracy sighed and looked up at me. The dark circles were still there.

"How, Randall?" She said, her voice froggy from sleep, "How will things get better? More and more people are dying and it doesn't seem like anyone's any closer to figuring anything out. I mean, I was there at the gallery when Mr. Lau was killed. I was there with *my parents* and there was a murderer there. And he knows who I am. And maybe he knows who my parents are too. I'm scared, Randall... Really scared. And I don't know how much more of this I can take. I don't know how much more I *want* to take."

She didn't seem aware of the tears that spilled from her eyes.

I set down my toast.

"God, I know this makes me sound like a total bitch but I didn't sign on for this shit, Randall. I like you. I like you a lot. And I want to be the girl who's there for you, the one who says, 'Go get 'em, tiger,' and who has your back during all of this... but you don't know what its like."

She looked at the ceiling and took a deep breath, steadying herself.

I just sat there and listened.

"When that bomb... when...before the ambulance arrived, I thought you were dead," she said. She began to cry harder then. I got up, knelt beside her chair, and took her hand.

"I didn't think things would end up this way. If I had, I would never have involved you at all. And I can't tell you that things won't get worse before they get better. I can tell you though that the bad guys made two fatal errors last night. They killed cops and they threatened my girl."

She snorted, and started to giggle in spite of herself.

I kissed her forehead, stroked her cheeks, wiped away her tears, and, with her face in my hands, said, "I'm going to make this right, okay? I promise."

I kissed her; she kissed me back. It occurred to both of us that it had been awhile since we'd spent any quality grown up time together. And even though there couldn't have been a worse time for it, we -

tentatively at first but then rather fiercely - did.

I only pulled a few stitches.

I'd live.

68

With an afternoon of shopping behind us, we met Tony Lau and Daniel at Marisol on Delmar. Tracy had mentioned wanting to try it, and I was up for something new. We were not exactly being discreet, but the more I thought about it, the less I saw the point in hiding. The baddies, whoever they were, weren't exactly shy about public displays. If they wanted to take a run at us, then by god I was choosing the battleground.

The restaurant, like most of the places on Delmar, was small, stylish, and filled with the almost terminally hip. I spotted them almost immediately, and we made our way to the table. Daniel and Tony stood to greet us. I handed Daniel a black case.

"My glasses?" He said, surprised.

I nodded.

He flipped the case open and said, "I am surprised, Dr. Lee."

"In my taste or that I keep my promises?"

"Both, to be honest," he said with a grin.

I shook hands with Tony. He kissed Tracy's hand. I did not growl at him.

"You look lovely, Miss Sandoval," he said.

He wasn't kidding. Tracy wore a dark purple dress she'd found while we were out shopping, a thin, black lace choker, and heels that matched her dress. Her long, pale legs were bare. Though they looked like smooth vanilla ice cream, I did not lick them.

Randall Lee – Master of self-control.

We all sat and checked out the menu. The place was billed as Nuevo Latino cuisine, whatever that meant. I read the names of dishes, then the descriptions. When the waitress came back around, we were ready to order.

I picked the Honduran Ceviche – tuna with coconut milk, lime, ginger, and pickled onion. Tracy ordered the Blood Orange salad and, to drink, a Mojito.

The rest of us ordered beer.

When the waitress left, Tracy said, "This is a little awkward, but I just wanted to tell you how sorry I am about your father, Tony…"

He gave a slow nod and said, "Thank you."

"Will there be a memorial?" I said.

"In San Francisco. Then my father's ashes will be sent home, as was his request."

"Where was home?" Tracy said.

"Hong Kong." Tony said.

"Oh? Randall used to live in Hong Kong," Tracy said.

"Really? Where, Dr. Lee?" Tony said.

"Kowloon Bay," I said.

Tony smiled and said, "My family lived just across the harbor, near the base of Tai Ping Shan."

The waitress brought our drinks. Tracy sipped her Mojito and grinned. "Small world, eh? I, for the record, know nothing about Hong Kong," she said.

Daniel said, "You are not alone."

"Oh, but you've got your own cool thing going on… Brazil, and Capoeira and all that? I've never been much of anywhere or done much of anything. I feel so plain and boring with you guys," She said.

"You're not plain or boring, whatever the company," I said.

She blew me a kiss and turned back to Daniel. "I had a few friends in school that did a little Capoeira, though. They always wanted me to try it, but I was too chicken."

"Tracy was a dancer, in college," I said.

"A dance *major,*" she said quickly. "I was a dance major. I learned a long time ago that if you say you're a dancer, people assume just you mean stripper."

Tony laughed and drank some beer. It seemed like a great idea so I joined him.

Daniel said, "If you dance, you would pick up Capoeira easily. My grandfather had the hardest time teaching me to relax enough to feel the rhythm."

I could sympathize.

"That's what Sombra said, that I would do well. I was always afraid of the flips and stuff."

"Sombra?" I said.

"That's what everybody called him. His real name was… Eric, I think. He was the teacher. Then there was Fava and Galinha. They were cool guys."

Daniel laughed.

Tracy grinned and looked around. "What?" she said.

"I thought my grandfather was harsh, but at least my Capoeira name is not 'Bean' or 'Chicken'."

Tracy laughed and said, "You should have seen Galinha, he did look like a chicken."

"I'm a bit lost," I said. "What's a Capoeira name?"

"In the old days," Daniel said, "Capoeira was outlawed, and it became the custom for the Mestre to give his students nicknames. In this way, the police could not find the other students through interrogation. Nobody knew anyone's true name or address, see? It became part of tradition, almost like an initiation… when the capoeirista reached some level of accomplishment, he would be awarded his name. Oftentimes, though, they are not the most complimentary of names."

"What's yours?" Tracy said.

Daniel drank some beer and shook his head with a small smile.

Our food came. Everyone took a minute to settle in and try their various dishes. Tracy happily ate her blood orange salad, bobbing her head and tapping her feet to a beat only she could hear.

"Good?" I said, grinning.

"*At least* as good as sex," she said.

"With lettuce," I said.

"And blood orange vinaigrette," she said.

I tried my tuna. I understood Tracy's enthusiasm, but it still didn't compare to sex. I suddenly felt very inadequate. Because of a salad.

"So, Daniel…" she said, "C'mon, spit it out. You're among friends."

He popped a sliver of beef tenderloin into his mouth and raised his eyebrows.

"What?" He said, stealing my favorite line.

Tracy grinned and chewed her lip a little. "You won't tell us your Capoeira name?"

Daniel shook his head, his braids rattled against the back of his chair. "I see no point in embarrassing myself during an otherwise lovely dinner, no."

"You're no fun at all," she said.

He took another bite of food, glanced from Tony to Tracy to me, sighed, and finally said, "Fada. You happy now?"

Tracy giggled and said, "That doesn't sound so bad. What's it mean, 'father'?"

Daniel kept his barely noticeable smile and, to me, said, "This girl has some power, eh? She make you say things you don't want to say?"

"On occasion, yes," I said.

He took another drink of his beer and, to Tracy, said, "When I was little, I was… what do they call it here? A mama's boy?"

He nodded to himself and continued. "Granddaddy decided one day that he would make a man out of me, see. Every day, when I couldn't do whatever new moves he showed, he would tell me, 'Get up, '*Fada,*' and do it again.' He always pushed just a little harder. I would practice for hours to be able to do the things he taught, and the next day, he push just a little past that. He would have me practice until I threw up. That was how I knew class was over. Then he would stand over me and say, 'Poor little *Fada* lost his breakfast.'

"When I was twenty-one, I beat him in the *roda*, the circle. I trapped him and he could not move. It made the old man happy. When we were finished, he said to his students, 'Today is the day I retire. From now on, look to Mestre Fada for your lessons.'"

"You were a teacher?" Tracy said.

"No. Hard to gain much respect from your students when everyone knows you only as 'Fairy', see."

"You never told me that," Tony said.

"Of course not. It does no good for my image as a tough guy. I tell nobody… it's silly girl's fault I bring it up now," he said, grinning at Tracy. "But if word gets around, I have to kill both of you."

Tony picked at his food, something with duck and corn cakes, and said, "Dr. Lee, have you found anything out about the murderers?"

I cleared my throat and took a drink before saying, "Well, there are a lot of things I needed to talk to you about… I was waiting for a polite way to bring it up. Thank you for saving me the trouble. There are some…difficult things I have to tell you, I'm afraid."

Tony frowned and said, "Go on."

"Certain details of your fiancé's death hinted that your father might have been involved. Clearly that is not the case, but it does seem that your father's business may figure into things."

"What details?" he said.

I cleared my throat again and looked at the millimeter of beer left in my glass. I flagged down our waitress and ordered another beer. I have found that a full beverage is essential when discussing unpleasant matters. It gives you something to do while thinking up tactful ways to word things. As my cup runneth dry, however, I had to just shoot straight.

"She was found in one of your father's massage parlors, where she worked, apparently. She lived in an apartment building with the other girls. In her apartment, we found a suitcase with over two hundred thousand dollars in cash in it. And pretty much every lead we've managed to find is either dead or comatose, so if you've got anything that could be helpful here, I'd like to hear it."

Tony stared at me.

The waitress brought my beer.

I drank some while he stared.

When he finally spoke, he said, "My father was a good man, Dr. Lee. He believed in something with all his heart. He believed in the Eight Tigers, said they were protectors of our heritage. He said they embodied the spirit of the *Han,* the Chinese people. More than anything, he wanted a successor. Someone who shared his dream. I was… a disappointment to my father in a great many ways… I see that now. When I return to San Francisco, I will put aside childish things. I will be the man my father believed I could be."

"And Luca Brasi sleeps with the fishes," I said.

"What?" Tony said.

"The Godfather. Don't tell me you haven't seen The Godfather, Tony."

He hesitantly shook his head.

"Go rent it. Tonight. No more speeches from you about family and duty and all that jazz until you watch it. Don't be a Michael Corleone, Tony. You're an artist. A damned good artist. Be that artist. Your father was proud of your art; he was proud of you. Whatever's going on, now is not a healthy time to be a gangster."

"The Tigers need me," he said.

"Listen, kid, getting yourself killed isn't going to impress him. And if you get capped, then what? Who runs the Eight Tigers then?"

He thought about that and remained silent.

"We need to consider the possibility that this whole deal could be a war for succession of the Triad… they took out your fiancé and child – the future – and your father – the past – and all that's left of the Lau interest in the Eight Tigers is you," I said.

He nodded and said, "We know."

"What concerns me, though… the part I really don't get…is Mei

Ling's role in all of this. What was she doing? Who was she running from? Where'd she get that kind of cash?"

Tony remained silent. Considering it was usually what I did when faced with any one of the ten billion things I didn't know in this case, I didn't blame him.

"When did you two meet?" I said.

"We were just children." he said. "It was an arrangement."

"Like an arranged marriage?" I said.

He nodded.

"How much time did you spend with her?" I said.

"Some, as children. When we moved to the states, I said goodbye to her. I didn't expect to see her again, really, but she came to San Francisco last spring."

I ate some more, and said, "And then what? You guys decided to keep the old arrangement just to keep dad happy?"

"She was a kind person. We enjoyed each other's company."

"So you hit it off and that was that," I said.

"More or less."

"And the money?"

"Perhaps…" he said, "it may have been some kind of dowry."

"I always thought those were paid from the bride's family to the groom," I said.

He nodded.

"So what, Tony, she was holding out on you?"

"I don't know," he said.

"You know something," I said.

He slammed some beer and said, "My father paid her to come, okay? At first, I didn't know, but eventually she told me. He believed she was my perfect match, and he very much wanted us to be together."

"Why? Why'd he believe she was your perfect match?"

"He consulted with several astrologers and priests. Our birthdays and signs made for a fortuitous match. I do not believe in those things, myself, but my father was very traditional."

"Your father was a Taoist," I said.

"Yes."

"I'm going to need to know the names of those priests," I said.

"Why?"

"Because the man who murdered your father and Mei Ling was very knowledgeable about Taoist rites."

"I'll see what I can find out," he said, sounding determined.

That made two of us. This was the closest thing to actual progress

I'd made in a long time. It was so exciting I barely contained a schoolgirl-like squee.

After dinner, Tracy and I took a walk down Delmar. The night was cold but beautiful. We had coats and fully functional immune systems, so we decided to live a little.

"I used to live here, you know?" Tracy said as we strolled along, arm in arm.

"No, really?"

"Mm-hmm. Right over there," she pointed to one of the stores across the street. "On the third floor. Total shithole, but I loved it. Every city has a vibe, y'know? A personality. For me, this is the soul of St Louis, right here."

I hadn't been in town long enough to know about that, but it was certainly a colorful area. A line of kids decked out in their finest punk threads wove around a music venue called The Pageant. "I used to go there almost every weekend. Didn't even matter who was playing," Tracy said.

Skaters zoomed past us, trying out tricks and nearly breaking themselves on the pavement. Yuppies talked $800 loveseats as they power-walked past; a homeless woman tried to sell me a hemp necklace.

"Right down here," she said, pointing to a nonspecific place down the street from where we stood, "there's this courtyard, and on the weekends they have swing dancing… so cool. You ever dance, Randall?"

"Not if I can help it," I said.

"Aw, why not?" She said as she huddled against my arm and shivered.

I shrugged and put an arm around her.

"Trauma," I said.

She stopped and looked at me with one eyebrow raised.

"When I was a kid, my dad hauled me off to Nebraska for my aunt's wedding. It was my first trip to the states, first time I'd met my aunt, even. At the reception, this girl – she was probably ten - grabbed my arm and dragged me to the dance floor. I got passed around among all the older girls – who thought I was cute, apparently – for the rest of the night. It was awful."

Tracy giggled and said, "A lot of guys would love that."

"Yeah, well, I was five at the time."

"Aw…widdle Wandall Lee," she cooed.

I rolled my eyes.

"Would you ever dance with me?" She said. "I promise not to drag you or pass you around like a joint..."

I shrugged again.

Dancing, for me, was an outdated and uncomfortable part of the mating ritual - Praying Mantises eat their mate's heads, humans dance. But, I'd learned a thing or two in my life; enough, at least, to know not to say that to her.

"Yeah. Sure. Sometime."

She narrowed her eyes and said, "But not now."

"Never on a full stomach... you can get cramps and die that way, y'know."

She leaned in close, put her arms around my neck, and touched her nose to mine.

"You are a poo, Randall Lee," she said.

I'd been called worse, and besides...this girl actually liked me.

"Shall we go home?" I said.

"You mean the hotel?" she said.

"Yes."

"I suppose."

"I lost points with the no-dancing thing, huh?"

"Big time."

"However will I get back in your good graces?" I said.

"I'll just have to think of something..." she said.

69

Too soon and far too early, I pried myself from the seductive warmth of Tracy and our shared bed and spent the morning in a freezing cold basement with a crotchety old man.

I had to get my priorities straight, obviously.

I practiced the entire form as Master Cheng watched. I went from movement to movement as slowly as I could, focusing on relaxing and keeping the 'spirit of play' Master Cheng spoke of.

When I completed the form, he grunted and walked away. I was left standing there in his basement, alone, for ten minutes wondering if I'd screwed up so badly that I hadn't even earned a dismissal. When he returned, he threw a broom at me.

"Follow," he said.

He drew a long, straight sword – a *jian* – and assumed a preparatory stance; I mimicked him as best I could with the broom. Small clouds of dust fell from the old bristles and hovered in front of my face. Cheng began to move; he was so subtle and smooth that he'd raised his arm to chest height before I realized he'd begun. I hurried to catch up and he said, "Ay! Slow, dickhead. This is why you have a broom and I have a blade… American mind does not grasp this sort of grace, this finesse. Too herky-jerky. Too rush-rush. Let yourself be slow. Let yourself float. Become… empty…"

He continued on through the form and I attempted to follow. I had not practiced Tai Chi sword in many years, and this form was different from anything I knew; I felt, again, like a beginner. Difficult as the movements were, I was distracted. I wanted to be checking out the things Tony Lau had told me, I wanted to be looking for the man responsible for destroying his family.

Cheng turned and his blade swept in a wide, slow motion arc. I was so focused on my broom that I was nearly very slowly decapitated. Master Cheng stopped and sheathed his sword.

"Even you are not normally this stupid. What is the problem?"

"I…"

"So scatterbrained. You still with the cops?"

"Yes," I said.

"Still poking around after young girls?"

I wasn't sure if he meant Tracy or Mei Ling, but I nodded.

"Aiya. You piss away too much energy. Better to focus on one thing, eh?"

I nodded.

"Okay," he said, wearily resuming his beginning stance. "Let's… Oh for Christ's sake, Lee… pay attention."

I wasn't sure how he'd known that I was recalling my dinner with Tony Lau, but I jerked to a ready stance. He stretched his neck like a turtle and settled back into the movements. I followed, but before long I was thinking of Mei Ling, and whether or not Tracy had been right. Was I really trying to compensate for—?

The broom in my hands exploded into a cloud of splinters before I saw him move. The tip of Cheng's sword pricked the soft underside of my chin, tilting my head back until all I could see were the cobwebs on the ceiling. I was balanced on my heels; if he moved forward as much as a hair's breadth, I would topple to the floor, powerless, if I was lucky.

Or have my skull skewered, if I wasn't.

I learned that I don't like feeling powerless.

"Too easy you forget. Tai Chi Chuan is life or death. Focus now?"

I couldn't open my mouth without upsetting my balance. I couldn't nod without skewering myself. I raised a hand, slowly, and touched my index finger and thumb together into the universal symbol for 'ok'. He lowered his sword, snipping off the top two buttons of my shirt as he did, and said, "Perhaps we talk about things on your mind, hey?"

I rubbed my chin and came away with a thin red smear on my hand.

"Don't be a baby… you do worse shaving," he said, seeing it.

Christ.

In an effort to economize his busy time, Master Cheng suggested that we talk and eat. Far from the exotic vegan diets my old teacher, Master Wu, prescribed for his students and patients, Master Cheng took me to his favorite restaurant – Burger King. He unwrapped his Ultimate Omelet sandwich with a look of unmatched bliss. I peeled back the plastic lid of my coffee and promptly burned my mouth with the first molten sip.

"Alright," Master Cheng said, lips smacking as he chewed, "what's your problem, huh?"

"Everything, I suppose," I said.

"Maybe you pick one thing," he said. Everything revolved around Mei Ling's murder, so I picked that. I told him about Jimmy Lau and Samson. I told him about the death threats. I told him about dinner with Tony Lau. He dabbed a bit of egg from his lip with a napkin and drank some Dr. Pepper.

"Who is this girl?" He said.

"Mei Ling Zhao," I said, "the girl I showed you pictures of, the one you…"

He screwed up his face and said, "I know which girl you speak of, turnip. What I mean is who is she?"

"Tony Lau's fiancée."

"Yes, but who is she? Why so much problem for this girl? You or gorilla cop-man think of that? This girl started something, eh? How many people hurt or dead here? All because of one young girl? Must be important girl, eh?"

70

When I left Cheng's, I called Tony Lau and got his voicemail. I left a short message, saying that I needed more information about Mei Ling.

Master was right; whatever was going on, it was quickly racking up an impressive body count.

I got in Tracy's car and, after spending five minutes trying to get the thing started, decided to take the long way back to the hotel. I was finishing up filling out the paperwork when Tracy called to make sure I wasn't dead.

"What are you up to?" she said.

"It's a surprise," I said.

"Well… death threats, living in the Ritz, having awesome dinners with terminally cute gangster types, I'm not sure my heart can take any more of this excitement."

I drove back to the hotel and called her back to tell her to meet me downstairs. She stood near the front doors, wearing an ankle-length denim skirt, a white Failure concert shirt and a maroon, thrift store cardigan. The doorman looked like he was on the verge of calling security.

When I pulled up in front of the door, Tracy's eyes widened.

"Uh… Randall? What is that?" She said.

"My new car. You like?"

She opened the passenger side door and climbed in, looking around like she'd never been in a car before. "Where's my car?" She said.

"At the dealership. We can go pick it up."

She kept looking around. She occasionally moved her mouth, but no sound came out. I kicked it into gear and we were off.

"I'm told it can go zero to sixty in less than four seconds, but I haven't tried that yet," I said.

"How?" She finally said. I didn't know enough about cars to explain. Luckily, I knew that wasn't what she meant.

"Your car was being a little grumpy in the cold, and I feel terrible for having to borrow it all the time anyway, so I went to a couple dealers looking for something like *my* dear old car… turns out, apparently they don't make the Stealth anymore. The salesman had me try this puppy out instead. It's a little more than I'd planned to spend, but what the hell."

"…It's a fucking Viper," she said.

"Yes. It's a convertible, too."

"Randall… aren't these, like, way expensive?"

"Maybe a little," I said.

"Okay, this is something I've been meaning to ask you, but I didn't know how to without seeming rude…"

"Shoot," I said.

"What the fuck, Randall? I mean, I haven't paid for a thing since we've been together. And then there's your little jaunt to San Fran, and the Ritz? Do you have any idea what room service cost…just for my breakfast this morning? And now this car…"

"It's alright. I make a decent living," I said.

She stared at me. We both knew that my business was not booming.

"Alright," I said, "Remember my dad?"

"The tax attorney," she said.

"Yeah. When he died, he left me a little money."

We stopped at a stop light.

"A little?" Tracy said.

"Yeah, around a hundred grand," I said.

"That's not *that* much, Randall."

"No," I said, "but he also left me his stock portfolio. And his real estate holdings. And I make a decent living poking people."

She sat very still.

The light changed, and we were the first car off it.

Vroom, vroom.

"…If you have money… why do you live in such a shithole?" Tracy said.

I turned and looked at her in shock. "I happen to like my apartment. Besides, I moved there for my shop. Good location."

She resumed her stillness, her silence. When she spoke, she said,

"…So… are you…rich?"

I grinned and said, "Oh, I dunno. You'd have to ask my financial advisor that."

71

We picked up Tracy's car and agreed to meet back at the hotel. I was glad. I didn't feel like talking about money any more.

She didn't get it.

Why did I bother with my practice?

Why not leave town till the trouble had blown over?

Why not live a life of luxury?

The fact was that there wasn't much that I wanted that I could actually buy. Every now and then, like today, I would splurge, but otherwise things were fine. Why make a big deal out of it?

I was an acupuncturist because it was the only thing I knew, and I suppose I liked doing it and it helped people occasionally. And as for the trouble, well, I was responsible for some of it.

I clean up my own messes.

Part of me worried that things would be weird between us now. I was not only older, I was – gasp – a sugar-daddy. All of it gave me a headache, so I turned up my new, expensive stereo and tried not to think too much.

For once it worked. Howard Stern was playing Lord of the Anal Ring Toss, and it's hard to think of much when that's going on.

Maybe I should blow money more often.

72

I was in the bath, waiting for my knotted muscles to work themselves loose, when the call came. Knox requested my presence at a meeting; he did not sound happy. I finished getting cleaned up and threw on a pair of jeans and a heavy grey sweatshirt. After kissing Tracy goodbye, I hopped in my new car and headed to the station. I found myself bobbing my head along to some freaky dance CD Tracy had left in the car.

At the station, Knox met me outside and mumbled a long trail of incoherent grumbles as he led me inside. We went to a large conference room. The enormous table was shaped like an oval with the ends chopped off square; as I sat, I wondered what the name of that shape was.

"Hey, pal," a voice said. I looked up to see a man of medium build leaning across the table, extending his hand toward me. I shook his hand and took the opportunity to check him out a little.

Blond crew cut; ugly scar above the left ear. Cold blue eyes. A nose that had been broken a few times. Efficient but cheap black suit. Shoulder holster bulge. Either that, or he was one of Knox's Abnormal Chest Tumor boys.

"Agent Mulder, I presume," I said.

He laughed and pointed a manicured finger at me in a 'you-got-me' gesture. "It's Janik, actually. Agent Janik. FBI Organized Crime Unit."

I sat and folded my hands on the table. Agent Janik sat across from me. Knox slouched in his chair at the head of the table. A bald dude with a prominently throbbing vein in his forehead sat at the other end. It just had to be the chief; he had the look of someone who yelled a lot.

Janik kept looking at me expectantly. I realized I hadn't introduced myself.

"Lee. Randall Lee," I said.

"Ah, Randall Lee the civilian," Janik said.

"That's exactly what it says on my business cards," I said.

"Shut the fuck up, smart ass," Baldy said. His forehead vein said, "Throb, Throb."

I stood. Janik stood with me. "Going somewhere?"

"Yeah. I'm gonna go shut the fuck up back home, with my very hot girlfriend. Thanks for the invite, though, I appreciate it."

Janik looked at Knox. Knox shrugged. "He does have a very hot girlfriend," he said.

Nice to know he had my back.

"Dr. Lee, your presence here today is needed. Please have a seat," Janik said. I watched the agent. He glanced away to shoot a look at Baldy. When he looked back at me, he said, "Please."

I sat.

"This is bullshit," Baldy mumbled.

"Do we need another time out, chief?" Janik said softly.

Baldy said nothing. He just sat there a-throbbin,' his arms crossed so tight you'd think he was trying to give himself the Heimlich. Agent Janik sat, adjusted the pleats on his pants and said, "Dr. Lee, it's my understanding that you've been quite helpful with this case."

I shrugged. "Quite helpful" seemed a gross exaggeration.

"Circumstances have dictated a federal interest, and I'm now the agent in charge here. I'd appreciate it if you would continue to lend your assistance to this investigation. I think we'd all like to see this matter wrapped up quickly and satisfactorily, yes?"

He looked from Knox to me to Baldy. I could've sworn that he even looked to The Vein, which I'd now nicknamed Throbby Von Grumpenstein. Stress, I've learned, makes me a little weird.

"I'm all about doing my civic duty," I said, "How can I help?"

"To start out, I'd like to hear – from you – more of what you and Detective Knox have uncovered," Janik said.

I nodded. "You mentioned that circumstances dictated an FBI investigation… what circumstances would those be?" I said.

"Privileged information," Baldy said, "You don't need to know that shit."

"I think I do," I said.

"I agree," Knox said. "He needs to know what's up."

"He doesn't *need* dick," Baldy said.

I said, "Now that's where you're right, chief, but I keep getting those spam emails anyway. You ever get those? 'Supersize your wang,' that sort of thing?"

From the look of him, Baldy was either going to shoot frothy milk out of the top of his head, or the Vein from Planet Eros was about to make its escape. He barked out short explosive bursts of verbal diarrhea until Janik silenced him by whispering, "Inside voices, children."

I leaned back in my chair. Who says murder investigations can't be fun? Once the chief was back under control of himself again, Agent Janik said, "I don't have a problem sharing this information, so long as I know I can expect complete confidentiality from you, Dr. Lee."

"Who am I gonna tell? Honestly."

"The press, perhaps?"

"Last time I talked to the press, they lumped me into an article on alternative healing next to an 'urban shaman' named Reggie Jenkins and some fat cat-lady who channeled fairies. You have nothing to worry about."

"Fair enough," Janik said. He turned on an overhead projector on the conference table and asked Knox to turn off the lights. The image projected onto the white wall was a photo of a crime scene in a restaurant. A fat guy in a brown suit was face down in marinara sauce. The back of his head was not in attendance. A yellow paper, tacked to his back by what appeared to be an ice pick, was inscribed with Chinese characters and a few hexagrams.

"Who's this?" I said.

"Giovanni Frichetti."

I gave my finest blank-eyed stare.

"One of the top dogs in the Candini crew out of New York," he said for clarification.

"Ah," I said.

"Can you read the note?"

"Yeah. Eight Tigers. They get around, apparently."

"Indeed they do," Janik said, clicking to the next photo, a man in white lying in the street. His eyes were vacant sockets. Same yellow paper tacked to his chest.

"This gentleman was Jimmy Antoneli of the Chicago Antonelis."

The third photo was a dark-skinned black man. A raw red crescent split his neck; his tongue had been pulled through the open wound. Another advertisement for Eight Tigers was pinned through the tip of the tongue.

"Vin 'Jooky' Williams, heavy hitter for the Crips in L.A."

"So…" I said, "We're looking at some sort of gang war?"

"Seems that way. Except the unusual thing about this war is that it seems to have started from within the Tigers, starting with the death of Jimmy Lau."

"…And the new Eight Tigers seem to think they can take on everybody. They're trying to absorb the smaller Triads, they're hitting the mafia, the gangs… it's like they're on friggin' steroids," Knox said.

I thought of Mei Ling. What was her part in this? That made me think of Tony Lau and his speech at dinner. About "putting aside childish things."

Tony and I were going to have to have a serious chat.

73

When I got back to the hotel, I found Tracy in the middle of some bizarre ritual. The stereo was on, and I recognized the song – Siouxsie and the Banshees' Cities in Dust – I was learning, little by little. I closed the door behind me and saw a bouncing flash of tantalizing pale flesh. I leaned around the corner and saw Tracy, clad only in lacy black unmentionables and thigh-high fishnets, grooving to the music as she leaned toward the bathroom mirror and applied mascara.

The last notes of the song faded and were soon replaced with unfamiliar, lilting strains. I walked over to the stereo and saw several open, empty CD cases littering the table. Most were Tracy's, but a few were mine. Clearly, she needed to fill space in the six disc changer.

Peeking over the couch, I had a perfect view of her. Her body swayed slower now, lithe and sleek. There was something to the way she moved, the roll of her shoulders, the arch of her back, the ripples of muscle in her calves, it was nearly maddening. But it sure made me happy to be a guy.

The song ended, and I heard her mumble something to herself. Then came the clacking of CDs changing, and the intro of Prefab Sprout's King of Rock and Roll blasted from the speakers.

I winced; this one was mine.

Peering over, I saw her shrug at her reflection and bop along to the beat. At the first chorus, though, she stopped and said, "What the hell is this shit?" She strolled out of the bathroom and stopped with a gasp as she saw me sitting there. "Christ, Randall, you scared the shit out of me," she said. The chorus repeated again. She made a face as if she smelled something foul.

"Randall."

"Yes?"

"What is this?"

"Prefab Sprout," I said, ever the helpful one.

"It may be the most irritating thing I've ever heard."

"It grows on you," I said hopefully.

"I try to stay away from things that grow on me."

The chorus repeated again.

"Ugh," she said, bending to reach the stereo. She turned off my CD and put in another of her own. I hadn't realized before that she was wearing a thong. I was acutely aware now, though.

"Hot frogs and jumping dogs… it's fucking stupid, Randall."

"Actually, it's 'Hot Dog, Jumping Frog,'" I sang.

She turned and cast a playful glare. Her naturally big, dark eyes looked bigger and darker than usual, and it wasn't just the makeup. With those eyes alone, she could make me feel like I was someone worth sticking around. With that gaze, I felt like Superman.

Granted, her other attributes helped too.

"Whatever, Randall. You need help. Don't feel bad…All men do. Usually, it's clothes, or cooking, or manners… you just have terminally poor taste in music. You can't help it. It's okay."

I raised an eyebrow.

"I'm not allowed to like what I like?" I said.

"No. Not when it's shit," she said.

"*De gustibus non est disputandum,*" I said.

"Huh?"

"'In matters of taste, there can be no debate.' Or something like that."

Tracy's CD clicked into place, and something that sounded like porno music came over the speakers. "*This* is good music though?" I said.

"This, Randall, is Prince. This is Great music," she said, effortlessly slipping into dance mode. The movements of her hips were probably illegal in most countries.

As she moved in close to me, her movements deteriorated into a simple back and forth two-step dance. She looked up at me expectantly. The two rocks I kept in my head clicked together and formed a spark; I understood what she was doing. She'd dumbed her movements down.

For dumb old me.

"No. No, no, no, no, no," I said, backing away.

"Randall…you promised."

"Yes, but… but that's not a dance."

"Oh?" She slipped back into her previous routine. Somewhere Salome was taking notes.

Tracy spun around and leaned her shoulders against my chest; the rest of her body rolled backward fluidly, crashing against me like a wave. Something somewhere below my waist short circuited.

"This isn't dancing?" She said, craning up to kiss the cut on my chin.

"Yes…very nice… dance. But me. I mean… I can't."

Get a hold of yourself, man.

"What I mean is that it's lovely for you. I can't do anything like that. I'd be fine with the standard old boring slow dance. I'm *king* of the standard old boring slow dance."

"You're a poo."

She walked back to the stereo and slapped the off switch.

"Trace--" I said.

She walked away and closed the bathroom door. After a few minutes, I went and knocked.

"What," she said.

"I do know one dance…" I said.

She opened the door a crack and leveled one lovely eye. I gave my most charming cheesy grin and said, "The Horizontal Hula."

Her lips rose ever so slightly.

"Until further notice, that's a solo number," she said just before slamming the door.

74

When she emerged, at last, from the bathroom, it was as though our exchange had never happened. She gave me a sly smile and wink and told me I should change.

"What, you don't love me just the way I am?" I said.

"Your clothes, dorkus."

My central nervous system finally finished processing her new dress and I nodded dumbly.

It was a pseudo-translucent, shimmery blue thing – gossamer in the extreme, and nearly indecent.

I said, "Guh," or some such thing.

She narrowed her eyes playfully and said, "It's not like it's anything you haven't seen before…"

"But the presentation is lovely," I said, "What's the occasion?"

"I'm going dancing," she said.

My heart sank. "Oh," I said.

There were two ways this could play out, and neither of them looked good. Either she'd had enough of Grampa Lee, or she expected me to go with her. For the first time in my life, I prayed for a night of dancing.

"Mm-hm," she said, "Me and Daniel and Tony. You coming?"

The effects of the dress were still short-circuiting portions of my brain.

I said, "Wait, what? Daniel and Tony? My Daniel and Tony?"

She giggled and said, "I didn't know you guys were an item."

"You know what I mean… Tony Lau. That's the Tony you're talking about."

"Mm-hm," she said, cocking her head and putting her hands on her hips.

"And how did this come about?"

"I called them. They're still in the hotel," Tracy said.

"Why would you do that?"

"Because something's been gnawing at my brain stem and I wanted a chance to… more fully test my hypothesis."

"What?" I said, "What?" Because I'm a genius.

"You just sit back and watch. Women's intuition," was all she said.

75

We met Tony and Daniel just outside of the club on Washington. Both men were dressed immaculately in tailored silk suits – Tony's white, Daniel's a dark plum; I was, according to Tracy, "kickin' it old skool" in jeans and a pullover. I'm pretty sure 'old skool' was actually some kind of code for "homeless person."

"Hey guys," Tracy said with a wide grin as she ran up and hugged each of them.

"I see your plan worked," Daniel said.

"Like a charm, baby," Tracy said glancing over to me.

Tony laughed and headed for the doors.

"Plan?" I said.

"She say you have a jealous heart, Doctor," Daniel said, the vaguest hint of a smile at the corners of his lips. I raised my eyebrows and leveled a look at Tracy. She winked and blew me a kiss. Looking to the club entrance, with its aneurysm inducing bass and its flashing lights and fog, my mind imagined the world's trendiest and most obnoxious UFO. I sighed and took a step toward my fate.

Right into a massive globule of regurgitated chewing gum on the sidewalk. "Aw, shit." I said, lifting my shoe to inspect the gooey damage. I heard Tracy giggle. Looking up, I saw that the others had already gone inside; she'd waited for me, which was nice.

"Well, Randall, it's official. You're an honest-to-God gumshoe now," she smirked and turned to go inside.

I sighed again.

76

There are many reasons to dislike dance clubs. Each person is an individual, and their reasons are as unique as the patterns of snowflakes.

Here, however, are some of mine:

For one thing, I tend to like songs that have a clear-cut beginning, middle, and end.

If I wanted to hear four hours of the same thing, I'd go home and throw on my Iron Butterfly album. I'm not big on smoke. Tobacco smoke, pot smoke, that wet-dog's-ass-on-fire fog that fills the dance floor, or the inevitable wisps produced by the friction of having 250 people rubbing together in a ten foot by ten foot square.

That brings me to another peeve.

Sweat.

I don't like my own, why would I voluntarily bathe in the fluids of a room full of Ritalin-addicted twenty-something ravers?

The answer is that I wouldn't.

Except that whenever I'd look over and see her eyes again they'd make me stupid.

Luckily for me, I was still about eight shots of vodka from donning a light stick and white-man's-overbite-ing my way into the Embarrassing Old Bastard's Hall of Fame.

After handling the gum incident in a very me fashion, I went in the club, got carded, got the typical double take I usually got when people saw my age, and found my party at a round table in a far corner overlooking the dance floor. I slid my way up to them and made it to the table in time to catch the waitress as she took our drink orders.

I sat next to Tracy in the booth and smoothly dragged my heels over the carpeted steps.

"For you?" the waitress mouthed over the thump and whir of the shit on the speakers.

"Jack and coke," I shouted.

She gave me a thumbs up and started to walk away.

"Agh!" she shouted loud enough to be heard over the music. She lifted her shoe and glared at the gum trailing from it to the carpeted step. "God-fucking-dammit."

I played it cool.

Looking around our table, I said, "Man. I sure am glad I didn't step in it."

77

"You want the first dance?" Tracy said, batting her eyes at me.

"Sorry," I said, "not nearly drunk enough."

She sighed and turned to Daniel. "I'd be honored," he said, taking her hand and whisking her away to the orgy of sweaty, bouncy stupidity below.

That left just me and Tony. He stared out at the floor. I decided to try it. I caught more than a few dudes checking out the highly visible parts of Tracy's figure. I fantasized about leaping over the railing and viciously chopping each of them in the forehead; it made me smile.

Tracy and Daniel went to town, quickly becoming quite the dance floor sensation. I half expected the crowd to part like it was Saturday Night Fever or something, but it didn't really happen that way. Thinly veiled beneath their movements, one could clearly see her pure sexuality and his lethal nature. Sex and death, the perennial twins of fascination.

"...Really something, eh?" Tony yelled.

I nodded, finished my drink, and thought, '...and she's going home with me, buddy.'

"Not much for dancing, yourself, though?" He said.

With my empty glass in hand, I remembered my rule about beverages and speaking.

And yet my mouth opened anyway.

"You can't possibly think you can take on everybody, Tony," I said.

He went with one of my lines. "What?"

I fondled my empty glass longingly and said, "Feds are involved now. I know all about the Tigers' big ole killin' spree. You're the new boss. You telling me you didn't order it?"

"...What? No!" He said. He stared at me with wide eyes and a slack jaw. Why didn't anyone ever just break down and confess to me? Why couldn't it, just for once, be simple and easy?

"C'mon, Tony. I'm not a cop. Just be straight with me. Your dad, your fiancée, and your unborn kid all get whacked by – probably - some rival gang. It's a natural reaction to want revenge. It's even natural to lash out at any possible enemy... but it's not smart. Somebody's already got a serious beef with your family. No point in making it worse."

"I don't even know what you're talking about," he said. Just then, my lovely returned. She slid into the booth next to me, her skin shone from the light and the sweat. She looked ecstatic.

Daniel came back too. He looked... like Daniel.

"How's it goin', party poopers?" Tracy said between sips of her drink.

"Fine," Tony said. Even with the pounding beat in our ears, it was easy to perceive that *his* fine did not mean fine. Tracy looked from him to me; she chewed on her straw.

Tony was staring at me. His eyes were cold and hard.

Something I said?

Daniel leaned over to Tony and said something close to his ear.

Tony shook his head very slightly.

Tracy picked up her water glass and fumbled it, soaking the front of her already revealing dress. Without averting his gaze from me, Tony Lau took his handkerchief from his jacket pocket and offered it to Tracy.

"Thanks," she shouted.

He nodded but still stared at me. I chanced a glance at Daniel, just to make sure he wasn't getting ready to spin-kick me to oblivion. The Brazilian sat with his head bowed. He might have been studying the table top or his hands; it was hard to tell with his dark sunglasses.

"All I want is the truth, Tony," I said.

"Are you sure?" Tracy said. It surprised me. It felt like everybody knew something I didn't. I didn't particularly care for that feeling.

Apparently I wasn't the only one. Tony Lau had turned his focus to Tracy too.

"How long have you two been hiding?" She said to him.

"Hiding?" Tony said. Daniel raised his head; it was pointed roughly in Tracy's direction, so I assumed she had his attention as well. Tracy nodded and regarded him calmly.

Daniel said, "Seven years."

Tony spun toward him and glared. Daniel bowed his head again. I struggled, in vain, to comprehend the exchange. Tracy glanced at me and smiled slyly.

"Who exactly is hiding from what, please?" I said.

Tony and Daniel were silent. Neither of them looked at me.

Over the music, Tracy shouted, "If you don't tell, I will, guys. He only wants to help. Really."

Tony didn't look happy. His mouth was a scrunched up sneer, his skin flushed a dark crimson. Tracy watched him for a minute and abruptly turned to me. As she opened her mouth to speak, Tony said, "Fine."

Tracy winked at me and leaned back in the booth, crossing her arms with satisfaction.

"Doctor Lee," Tony said and stopped, searching for words, "my father was a great man. You may not believe it, but he truly was. Throughout my life, his primary concern was my happiness, my safety. Life in a Triad in Hong Kong is not easy. Not safe. He brought the family to America so that I would not have to live the kind of life he'd had. He brought Mei Ling to the states for me… to protect me."

He stopped and stared at the table. Better the table than me, I thought. I waited, knowing he'd speak when he was ready. The music still battered my central nervous system, but in that moment, the club felt very quiet, very still.

"He understood, right from the first. I was so afraid, but he just… he took me in his arms, y'know, and he said that - no matter what - I was his son. I wanted to just tell the world, I was so happy then… but he told me how dangerous that could be. For me, for him… for the family. Some things are still seen as weakness. The Chinese are an old fashioned people."

There was a tightness to Lau that I'd never noticed until now, as it loosened and unwound the muscles around his eyes and jaw. Whatever he was confessing to, it was a profound unburdening to him.

"I told you the truth about Mei Ling. As children, we were best of friends. My father hired the astrologer who compared our signs. He was convinced that we would be a perfect couple. Years later, even though he knew, he paid a great deal of money to bring her here."

He slumped in the booth, his eyes cast now at the floor.

"There had been rumors, however careful we'd been. My father paid her… to help alleviate the shame. Mei Ling did not care. She was still my friend. Perhaps she even loved me a little."

"You didn't love her," I said. The three of them looked up at me; I felt very dense, but I didn't know why. There was a fuzzy sort of sensation in the back of my brain, as if the connections really wanted to click but just couldn't reach. Tracy gave me a sympathetic smile and patted my hand. Imitating Daniel's accent, she said, "You 'ave a jealous 'eart, yes?"

"Apparently, yes."

"Yet you let me dance with Daniel," she bit her lip and lowered her chin a little.

"So?"

"Would you let me dance with one of the guys down on the dance floor?"

"Well, I don't really have anything to say about it. You can dance with anybody you want to dance with, but I wouldn't like it."

"Because you'd be jealous," she said.

"Damn right," I said.

"But you're not very jealous of Tony or Daniel?"

"No, not really," I said.

"Why not?"

I shrugged. The techno was starting to really give me a headache.

"Might it be because they don't look at me the way some of the other guys do?" She said.

I shrugged again.

She leaned in close and said something. I knew I couldn't have heard it right.

"What?" I said.

She got in very close and yelled. This time there was no mistaking it.

"They're gay, dear," she said.

78

"Oh, just because they don't ogle you, they're gay?" I said. "Aren't you being a bit full of yourself?"

She smirked and said, "Randall, I've caught our waitress staring at my tits tonight, okay? I've gotten glances from just about everybody here. Same with the last time we all went out. It may sound like I think I'm all that, but that's not it… a girl just learns to feel when people are staring. Usually, if I show a millimeter of cleavage, I'm dealing with looks all night. Besides, that's not what cinched it for me. Body language, conversation, hell, even Daniel's Capoeira name…"

"Still," I said, "That doesn't mean they're gay, for god's sake…"

I glanced at Daniel. He didn't seem to be paying attention. "Tell her, would you?" I said.

"What would you have me say, doctor?" Daniel said.

I looked at Tony Lau. He still stared at the floor. I looked at Daniel. I saw myself reflected in his glasses.

"Oh," I said.

Well, shit. Some fucking detective I am.

79

We went back to the hotel. Over coffee, I heard the whole story. Tony had been hiding, really, his whole life. He'd been a sickly child, but Jimmy Lau had gone to insane lengths to show the rest of the family - and the Eight Tigers - that his son was strong. The older Tony got, the more important it became. To be a future leader of the Eight Tigers, he had to be tough. He had to be a 'real' man. Jimmy Lau had even threatened to throw several of his 'brothers' out of the gang for suggesting that Tony might not be up to snuff.

When Lau arranged for his son's engagement, many of the rumors ceased. With Lau's acceptance and involvement in his son's art career, the whole point became more or less moot.

Jimmy Lau had protocols in place for choosing a suitable heir to the Eight Tigers. Unfortunately, now that he was dead, none of the other 'brothers' wanted to follow them. Each had their own claim of seniority; each had supposedly received Lau's blessing.

For Tony, the whole affair had been painful. The kid just wanted to live his own life.

Chances were good that he would never truly be able to.

80

After Tony and Daniel left, Tracy and I sat in the living room area of the suite. She'd pulled those long, magnificent legs of hers up under herself in the chair and sat sipping cocoa.

I cracked the top of a bottle of Glenfiddich, poured two fingers worth (if those fingers belonged to The Thing from Fantastic Four), and sat across from her on the couch.

For a long while, we were silent.

Pain still lingered in the room, and it was hard to ignore. I couldn't imagine what it had to be like to be Tony Lau, on so many different levels. To lose your fiancée, your child, and your father in the space of a month; to live a life being groomed for something you couldn't care less about; to be unable to love, truly love, freely.

I looked at the goddess across from me – with the dot of marshmallow fluff on the tip of her nose from a particularly ambitious gulp of cocoa – and imagined a life in which I had to measure my glances, conceal my touches, and keep my mouth shut.

I couldn't do it.

Nobody should have to.

"… I love you," I said. The words surprised me, but they hit Tracy as if I'd fired a gun at her.

"What?" She said.

"You heard me."

"Say it again," she said, her eyes shining.

I said it again and felt some of the ache in my heart dissipate. Setting my drink on the coffee table, I got up, went to her, and knelt in front of her. She slid her legs out, unfolding them, and wrapped them around my waist. Her hands slid through my hair and intertwined on the back of my neck. Our lips met, and I felt droplets hit my face. When I looked up at her, the shine of her eyes had brimmed over, painting crystalline lines down her cheeks.

She sniffled and shrugged, laughing a little. "Nobody's ever said that to me before," she said. "It's a little disarming."

"Tell me about it," I said.

She wiped at her eyes and leaned back, breathing slowly and deeply several times before saying, "I've… never really said that to anybody either."

"It's okay," I said. "You should only ever say it if you really mean it."

She was staring down at our hands which had somehow come together. Her eyes rose to meet mine and she said, "…and you really mean it?"

I nodded and kissed the marshmallow from the tip of her nose.

81

In our moonlit bedroom, with the sounds of the sleeping city beneath us, we laid in each other's arms, skin against skin. I listened to the sounds of the wind against the building, the occasional passing car, and the steady tide of her breath.

As I was drifting off, Tracy said, "Randall?"

"Hrmf?"

"…I love you too."

I smiled, kissed her hair, and fell promptly asleep.

I didn't dream.

I didn't need to.

82

After breakfast and a water conserving shower, I kissed Tracy goodbye. She was off to visit her parents, and I was heading for a morning of punishment. Master Cheng answered the door in his pajamas – yellow footies with small Howdy Doody heads dancing in random patterns.

"Am I early, Master?" I said.

He blinked at me several times and said, "No, why?"

Before I could answer he turned and disappeared into the house. He'd left the door open, a sure sign I was invited in. I closed the door behind me and went through the antiquated kitchen and down the basement steps. Cheng promptly slumped into his easy chair.

The open concrete floor was filled with his students. They practiced their various sets without any semblance of order, sometimes crashing together in the cramped space. Master Cheng said something, and for the first time I noticed the older man sitting in the other easy chair. As the students labored, the two older men appeared to be playing *Xiangqi* – Chinese Chess.

I looked around, seeking some small open space in which to warm up.

Cheng immediately said, "Lazy American asshole, get to work…stop wasting my time."

I wasn't sure how I was wasting his time, since he'd barely noticed me since I'd arrived, but I wedged myself into a small alcove by a metal shelving unit covered with moldy issues of National Geographic and Playboy and began to practice the Silk Reeling exercises.

When I was finished, several of Cheng's students approached, bowing slightly, and asked to push hands. I did, feeling beady eyes on my back from the direction of Cheng's chair.

"Ay, Frankenstein! What, you eat too much French fry? Too much Big Mac? Why so lumbering? Why so heavy? Be light, be a crane!"

And, to my partner, "Jiong Lu, do not hang off the American… he is not a meat hook."

As I practiced more, circulating among different students and occasionally stopping for small breaks, I felt eyes on me more and more frequently. From the corner of my eye, I saw Cheng's guest rise and approach the class. Cheng was not far behind.

The man was almost a foot shorter than me. His hair was severe and short, plastered to his head like a helmet. His eyes were a pale grey. He wore the same long, wispy beard I was used to seeing in kung fu movies.

The guest went to one of Cheng's top students and assumed a deep pushing hands stance. The boy mirrored him. Moments after touching forearms, however, the boy was launched from his feet and into several of the other students. When the boy stood again, he held his arm gingerly.

The guest paid no attention, but went to the next student. He yielded to the student's first push, flowing around the kid like liquid, and delivered two knifehand strikes to the kid's hip, knocking him into a shelf of old newspapers.

Without a word, he moved on to the next student – Jiong Lu, the kid I'd been practicing with. I pushed the kid back and said, "My turn."

Cheng stepped in and said, "Ay, American asshole-head have no manners. Pardon, sir, pardon."

The guest just stared at me.

I stared right on back.

He sank into a deep stance as easily as if he were sitting on a chair. With his thighs parallel to the ground, he raised an arm as an invitation. I dropped down to his level and mirrored his stance. As I raised my arm, he made a slight shaking movement with his waist; I turned and yielded, barely avoiding the same *fa-jin* strike that had almost broken the other student's arm.

I moved in, stepping behind his right heel with my left foot, and pressed into his floating ribs with my forearm. Without moving, he absorbed the strike and then seemed to puff out like a blowfish. I kept my footing, and my position, only because I had not yet committed weight to my left foot.

I withdrew, seeking a more strategic positioning, when, with a violent shake, his arms flew like steel whips at my head and torso.

In the millisecond given, I had no Tai Chi defense; I simply raised my arms and tried to keep my head down. The strikes numbed my arms and sent shockwaves of agony through my skull. I was barely aware of his arms looping around, driving my defenses down, and looping up to strike – with the knuckles of his index fingers – my exposed temples.

Before he struck his target, I saw something slide in, catch his arms, and push him back.

Something hard and gnarled jabbed an acupuncture point in the side of my neck and moved down to stab at points in my chest.

In seconds, the feeling returned to my arms and the spider webs in my head cleared.

I saw Cheng, his bony fingers still poking me, warding off his guest with a broomstick.

"Cannot have you killing my students, Ang," Cheng said mildly, "Bad for business."

The guest – Ang – showed no emotion. He turned, as if to leave, and whipped his shoulder back into the tip of Cheng's broomstick. The stick cracked and shattered, but Cheng held his position.

Ang mounted the stairs and disappeared.

I held my chest and struggled through a few breaths before managing to say, "Who the hell was that?"

"Ang Su Chan. Very famous practitioner from Hong Kong. In town on business. I am surprised you have not heard of him. I invited him as guest instructor… To bruise students is good, to break them is not so good. Plus he is an asshole."

I swallowed with some difficulty and said, "I think he was *trying* to kill me."

Cheng turned, scratched his belly through his Howdy Doody pajamas, and said, "Of course he was, numb nuts, he is the man you've been looking for."

83

"What?" The old man said.

Apparently, I'd been staring. "...What do you mean?" I said.

"Your killer...it's him. I find out he's in town, I invite him, see his technique..." he said, shrugging. "Now I know for certain,"

Spitting a curse, I bolted for the stairs, fumbling for my cell phone as I ran. I jammed Knox's speed dial number with my thumb and wove through the house, knocking over stacks of newspapers and crashing through piles of aluminum can-filled plastic bags. Knox answered just as my foot tangled in a strand of orange twine leftover from bundling newspapers and sent me sprawling across the floor.

"Lee? That you?" He said.

"Get over here. Now. Olive and 82nd." He knew I wasn't screwing around, at least. He hung up and I scrambled out the front door, scanning the street for some sign of the killer. A huge grey Lincoln pulled out of a side street and made a left onto Olive. In five minutes, he'd be on the highway and gone.

I thumbed the remote start on my key chain, unlocked the doors, slid into the driver's seat, and pulled out into a tight U-turn. I stomped on the gas pedal and flew after him.

84

"So…you - a civilian - pursued a dangerous murder suspect."

"That's right," I said.

"And at what point, exactly, did you collide with the detective's car?"

"Oh, pretty much right away," I said.

The captain was enjoying the hell out of this, I could tell. Agent Janik leaned back in his chair and crossed his arms. Knox scowled at me. The bandage on his forehead really brought out his eyes.

Luckily, I was unscathed. For once.

My new car on the other hand…

Jesus wept.

Guess I'd see just how good that 'bumper-to-bumper' warranty really was. I scowled back at Knox. His car was a piece of shit.

Captain Baldy, meanwhile, rambled on for another fifteen minutes about how I should be arrested and how Knox should be yanked off the case. Janik leaned forward and said, "Not so fast, captain. Where would we be without the work of these two gentlemen? Considering the resources at their disposal, I think they've done a fine job. That includes Dr. Lee. Nobody's being pulled just yet."

"You're not pulling rank on me, dammit. I still say what goes around here," Baldy said.

The vein pulsed once, like an exclamation point. Dong!

"I'm not even sure what the hell you're doing here, Janik. I don't see how this is a federal matter."

Janik raised an eyebrow and leaned in. Something in his eyes darkened and changed – this was the face normally reserved for the interrogation room, I imagined. "Normally, *sir,* I wouldn't think of pulling rank on anybody, but seeing how your only involvement in this case has been to obstruct, interfere, and generally fuck things up, that's exactly what I'm going to do. This is my case, captain, so from now on your presence in these proceedings will not be necessary. I will email you my progress reports – as a courtesy, you understand – but that's all the involvement I'll need from you. Do we understand each other, Captain?"

Baldy just stared. I watched the pulsing in his head and remembered my favorite scene from the movie *Scanners.* Janik took a toothpick from his inner coat pocket, slipped it between his teeth, and began to chew. After a moment, he looked up at the captain and said, "Okay, obviously not. Get the fuck out, please."

"You're throwing me out of my own goddamned conference room."

"That's correct. Was there a question?"

Captain Baldy stood slowly – I thought he might actually burst if he made any sudden movements – and walked out of the room without a word. I could foresee much unpleasantness in Knox's future.

For now, though, it was time to get down to business. Janik fiddled with the USB cable on his laptop, checked the connections to an old overhead projector the size of a tank, and grunted as an image sprang to life upon the conference room wall – a photo of our boy.

"Ang Su Chan," Janik said. "Sixty-eight years old. Citizen of Hong Kong. Only prior conviction – Involuntary manslaughter wheedled down to self-defense… in 1974. He leads a senior's Tai Chi Chuan class at the Tai Chi Garden in Hong Kong Park. You sure this is the guy, Lee?"

"Yeah, that's him."

Janik leaned back in his chair and clamped a toothpick between his jaws. "This old man is the killer," he said. It should've been a question, but his voice didn't go up at the end.

"Yes," I said.

"Huh."

I looked at Knox. He stared at the table and scratched at the stubble on his cheek.

"I'm not making it up, guys," I said.

Janik raised his eyebrows as if he were surprised at my statement. The toothpick bobbled between his teeth. Knox kept on staring and scratching. I slid the sleeves of my shirt up to my elbows and held out my arms. The bruising was already worse than I would have guessed; I made a mental note to stop by the shop on the way home and grab some more needles, some *dit da jow*, and a few herbs for tea.

"Holy shit." Knox said, leaning in to study the muddy yellows and maroons splotched across my forearms. Janik said nothing. He just sat there, staring, with the toothpick jutting from his teeth like an exclamation point.

"What we need to find out," I said, sliding my sleeves gingerly back down, "is where the hell he is and what his connection is to Mei Ling and the Eight Tigers."

Janik got on the phone. Within fifteen minutes he had a surveillance detail assigned to the airport, a team researching names and possible aliases cross-referenced to hotel registries throughout the bi-state area, and lunch in thirty minutes or it was free.

Ladies and gentlemen – your tax dollars at work.

85

While Janik and Knox did the whole cop thing, I went back to the hotel, made some phone calls, and sat around looking clueless; in other words, I did my thing. I called Tracy's cell and got her voicemail, so I left a message telling her to beware of sinister old Chinese guys. I called Tony Lau, found out he'd returned to San Francisco, and gave him an update. The name Ang Su Chan didn't ring any bells with him, but he promised to look into his father's records.

That concluded my limited usefulness for the day. I kicked back on the couch, turned on the television, and promptly fell asleep. Six hours and some change later, the sound of keys in the lock rattled me awake. I slid from the couch and slinked over behind the door, ready to pounce if necessary.

Seeing the peach Converse All-Stars, the baggy cargo pants – concealing what I knew to be the finest legs in the free world – and the holey, faded Bjork T-shirt, I knew that pouncing would be absolutely necessary. With all that was going on, though, I opted for the straight forward approach; I could just imagine jumping out to surprise her and getting a ring of keys raked across my eyes.

After the day I'd had, I didn't think my fragile male ego could take it.

"Hey," I said.

She started, but relaxed when she saw me. "Christ, Randall, what the hell are you doing?"

"Waiting for you, hot stuff. How're the folks?"

"Lecturey. As usual. I had to tell them I was getting a tattoo just to draw the fire off of you."

"I almost got beat to death," I said.

"The worst of it is, I had to feign a full-sleeve design before they'd actually listen… wait, what?"

"Master Cheng found the guy who killed Mei Ling."

"That's great! You got him?"

"No. That's where the part about almost getting beat to death comes in."

"He got away? You didn't kick his ass?"

"Sadly, yes. And no, he received no ass kickings from me."

She studied my face and systematically moved her gaze downward. Her eyes widened and stopped; I looked down at my arms. They hurt to move.

The bruises had gone from purple to black in a few hours.

I winced as I raised my arms to look closer. She gasped.

And grabbed them.

After convincing myself not to vomit or pass out, I asked her nicely to stop squeezing the deep-tissue bruises. "Oh shit…sorry," she yelped.

"S'okay," I managed through clenched teeth.

Together we went to the kitchen, took two very cold Heinekens from the fridge, and got to the business of making things all better. The beer was good, the kisses were great. The way a faded, holey Bjork looked on, crumpled, from the floor was a little creepy but I got over it with proper distraction, of which there was plenty.

86

"What're those?" she said, later. She was perched on the edge of the tub, wearing only her Bjork shirt and a pair of sheer (what-the-hell's-the-point-honestly?) panties.

I opened the glass case, took one of the nine instruments from it, and put the rest back on the sink. "These," I said, "were my teacher's. Actually, they were handed down from his teacher's teacher's teacher. Back in the old days, doctors carried these around instead of the little flimsy needles you're used to seeing."

"And they *used* those?"

"Yeah. Each one has a specific purpose. A lot of modern acupuncturists wouldn't know what they're for, but my teacher was very traditional."

I held up the long steel tool – a thick, edged needle – and Tracy eyed it nervously.

"And what is that one for?" She said.

"A few things. What we're going to do today is this..." I said before pressing the edge against the darkest part of my left forearm. With a flick of the wrist, I opened an inch-long furrow in the skin. Thick black blood welled from the slit. Tracy sucked in a deep breath and looked away.

"It's better like this, trust me," I said, squeezing the wound gingerly. More sludge spilled out.

"*Why?*" She said.

"When somebody like our killer hits you, it's not like taking a punch from some guy off the street... Joe Dipshit punches and he might cause some minor problems, bruises, maybe a broken bone.

Somebody like our boy Ang hits you, he's out to shut down whole organ systems. Sometimes, even when the main goal – death – isn't met, the body is still sent into a kind of toxic state. What you see now is proof of that. This blood, if left untreated, would eventually have to be processed and filtered and cleaned by my body. If I wasn't the strapping, relatively young lad that I am it could cause serious problems in the liver and kidneys. Better to just let it bleed out."

"Oh. Good times," she said, glancing at the blood with a look of disgust.

I squeezed again, and before long the wound ran bright red. I twisted the top off a bottle of peroxide with my teeth and poured the liquid over the cut. Tilting my arm, I let the pink froth fizz down the drain. I looked up into the mirror, smiled at Tracy, and said, "You learn something new every day, huh?"

"There are some things I never needed to know, but thanks."

"...But not *all* things," I said with a wink.

She blushed and hid her face behind her knees. "No," she said, "not all things. Some educational things are nice."

She knew just what I was talking about. Earlier in the evening, I introduced Tracy to the art of sexual alchemy. Those crafty Taoists... they came up with acupuncture points to stimulate everywhere.

Yep, everywhere.

I tore open a bandage and attempted to apply it one-handed. Tracy sighed and slapped my hand away. As she got the bandage in place and taped it, she said, "Why do you do that? Just ask for help. You can't do it all yourself, you know, and you shouldn't have to. It's all part of the deal, Randall... you and me. Comes with the territory, so get used to it."

I took the steel blade and spun it across my palm until the handle pointed to her.

"Wanna do the honors then, honey? There's still my other arm to do."

"Oh, hell no," she said, leaving and closing the door behind her. I finished my third beer of the night and did what had to be done.

But when it came time for the Band-aid, I actually did ask for help.

87

At 2:45 in the morning, with the TV's black and white flickers illuminating the aftermath of our midnight Chinese take-out picnic, and the sounds of Phillip Marlowe being hardboiled, Tracy and I talked. There were just too damned many pieces to this puzzle, and it seemed like I hadn't put any of them together without her.

We talked about Ang and his background. About the organized attacks on crime syndicates throughout the country. About Tony and his place in all of it. Tracy bit her lip, frowned, and climbed out of bed. She wore a thin black tank top and some lacy black panties, but I managed to keep my mind on the case.

Mostly.

She returned with another round of drinks. As she popped the tops of the glass bottles, she said, "So… somebody decided to take over the Eight Tigers. This much we know. They whack Mei Ling, Tony's future wife, and Jimmy, Tony's dad… but they don't hit Tony. Why?"

I grinned at her terminology – my girlfriend the Mafioso.

"At first I thought he was in on it. Now, I don't know," I said.

"Whoever it is, they're *pissed.*"

"Why do you say that?"

She shrugged and said, "Everything you've told me… these guys are like out to wreck Tony's life."

"Maybe that's why they haven't gone after him. They want to make him suffer first?"

"But why?"

"No idea."

Tracy crossed her arms and rested them atop her knees. She leaned her chin on her crossed arms and closed her eyes. Except for her toes, which bobbed to some rhythm the rest of the world couldn't hear, she was perfectly still. Her toes suddenly stopped; her eyes shot open.

"We're so fucking dumb, Randall."

"We are?"

"Big time. What did Tony say? The wedding was supposed to quiet the rumors… there were guys in the Tigers who'd been talking shit… Mr. Lau had to threaten some of them…"

My chest tightened. Exhilaration and sickness mingled.

"So these guys decide Tony's too much of a pansy to run the gang, they plan their own little hostile takeover, and they declare war…" I said.

"Something like that." she said.

"What about Mei Ling? Why her? Why the elaborate rituals?" I said.

"To let the Lau family know that they weren't fooling anybody with their little charade?"

I frowned.

"Seems a little thin," I said.

She joined me in frowning.

"You got something better, I'd love to hear it."

"Jimmy Lau was a Taoist… maybe it was supposed to rattle him."

"But he'd never see it. Besides, how'd Mei Ling end up in his massage parlor?" She said, a trace of a smirk playing at the corners of her lips, "*Whose* story is thin?"

I felt the twinge in my chest again.

I picked up the phone.

It was almost 1 a.m. in San Francisco, but he picked up on the second ring.

"Sorry to disturb you, Tony," I said.

"Just painting. What's up, Dr. Lee?"

"This will undoubtedly seem random as hell, but… well, are you a religious man, Tony?"

There was a laugh on the other end. "No, Dr. The historical practices of my people are interesting to me, but I am proud to be a devout atheist."

I knocked the receiver against my forehead and nearly missed what Tony said next.

I looked at the phone and said, "Wait…what?"

"I said it was the only thing father and I ever really fought about… he was always sure Mei Ling would change me. In more ways than one,

I imagine."

"She was Taoist," I said.

"Very much so."

I mumbled some sort of goodbye and hung up. "Fuck." I said, slamming the phone onto the nightstand.

Tracy stared.

"What?" she said.

"It wasn't a show."

"What wasn't?"

"The whole damned thing… the crime scene. Ang wasn't showing off. He wasn't out to get attention. That ceremony was strictly for Mei Ling… because she believed. Because it would be the most terrible thing she could imagine. Because she would fear not only for herself, but for her unborn child."

"And this Ang guy knew her enough to know that," she said.

"It would seem so."

"What a bastard."

The encounter with him was still fresh. I remembered his eyes and wondered if they'd been the same – cold and vacant – when he issued the strike that killed a young mother and her baby. I wondered how a man could kill like that. No emotion, no remorse.

Sticky warmth spread through my arms and surged into an intense, burning heat. Looking down, I saw my fists were clenched and shaking from the force; the warmth formed matching scarlet blossoms that seeped through the gauze pads on my arms. A numb throbbing filled my ears; my jaws ached. With some difficulty, I willed my hands to open. They still shook and hummed.

"Randall?" Tracy's voice came from ten thousand miles away, echoing down the empty spaces that lurked between me and my rage. I made no move to shrink away from her. The truth was that I don't know that I could have moved if I'd tried. The fullness of everything had settled, and its weight was more than I could bear.

Her hands felt light and cool and smooth on my back.

"Hey…*hey*…What's wrong? Are you hurt?"

The truth - and the language necessary to express it – was too sharp, too ragged, to release.

The images seared my eyes – the girl, in life, in photos, smiling, happy; in death, cold and blue.

She'd been little more than a child.

Carrying a child.

I pressed my palms hard against my eyes but, hard as I pressed, it still came – memories that raked my mind like bits of broken glass - sable hair, lovingly braided and tipped with pink bows; delicate eyes, almond-shaped like her mother's but grey like mine; tiny giggles like the sound of wind chimes in spring.

So many times, I made her cry.

Pick up your goddamned toys. I'm not going to ask you again.

Quiet, you don't have anything to cry about.

Do not make me repeat myself. Sit still, dammit.

Daddy's busy, go watch TV or something.

Listen to your mother.

I'm too busy.

Later.

I'm busy.

So many times. Too many times.

And in our final moments together, in the quiet, clean place, she looked so very small tucked under the sky blue sheet.

Here, she was perfectly behaved. Here, she was quiet, and polite, and she never interrupted or caused trouble. Here I could be bothered to be with her.

I cannot recall the face of the coroner. In my mind I see only his white coat and his hands – thick, with tufts of grey hair sprouting from the backs and from the fingers. I remember the cheap gold watch on his wrist, and the green-stained skin peeking from underneath it.

I remember him drawing back the sheet.

Covering her forever.

And the world did not end, though it should have.

There, there's and a truckload of condolences. Acquaintances that look away or downright ignore your existence. Because tragedy could be contagious. Sedatives and pain killers and sweet, sweet liquor. And the unbearable emptiness and silence that is the reward at the end of the day.

There's too much quiet, though, too much space – more than two people can take, especially when any feeling for each other has leaked out of the gaping hole that lies where their life used to be.

I have forgiven Miranda for nearly everything, but there is one thing I can never absolve–

She never had to see.

She can remember Grace as she was.

For that, I hate her.

I'm good at hating. In the purity of the moment, I had wanted nothing more than to hit the streets; to search, to hunt, to ask around… anything. I wanted to find Ang Su Chan.

Instead, I asked Tracy to get me another drink.

Something stronger.

And I sat back, and I drank, and I did what cowards do.

I did nothing.

88

After watching the sky's colors change from gunmetal grey to peach and salmon and crimson, I slid out from the warm comfort of the bed and showered. I felt every scrape, every bruise, and every cut under the barrage of hot water.

Ain't life grand.

Tracy slept; I envied her.

My hair was still wet when I arrived at Master Cheng's fifteen minutes later.

The old man rubbed his bleary eyes with a liver-spotted hand and said, "What the hell?"

"We need to talk."

He waved me in and retreated into the house, the plastic bottoms of his pajamas slapping the floor like duck's feet. I followed him into the kitchen and sat at the table while he took a two liter bottle of Dr. Pepper from the refrigerator and poured some into an old Big Gulp cup. He took a sip and offered me some.

I nodded. While he poured my drink, he said, "What is the problem now?"

"You found him. How?"

He turned, a plastic cup in each hand, and waddled to the table. With a groan, he sat, smacked his lips, and said, "Who, Ang Su Chan?"

"Yes."

"He find me. Call on telephone."

"You run a closed school."

"Closed to idiot Americans, sure. Last thing I need is flabby yuppie girls in my basement. Talk Yoga. Talk Oprah. Aiya. Mr. Ang, he is a colleague of sorts. His reputation was good."

"So you invited him based on his reputation."

"And background. That he teach Chen style seemed curious."

"You had some suspicion, then."

"Always. Old Chinaman here in America? Suspicion becomes closer than your own underpants."

"When did you know?"

Cheng drank some soda and reached across the table for a half-full bag of Cheetos. He crunched on a handful before speaking. "He ask too many questions… want to know all about my students. You come, suddenly he want to know all about you. Questions, questions, questions… worse than my wife, rest her soul. Finally, I tell him to practice with students if he so interested… the rest you know."

He grinned; orange film crusted his teeth.

"You set me up," I said.

His smile faded. "In China," he said, "this is the way – a challenger approach, the master sends top disciple to fight. Nobody calls that a set up."

"So, I'm your top disciple?"

"Not after that piss-poor showing. I see I have wasted my time with you."

"What? You said yourself that he was good…"

Cheng threw down the bag of Cheetos. "I said his *reputation* is good. His skill is shit," he spat. Cheeto bits flew through the air, narrowly missing me.

Must be my lucky day.

Turning my attention back to the old man, I said, "He seemed pretty damned good to me."

"Of course. You are two peas in pod. Two dummies trying to out-dummy each other. Not a glimmer of Tai Chi Chuan between the two of you. Embarrassing."

"Listen, you old bastard, I was fighting for my life out there… He damn near killed your students, and he damn near killed me. He's better than me, alright?"

Cheng's face became deadly serious. "This is exactly what I say. You were *fighting*. You cannot fight this man. How did I best him? I care not for his hatred. It means nothing to me, so it cannot cling to me.

"Ang Su Chan is nothing. A child. No… a beaten dog who only know how to snap. You, Randall, are a *man*. A man does not soil himself in the presence of a child or froth at the mouth to prove something to a beast. You must be better than this. Your master did not teach you to be nothing more than a clenched fist, capable only of lashing out. Whatever this darkness is that you feel, you must let go of it, boy. If you do not, then you are correct: You will fight for your life, and you will certainly lose."

89

"No fucking way." Tracy backed away as if I were trying to give her a flaming bag of poo.

"C'mon… I'm told it's very easy. Point and shoot. That's it."

"No, Randall. I'm not taking that thing."

"Tracy…"

She walked away to the bedroom, leaving me holding the 'gift' I'd bought her – a Smith and Wesson 36LS Ladysmith revolver. It wasn't as well received as I'd hoped. Not that I blamed her, really. In the store, I'd looked at several firearms for myself, but I was surprised by how unnerving it was to hold one of those things, how final. A gun just wasn't for me, but I wanted Tracy to have *some*thing.

Just in case.

With a sigh, I put the pistol back into the brown paper bag I'd transported it in and tossed it onto the couch.

And the phone rang.

"Got our boy," Knox said. "Seems he's at the airport, attempting to get a ticket back to Hong Kong… under the name Jakob Smith. He's with a group of – I quote – 'unsavory Chinamen'… I'm thinking maybe the crew that set the ambush for the cops… Anyway, I'm meeting Janik's team at the airport. Thought you should know."

"I'll be there in ten minutes. Which gate?" I said.

"Whoa, it wasn't an invitation, partner. Might get ugly. No civvies allowed, man, sorry."

"You'll still need a translator," I said, hurriedly, frantically, "And with Ang, you don't know what you're dealing with. Don't get in close. Don't let him touch you. If you have any reason to at all, just shoot the bastard."

"Listen Lee, I appreciate the concern, but I think we can handle an old man, alright? I'll call you when it's done."

And he hung up.

I dropped the phone and grabbed the keys to my loaner car – an 89 Ford Escort from the used car lot.

"Trace? Gotta go. Stay in, lock the doors. Gun's on the couch. See you later."

Tracy peeked out of the bedroom looking confused.

"Wha-?" she said.

I pulled on a jacket and said, "Off to catch some baddies. Stay safe."

With a quick kiss, I left the hotel. The drive should've taken ten minutes. With my speedster it took closer to twenty.

90

I parked in the 5 minute passenger pickup lane, ignored the screaming parking attendant, and ran inside. The woman at the information booth was very friendly. She was also old enough to personally remember the Wright brothers. In the time it took her to locate the map on her console, I spotted a directory across the way. I thanked her and jogged over to the display.

It didn't tell me anything. Looking around frantically, I realized Info Booth Lady was my only choice. Four and a half minutes later, I knew that a) there were no direct flights out of St. Louis, b) Continental flight 214 left in twenty minutes for Newark and caught a connecting flight to Hong Kong, and c) Eunice – the Info Booth Lady – had Irritable Bowel Syndrome.

There must just be a sign on my forehead, I swear.

I made my way to the gate – naturally, it was the one furthest from where I stood – and was about halfway there when a pack of uniformed cops ran past, hands on holsters, radios squawking.

I picked up the pace and followed.

91

The first shot rang out as I passed Starbucks. It was quickly followed by screams. Frightened travelers surged toward me. I ducked into the coffee shop until they passed. I heard someone bark an indistinct order; I heard snippets of Cantonese.

More shots.

A scream. This time it was filled with pain, not fear.

More sirens in the distance.

I slid around the wall and peeked carefully around the corner. If ever there were a place for a stand-off, this wasn't it. The area was open; the only – limited – cover was the baggage carousel. Cops stood together in a defensive cluster, guns drawn. The "unsavory Chinamen" stood opposite them. It was like the shootout at the O.K. Corral.

Except for all the luggage.

And the hostages.

There were six young-ish Chinese men in black silk suits. Each had managed to snag their own human shield from the crowd. Except for a seventh member of the group who lay in a pool of something dark on the floor.

It wasn't Ang. In fact, Ang was nowhere to be seen.

The kid in front – maybe 22, shoulder-length hair, Don Johnson style stubble – peered out from the elderly woman he was holding long enough to say something to the cops.

They didn't understand, but I did.

I stepped out with my hands raised and replied, "Do not kill the woman. I am the police translator. They do not understand your demands."

In less than a second, I had a room full of weapons pointed at me.

I could see where one's bowels could get a little irritable.

Somebody said, "Aw, fuck."

I knew the voice. In other circumstances I would've grinned. At the moment, though, I was thinking that, out of all the stupid things I'd done in life, this was probably the stupidest.

Lambert Airport is a shithole. I don't want to die in a shithole.

Chinese Don Johnson called me over. I went, since he made it clear that I'd be shot otherwise.

"Tell them to lower their weapons," he said.

I did.

The cops didn't move.

"Work with me here, guys," I yelled.

A few lowered their guns. Most didn't.

It's good to know you're loved.

Chinese Don Johnson grinned and said, "Too bad for you, eh?"

He raised his gun.

I stripped it from his hand and shoved the barrel into his eye socket. It happened so quickly that the others didn't see it immediately.

"Let the woman go," I said.

He did.

The rest of the crew now saw, and they were pissed. Guns waved, curses flew. I pushed the gun deeper, enough to almost knock him down, and said, "Tell them they need to calm down. They're making me nervous."

He did. He sounded a lot more nervous than I did. That was okay by me.

"Tell them to let the hostages go," I said.

"They will not. Not even for me."

I knew he was right. I didn't push it. "Where's Ang Su Chan?"

Something flickered in his eyes.

"Yeah, that's right. He's the one I want. I don't give a shit about you or your buddies. Where is he?"

"He left. Just before the cops came," he said.

"What do you mean, he left?"

"We had our boarding passes. He gave me his and said he'd be back. I don't know where he went."

Shit.

"Janik?" I yelled. From across the room, the agent responded.

"You got guys at all the exits?"

"All secure, yeah."

"Ang's here. Somewhere."

"Lee?"

"Yeah?"

"You're a real shithead you know that?"

"Yeah. I know. Hey, any ideas of how I can get out of this?"

"Not especially. Cool maneuver you did with the gun, though."

"Thanks."

The rest of the crew still had me in their sights, though. As if he read my mind, Chinese Don Johnson said, "You cannot hold me here all day."

"That's what you think, chief," I said, loud enough for the whole crew to hear. "Besides, I won't have to. See the ugly dudes in the suits over there? Feds. Look up there on the balcony… Snipers. You know why they're here? Look around you. You're in an airport. You have guns. You have hostages. That means you've been promoted from low level thug to full-fledged terrorist. That means the airport is surrounded by more cops than you've ever even imagined. You're not getting out of here. You see that, right? One of your boys shoots me or one of the hostages, and you all die. You want that?"

He couldn't shake his head, but I could tell he didn't.

"Tell your boys to stop this before it gets out of hand."

He glared at me with his one free eye. I pushed the gun a little more. He gave the word, and the others lowered their weapons.

Somehow the cops were there – guiding away the freed hostages, separating the gangsters, frisking them, cuffing them. Knox laid a hand on the top of the gun I had pressed halfway into Chinese Don Johnson's skull and told me to let go.

We'll take it from here, he said.

Upon releasing my grip on the pistol, I felt a wave of weakness travel from my fingers, up my arm, and throughout the rest of my body.

The adrenaline washout. I felt shaky and cold, so I worked my way past the frantic cops and feds, past the gawking and fearful would-be travelers, and planted myself on a padded bench by the baggage carousel. As I sat and tried to regain control of my motor functions, Ang's crew were taken out in handcuffs and loaded into the back of a couple of police cruisers.

"We've got men posted throughout the route."

I looked up at Agent Janik and nodded.

"In case… anyone tries anything like last time."

I nodded again.

"Ang?" I said.

"We'll find him." he said.

Knox came over, carrying a bag, and said, "We got this, at least."

He laid the bag, a black briefcase, on the bench next to me and said, "Tag says Jakob Smith… be a shame if the lock on it didn't work…"

Agent Janik said, "What?"

"You got a paper clip?" Knox said.

Janik looked through the thick stack of reports in his case folder and slid one free.

"Why?" he said.

Knox tossed it to me. I straightened out the metal, slid it into the first lock on the briefcase and, after a moment of jiggling it around, heard a click. The second lock opened as easily. Before I could open the case, Janik said, "Hold on just a damned minute."

I stopped and looked up at him. Knox looked from me to Janik and back.

"Broken lock or not, I can't have a civilian tampering with evidence," Janik said with an almost imperceptible wink. He slipped on a pair of latex gloves, knelt in front of the case, and gingerly opened it. There were Cantonese-English phrasebooks, neatly folded maps of the city, a stack of postcards from various tourist sights, and a small manila envelope. Janik took the envelope and tipped it, pouring a stack of photos onto the bench.

The top one I recognized.

I'd taken one just like it from Mei Ling's apartment. It was her, smiling, arm in arm with a guy who was not Tony Lau. It seemed faded somehow, and the color was off, but otherwise it was the same picture. I asked Janik to spread the pictures out; I was impatient to see them all, but, without gloves, I was at his mercy. The other photos were all of Mei Ling as well, but in much younger days. School pictures, snapshots taken at sporting events, a few birthday shots. She was just a kid in most of them.

Only the first really showed her as she had looked just before her death. After several minutes of futile study, Janik gathered the packet of photos and moved to put them back into the briefcase. A few slipped from his grasp and fell, swirling like leaves, to the floor.

Out of habit, I leaned forward to retrieve them and froze. Scribbled characters across the back of one photo read *Kwun Yam Beach, 1968.* I picked up the photo, despite the protests around me, and flipped it over.

92

The search was fruitless.

After six hours, and with a great deal of pressure from the local authorities, the airport was reopened. Those who had been detained and questioned and searched and put through hell left threatening lawsuits and exclusive interviews to the media.

Janik looked miserable.

Understandable, considering the abuse he'd taken from damn near everybody. At the end of the day nobody really remembered the successful arrest of six suspected cop killers - the media, the public, and most of the cops just labeled the operation a giant screw up.

So did I, but not for the same reasons. Ang Su Chan had been here and, somehow, slipped through our fingers. I called the hotel and left a message, and then called Master Cheng to let him know what was going on. I told him to be careful.

Cheng told me to go fuck myself.

After hanging up with him I checked in with Janik and Knox, made sure there wasn't something else I could fatally screw up with my presence, and told them to have a good night.

I knew they wouldn't. Neither would I.

It was after eight, and dark, when I left the airport and found one bit of good luck – my car had only received a parking ticket and had not been towed. I unlocked it, got in, and started the engine – all without incident. Apparently, the universe thought I'd had enough crap for one day.

I drove.

Maybe it was the absence of a working radio in my loaner car, or the remaining bit of adrenaline sharpness to my vision. Maybe it was boredom, dumb luck, or some secret sixth sense.

But by the time I reached the highway, I *knew* that I was being followed.

93

The vehicle was a white station wagon. Missouri plates. The silhouette in my rear view mirror lacked any identifying traits, but I was certain it was not a well-wisher. I didn't particularly care. I took the exit for the hotel, and watched the station wagon pull off behind me. I let the valet park my shitmobile, and I went inside before my shadow got too close.

In the elevator, I started feeling strange. Sick.

If it was Ang, he had no reason to follow me. Slick as he was, he could've gotten to me pretty much any time he wanted. So what was going on?

It tickled the back of my brain and the elevator dinged as each floor passed. The sickness solidified into a ball of lead in my stomach as the elevator doors opened on our floor. I ran down the hall, to our room, and knocked frantically.

When there was no answer, I fumbled the key card from my wallet and slid it in the lock. The strength vanished from my legs as soon as the door opened.

A chair lay on its side in the middle of the room – the only thing really disturbed – but Tracy was gone. It wasn't until I turned around, back toward the door, that I saw the gun.

She must've tried to get it. Must've tried to use it.

The paper bag lay, torn, beside the couch. The small pistol was twenty feet away, lying alone on the carpet. Somewhere, Tito mewled.

The phone rang.

94

I picked it up. My hand felt ready to crush the receiver.

"*Dr. Lee?*" Ang said in Cantonese.

"Ang Su Chan," I said.

"*I tried to make you stop, Doctor. I am sorry that it has come to this.*"

"You have Tracy?"

"*As I said. I am sorry.*"

My stomach dropped.

"Is she alright?" I asked, my voice quivering.

Silence.

"Is she, you fuck?" I screamed.

More silence.

Then, *"Let us be civilized, Dr. Lee."*

"What do you want?"

"*I want what you want, Doctor. I want this to end.*"

"Alright, Ang. How do we end this?"

"I think you know how this ends, Dr Lee."

Yes. But if there was to be a meeting, I would – at least – choose the place.

"You know Millar Park? Off of Olive?"

"Of course."

"Meet me there, in twenty minutes."

He hung up.

I hurried to the car and drove to the park where I first met Master Cheng. Set back from the street, I found an area far from the streetlights, and parked in the darkness. I got out and moved to a grouping of small pine trees fifteen feet from the car.

And waited.

And watched.

Headlights rounded the bend and approached slowly.

I shoved my hands in my jeans pockets for warmth and shivered a little. The air carried the steam of my breath in billowing clouds. The station wagon parked next to my car, and the headlights turned off.

I thought of Tracy, and felt the sickness return. Whatever had happened to her… I should've been there. I should've protected her.

Not the first time for this, my mind said. *You're not too great with the whole protection thing, are you?*

The door opened and the driver emerged. The natural grace of his posture, the loping sort of stride, the harsh sharpness of his movements – I wouldn't have searched so hard for my enemy if I had only known he would come to me.

He peered into my driver's side window, opened the door, and cursed under his breath.

My stomach roiled.

What has he done to her?

He looked around, cursed again, and checked the back seat.

Was she suffering, was she crying out for me to save her?

My fingernails dug into the palms of my hands. My jaws clenched so hard that my teeth ached.

I called out his name.

Turning, he sank into a defensive pose like a cat. I watched his head sway back and forth, searching the darkness. I stepped out of the trees slowly, without making a sound. He could not see me but, backlit from the streetlights, I still saw him.

"*Why don't you come out in the open*?" he said in Cantonese.

"First tell me about the girl. Why did you kill her?" I replied.

I could not make out his features, but his swaying stopped.

"What does it matter?" he said.

"I have to know," I said.

He seemed to shrug. He walked toward my voice and said, "*Duty, though that word means nothing to you, I'm sure.*"

I stayed on the move, flanking him to the right in case he had a weapon. "I understand duty. I don't understand murdering a pregnant woman. I don't understand terrifying her with damnation before killing her like a coward…"

"You think I enjoyed it? You are wrong, boy. You do not understand duty… in life we must sometimes do things, horrifying things… not because we wish to."

"And this 'duty' makes it okay? It makes what you did right?" I said.

He laughed a short, harsh laugh and said, *"No. Never right. There is a special hell reserved for men like me."*

"So now you've come to kill me, now. To clean up one more loose end?"

"I come to put an end to this," he said quietly.

95

I took a deep breath and stepped into view. Ang Su Chan remained a shadow silhouetted by the street lights. He surprised me by raising his right fist and covering it with his left palm – a traditional salute among martial artists – and bowing slightly.

I returned the gesture and waited, unsure of what would happen next. The old man exploded into action, arms coiling and twisting. In one second, the strikes were loose, whip-like tentacles, in the next moment, they were solid, thrusting punches.

I let him come, deflecting the lashing barbs and cannon fists. The strikes slammed against the wounds in my arms, sending jolts of pain through my body. I felt something tear, and a warm wetness began to seep into the sleeve of my jacket. Fear tugged at my mind. Fear, and doubt.

I can't do this.

No. You have to. For her. For them.

Why?

Because you're the only one who can. And because this fucker deserves to die.

I thought of Tracy. I thought of Mei Ling and her child, of Madame Chong, and Jade. I thought of Jimmy Yi Lau and Samson, of the policemen who fell.

I thought of Grace.

And I howled as I rushed in for the attack. I saw Ang's teeth in the streetlight; a smile. He easily parried my strikes, opening up my chest, and struck out with his fingertips.

I leaned back and rolled away from the strike. Ang managed only a glancing hit, but it was enough to make my heart skip a beat. He moved in again, and the back of his wrist cracked my cheek.

He's too strong. I can't fight him.

The words of my teacher echoed in my mind as Ang's blows tested my abilities. I fended off the strikes as best I could, but my body felt heavy, tired.

I breathed in the cold night air and said a silent apology. To Tracy, to Knox, to Mei Ling.

To Grace.

Because, just for now, I couldn't hold on to them anymore.

I exhaled.

I let go.

My body relaxed, and, as Ang moved in with renewed attacks, I began to parry him with touches light as the flecks of snow that began to fall. And with every point of contact, I stuck to him, following his movements, smothering them. His fury was a terrifying thing, a physical presence, and his every movement then was designed only to kill.

The space around me was mine, though, however much the old man tried to take it. His punches and kicks became deadly feints, they were supposed to make me react, make me move. I was supposed to attack or retreat; I did neither.

Instead, I played.

The old man presented an opening in his stance – an obvious trick to get me to attack low; I slapped him in the face. He reeled and covered himself clumsily, expecting me to follow up with another strike; I didn't. He lunged, stabbing fingers toward my vital points.

I shifted my weight backward, just out of his reach. In his anger and overconfidence, he overextended by perhaps an inch.

Capturing his wrist with my left hand, I stepped backward and pulled him into my right knifehand strike – a technique from the form known as 'Repulse the Monkey.' I had done so playfully, but as I struck his right shoulder at the joint, I felt it separate. He howled from the pain and shrank away.

I let him.

He stumbled and, with deceptive speed, lashed out with a kick to my ankle. I winced and barely dodged a wide, arcing strike aimed at my eyes; his knuckles glanced off my split cheek, sending sparks of white heat through my face.

Shaking off the pain and anger and fear, I realized I had become perhaps a bit overconfident as well. Ang Su Chan circled, pacing, looking for an opening. His right arm hung uselessly; his eyes flitted around, huge and panicked, wild.

Ang made snarling whines of pain between his teeth as he struggled to breathe. Blood and saliva trailed from his lip and fell to the ground to freeze.

His feet shifted, rooting.

His stance deepened, solidified.

In the madness of his eyes, I saw Mei Ling.

And in Mei Ling, I saw Grace.

Cold and blue.

Lifeless.

So small, tiny fingers and toes.

Those eyes, just like her mother's…

It would be so easy. No more pain. No more guilt.

All I had to do was nothing.

The man before me moved, his fist shooting out like an arrow. Something in it glittered in the dim light.

I regained my center and shifted, sitting back on my left leg. I avoided the incoming attack by inches.

In that timeless time I thought of nothing – not Mei Ling, not Grace, not winning or losing or living or dying.

There was only the game: this dance, this moment.

The palms of my hands connected to his arms, one in front of his elbow, and the other on his tricep. I felt the *chi* of his attack, the black surge of anger and hatred fired toward me through that arm. I turned my waist; my arms followed the motion, palms sliding in opposite directions down the length of Ang's arm, redirecting – reversing – the flow of poisonous intent back upon its wielder. Ang Su Chan's eyes widened and his breath caught in his throat.

And he fell.

Snowflakes lit upon his open eyes, melted, and trickled to the ground. A small, thin-bladed knife glinted from the palm of his hand.

I called Knox.

96

There would be no need for an in depth investigation. It was a clear cut case of self-defense. That a 68 year old man would have a massive heart attack in the midst of a fight was not suspicious.

I kept it together okay until Knox told me that they'd found Tracy.

In the back of Ang's station wagon.

Alive.

And pissed.

Ang hadn't wanted to hurt her, not really. She'd been simply bait.

Unwilling bait.

At least she hadn't made it easy on him.

97

On the drive from the police station to the hotel, my muscles began to tighten and lock up. It was to be expected; my body had absorbed more abuse that month than the previous ten years combined. The pain at least kept my mind off of things.

Killing an old man, murderer though he was, did not make me feel like a tough guy. It did not make me feel very smart either, considering I still didn't know the why of everything.

A small voice in the back of my head seemed to suggest that I did, but it was the same voice that suggested I'd like the movie Moulin Rouge, so I didn't take it very seriously.

I parked and took my time getting out of the car. Tracy helped as much as she could, but she was pretty battered herself.

We needed a vacation.

On the way to the room, every minute of every year of my life weighed on the muscles of my back and legs; each cut, bruise, burn and scrape sang; the lanced wounds on my forearms throbbed.

After promising myself that I'd cut down, all I could think about at that moment was a tall, stiff drink. We got into the elevator, pressed the button for our floor, and, when the doors closed, leaned against the mirrored walls for support. Talking took energy we didn't have.

My ankle wouldn't accept my full weight; my cheek and jaw felt like an overcooked sausage. Ang hadn't managed to strike any specific acupuncture points, but the effects of his rage were impressive. The elevator doors opened, and together we limped down the hall to our room.

Once inside, we helped each other undress. I inspected Tracy's bruises, gave myself a quick once-over and, convinced neither of us had been "Death Touch-ed," went to bed.

Just before dozing off, I realized something.

A drink would've been nice, but the only thing I really needed was her.

98

Sometimes life takes on a certain quality, a lucidity and clarity that encompasses and surpasses and crosswires the senses together. Moments we know will be cherished memories even as we live them.

That night, at the hotel, was such a time.

To hold and be held, silently, and to relish the silence as much as the touch… tracing the planes and lines of the one I know so well and yet hardly at all… night deepening, reaching its apex, and receding… drowsing through the dawn, entwined together as though fused…

…even the peach fuzz gargoyle thing coiled upon my head…

Moments in time, captured forever.

This was home, here with her; this was peace.

When at last we rose, we reached a decision. I gathered our things while Tracy snuck Tito out to the car. I paid our bill and turned in the room keys.

They weren't necessary anymore.

99

The next week or so consisted of attempts — some successful, others not so much — to return to normal life. Tracy returned to work, at first picking up only a few shifts until she was ready. I cleaned up the shop, checked my machine, and dutifully called back the patients who apparently thought I'd died.

I had no patients. Really, though, that was okay. I wasn't in the headspace to be much help to anyone anyway.

Then there was the apartment. I'd missed it, of course, but now…

I never thought I'd miss Tito.

As for the case, Knox and Janik were still working hard to put together the pieces and figure out the missing bits. I left them to it. As far as I was concerned, my part in it all was finished.

Mostly.

100

The ceremony took place outside, in the sun. 68 degrees in January. Even for California weather, it was exceptional. Massive sticks of incense burned at points around the area; a thick musky sandalwood that clung to the nostrils long after the smoke was gone. The priest paced around the perimeter, chanting mantras and waving a blessed mirror about. He wore a flatboard hat that Tracy said made her think he was graduating from high school.

I stood near Tony Lau and Daniel D'Avila; their suits made me feel woefully underdressed. Tracy insisted that I looked perfectly respectable in black Dockers, a wine-colored shirt and black jacket, but I just felt shabby.

So far, it was just the five of us; no one else had shown up yet. Tony glanced over at me and gestured slightly. He turned away and walked to the railing overlooking a small pond. I followed. We both leaned against the rail and looked out at the water.

"I don't know why you've insisted on this. I would've been more than happy to pay--" he said.

"It's just something I'd like to do," I said.

He flashed me a look that said he didn't understand.

That was okay.

Looking down again, he said, "It was an accident, you know…just… well, it's amazing what tequila can do…" He laughed bitterly.

"It was her birthday. Daniel went home. We all figured it would be good for me to be seen out with women… We were talking and drinking and it got late and there was more drinking… I guess a part of me wondered if father was right… I don't even really remember it. Just flashes, really. Horrible, clumsy flashes. For all the hurt it caused, you'd think it would be clearer. It should be, y'know? I should have to feel it…just like he did."

"Daniel," I said.

"He never complained. Never said a word. He knew… but he just wanted the best for me, you know?"

I nodded.

"I still can't believe the one time she and I…" he shook his head, there were tears in his eyes.

"Fathers everywhere have had that same feeling, believe me."

He looked up again and said, "You have done so much for us, for her, you shouldn't have to do this… please…"

I shook my head. "Tony. I want to."

Mourners began filtering in, finding seats near the gravesite.

"Looks like it's almost time," I said.

He nodded and together we went back to our seats. I scanned the crowd. There was no one I knew. Yet.

The priest chanted some more.

Tracy put a hand on my wrist, leaned in, and whispered, "What's he saying?"

"He's explaining to the gods that the grave is consecrated, the body is cleansed, and the offerings are in place. He's asking that they welcome her home now."

"Oh," she said, her eyes moist and shining, "…Baby too?"

"Baby too," I said quietly.

She nodded. I offered her a tissue. She took it and wiped her eyes. Traditionally, the bodies would be displayed; time had made that impossible. The casket stood before us – a small, grim reminder of the horrors of the world and the chance of redemption.

I wasn't sure of what I believed, but if Mei Ling's spirit was around then perhaps she could yet find the peace she deserved.

Perhaps we all could.

He arrived just as Tony rose to say a few words. I recognized him immediately. Aside from the grey at his temples, he looked just as he had the last time I'd seen him. He stood far to the back of the gathering, well away from the rest of us.

I took Tracy's hand, squeezed it, and excused myself from the services. As I worked my way over, I saw him notice me. He immediately looked away. When I was close enough, I said, "I believe I have something of yours."

He didn't pay any attention. Just when I was about to repeat myself, he said, "I am not interested."

"Are you sure?" I said, taking the photos from my jacket pocket. "They're a memorial too, in a way."

He stopped, stared at the pictures and slowly raised his eyes to meet mine.

"I retrieved them from a man named Ang Su Chan. I believe you knew him?"

"No," he said, turning to leave.

"Oh come on, Zhao… you expect me to believe you'd trust a complete stranger to murder your daughter?"

He stopped.

"Is this the part where you do the whole denial thing? Because then I go through how the killer had intimate family photos of your daughter and you and your wife… presumably because Mei Ling is the spitting image of Mrs. Zhao… and how funny that all is. Then you give a weak explanation and I tell you how my cop friends traced a $50,000 deposit into Ang's account back to your bank. So let's just cut out the middle man, alright? You did it. We both know it. I just can't, for the life of me, figure out why."

Pei Jin Zhao stared at me with disgust. I stared back, giving him a taste of the ole I'm-rubber-you're-glue look.

"The Eight Tigers are an evil organization," he said.

I blinked. "And?" I said.

"Ang Su Chan sought revenge… his niece was one of Lau's little whores."

"Jimmy Yi Lau brought her to America," I said.

"Yes. She died of heroin overdose within a year."

"So?"

"He came after me," Zhao said, straightening his jacket.

"Why?"

"I was once the head of the Tigers' prostitution interests in North America."

"What happened?"

"I was given a second chance… to repent, to live again," he said.

"How so?"

"Through the holy blood of our Lord, Jesus Christ."

I stared at him for a long time. Part of me wanted to laugh, the other part wanted to throw up.

I kept it cool, though.

"So you saw the light. Then what?" I said.

"I resigned and begged Jimmy to do the same. We cannot oppress our own people and call it freedom."

"He turned you down."

Zhao nodded sadly. "He was a pagan."

"Right."

"Years passed, but he came to me – in my home – as if I were still his partner in filth. He offered me money… money… for my daughter to marry his damned sodomite son. Naturally, I refused and sent him away."

"Naturally."

Something darkened in his features, as if a shadow overtook him. "You cannot know what it is like to be a father… to have a… disobedient child. A pagan… She went to that gangster and she took his goddamned money just like the whore of Babylon! I ask you, what is a father supposed to do?"

"Talk to her, get some family counseling, maybe try the whole tough love deal… I can think of a lot of options… none of them involve murder."

"As I said, you cannot know what it is like."

I took a deep breath and said, "So Ang comes after you. What then?"

"He sought redemption, but would not give up his pagan ways. I explained that I was no longer with the Tigers. He and I both sought to destroy their evil organization."

"And you gave up your former friends and your own kid."

"Let pagans kill pagans. It means nothing to the Lord," he said.

"And you think Jesus is cool with you paying and orchestrating murders."

He smiled beatifically and said, "I am forgiven of all my trespasses. All that I have done and will ever do. You too can know His love…"

And he reached out for my shoulder like a mentor, or a brother, a best friend.

I don't know exactly why, but something inside me knew that I couldn't let him touch me, as if that one small act would mean something horrible, something I could never take back. Without thinking, I shifted my weight away and turned to avoid his touch. Simultaneously, I reached out and slapped his chest with the fingertips of my left hand.

Pei Jin Zhao sat down hard and looked up at me with genuine shock. "Do not fear Him, brother. He accepts all! He forgives all! But reject him and you face the fires of hell. The wages of sin is death, brother!"

I threw several of the photos of Mei Ling onto his lap and said, "Remember that, then, and remember her… every day for the rest of your pathetic life. And, for your sake, I hope to hell that your 'heavenly father' is a better dad than you ever were, you fucking piece of shit."

I turned away and started back to the ceremony.

"You're…not calling the police?" he said.

I stopped, turned, and looked at him. "No need," I said.

101

After the ceremony, Tony came over and shook my hand. He thanked me again. Together, he and Daniel left. There was so much left for him to do – the reuniting of the Eight Tigers, if he still chose to do it, the beginning of a promising career as a painter, and, perhaps the most difficult, the act of living his own life for once. I wished them the best of luck, but I did not tell them goodbye.

Fate would cross our two paths again, I was sure of it.

Tracy and I went out to dinner, caught an early movie, and boarded our plane by 9 p.m. We could have stayed for a bit, but both of us were sick of hotels and, frankly, the unnatural California weather was freaking us both out. We'd been conditioned to the hell that was the Midwest.

We landed in St. Louis just after 5 a.m. after circling the airport for over an hour…

Thunderstorms and a chance of sleet.

Now that's more like it.

As late as it was, we decided to stay together at my place.

I drove.

In my repaired Viper.

Happiness.

I took her up to the roof. There, with a pyrotechnic display in the sky and a battery powered stereo, I asked her to dance with me. Me, the king of the boring old slow dance.

I put The Flamingos' I Only Have Eyes for You on the stereo, and we danced.

Slowly.

A little stiffly.

A little painfully, still.

It was one of the best times I've ever had.

In the morning, we got up and got to work. There was much for us to do as well – rebuilding my business, redecorating my apartment (Tracy says it "screams for a woman's touch"), and, perhaps the most difficult, the act of living *our* own lives for once.

Sonic Youth blared on the stereo as Tracy bebopped into the living room carrying a cardboard box. She wore cut-off sweats, a Dresden Dolls T shirt, and a red bandana to keep her hair from her eyes.

Her bangs were now back to purple again.

What can I say? I love the girl.

"You know you have, like, a whole closet of these?" she said, gesturing with the box.

"Yeah," I said. My chest felt tight. I could practically hear the words of my teacher, "*Fang Song, fang song.*"

Relax. Release.

So I did.

I let go.

I finally let go.

"C'mon, we'll do it together," Tracy said, putting down the box and sitting in front of it.

I crouched beside her and peeled away the packing tape. Unwrapping the first newspaper-covered frame, I said, "Trace, this is my daughter, Grace. This was taken just before her third birthday, when her mother and I took her to the carnival for the first time."

Together, we unwrapped each photo and I told her the stories that accompanied each one.

She listened.

Sometimes we laughed.

Sometimes we cried.

I couldn't have done it without her.

102

A week later, on Sunday, John Knox showed up at my apartment. He wore ratty jeans and a sweatshirt. Clearly, he was not on duty.

"Got a minute?" he said.

I let him in and offered him a drink.

He had a scotch; I had a bottled water. We sat in the living room. He was on the couch and I was in one of the new plush chairs Tracy picked out. He looked around the room at some of the photos and remained silent.

"Business or pleasure, Detective?" I said.

"Janik faxed me this earlier this morning," Knox said, leaning forward and pulling a folded sheet of newsprint from his back pocket. "He thought I'd find it interesting."

He passed it to me.

I read it.

"Huh." I said.

"Huh?" He said.

I nodded and repeated, "Huh."

"You read the story, right?"

"Yeah."

"I don't think you did. Because, for me, a story about a 250 pound man starving to death… even though by all accounts he ate like a pig… and even though he was hospitalized and treated and given upwards of 4,000 calories a day by IV… for me, that story would elicit more than a 'Huh.' Top it off with the fact that said man was our money man in the murders of a whole fucking lot of people and I'd say it's downright suspicious, wouldn't you?"

I shrugged.

"I showed this around town a bit… Would you care to know the word that kept popping up?"

"Hm?"

"Just like the Madame… *deem-mok, deem-mok*."

I grinned and said, "Dim Mak, detective? The 'Death Touch'? I thought I told you… it's a fairy tale. Doesn't exist."

"Good thing. Because if it did, I'd have to investigate and probably arrest somebody. There are those around town who don't see the difference between this and what Ang Su Chan did…"

I ran a thumb down the ribbed edge of my water bottle and exhaled slowly.

"Hopefully there are those around town who do," I said.

Knox seemed to study me for a while.

Finally, he said, "Yeah. Yeah, I guess there are."

He stood and said, "Well, I guess this is it, eh? No more Triad shenanigans. I'll be sure to give you a call if anything else goes down with the 'Orientals'…"

He grinned.

I said, "You do that. And if I ever need a Polack cop, I'll give you a ring."

He chuckled and nodded and offered me his hand.

I shook it.

"You take care of yourself, Lee."

"You too, John."

I closed the door behind him. The article still sat on the coffee table. I wadded it up and threw it away.

I went into the bedroom, to the small Taoist altar Tracy and I had set up along the east wall. The low table held photos of my first teacher, my mother and father, Tracy's grandmother, and, of course, my little girl. In the back right corner, behind an incense burner, I'd tucked a photo of Mei Ling Zhao -- age 7 -- practicing martial arts. Behind it was the photo of her parents on the beach in 1968, the photo Mei Ling had had retouched and framed.

I took it, crumpled it, and added it to the article in the trash.

As for the other picture, the one of Mei Ling, I kept it right where it was.

103

"What are you do? So Clumsy! Ay! Ay! Stop! Stop, stop, stop. You break old man's heart."

I grinned. It was nice to have somebody else taking the heat instead of me. Tracy, on the other hand, looked miserable. And Cheng, well, Tracy had him so flustered he could barely speak English. I knew the feeling.

"I'm doing exactly what you told me to, you old bastard," she shouted.

"I never say to flap your arms like a chicken!" Master Cheng shouted back.

Tracy got in his face and growled, "I'm right in the exact same position you put me in, asshole."

Master's eyes widened and he stepped back to look at her again.

"Ah," he said. I tried to suppress a laugh and didn't quite succeed. Cheng heard it and shouted, "What you looking at, dickhead? Maybe you worry about own sorry ass, eh? Oh, you damned Americans, you suck my will to live, you know this?"

Spring had arrived at last, and it was a perfect day – blue skies, cool breeze, and no worries.

Tracy stood in the posture 'Ward off left,' one of the first movements in the form. I rolled leisurely through each movement, watching her struggle and shake, knowing just how badly her legs must hurt… it was just a part of the process. She'd work through it.

And, until then, I got to rub her sore muscles after class.

I was halfway through the third and final section of the form when Master Cheng turned his attention to me. He crossed his arms, frowned, and watched silently.

"Snake creeps down" into "Step forward seven stars."

"Step back and ride the tiger" into--

"Ay, hold!" He barked. I froze in position and waited. He scuttled over, made a correction in my posture – moving my arm to a position I knew it didn't belong in – and yelled, "Stupid asshole- head! Ay!"

He quickly moved my arm back into the position I'd had it in originally and said loudly, "*This* is correct!"

I stared at him dumbly before moving again into "Turn body and swing over lotus."

Leaning in close, Cheng said, "Dear boy, in all ways, you are my perfect student, and you make your master proud. But this you cannot tell the others… it is bad for morale."

He winked and went back to torment Tracy some more.

I continued on with the form, through "Apparent Close," and into "Cross Hands," feeling the warmth of the sun on my face and enjoying it. For now -- just for now -- all was right with the world.

In the background, I heard Tracy call Master a "shriveled old tyrant."

I smiled and kept on moving. While they continued to squabble in the background, I came to the end of the form, slowly lifting my hands and letting them glide back down to my sides.

Shou Shi – Close.

So, What's Next for Randall and Tracy?

Pressure Point -- A Randall Lee Mystery (Available Now!)

Stay up to date with Randall Lee's adventures, and my other projects, by signing up to my newsletter! It's fast, it's free, and I promise not to bomb your inbox with lots of junk. Send an email to charlescolyott@gmail.com. Be sure to write "Newsletter" in the subject line. Members will receive exclusive news, previews of new books, and, quite possibly, some free stuff!

Support Indie Writers!

If you enjoyed this book, please tell your friends! Word of mouth and good reviews are crucial for new and indie writers. A quick review on Amazon, a mention on Goodreads or even a shared link on Facebook can mean a lot to get the word out about the books you love!

About the Author

Charles Colyott lives on a farm in the middle of nowhere (Illinois) with his wife, 2 daughters, cats, and a herd of llamas and alpacas. He is surrounded by so much cuteness it's very difficult for him to develop any street cred as a dark and gritty writer. Nevertheless, he has appeared in *Read by Dawn II*, Dark Recesses Press, *Withersin* magazine, *Horror Library* Volumes III & IV, *Terrible Beauty*, *Fearful Symmetry*, and *Zippered Flesh*, among other places. He also teaches a beginner level Tai Chi Ch'uan class in which no one has died (yet) of the death touch.

You can get in touch with him on Facebook, or email him at charlescolyott@gmail.com.

Unlike his llamas, he does not spit.

CPSIA information can be obtained at www.ICGtesting.com
Printed in the USA
LVOW12s0757170214

373983LV00001B/275/P